RISKS AND REWARDS

Duncan Pell

authorHOUSE®

AuthorHouse™ UK Ltd.
1663 Liberty Drive
Bloomington, IN 47403 USA
www.authorhouse.co.uk
Phone: 0800.197.4150

Published by AuthorHouse   07/21/2014

ISBN: 978-1-4969-8588-0 (sc)
ISBN: 978-1-4969-8306-0 (hc)
ISBN: 978-1-4969-8589-7 (e)

My thanks to the Author House Team for their support, help and professionalism. Thanks also to Joe for providing feedback, constructive advice and encouragement.

"To my daughters Mollie and Annie.
You are always in my thoughts"

PROLOGUE

He arrived as usual: on a Sunday, at gate C-12. And he followed the arrivals signs down to the baggage hall and out through the *nothing to declare* area. He exited the terminal through some revolving doors and turned left for the car park pay machines. A charge of sixty-two euros to his credit card provided precise evidence of when he left the airport building. He climbed two flights of stairs with his parking ticket ready in his shirt pocket. He was an old hand. He always parked the car on the top floor in more or less the same place – that way there was no danger of forgetting where it was parked.

Everything he had done since leaving aisle seat 3C on KLM flight 1312 had been conveniently recorded for the future investigation. His passage through Schiphol Airport Amsterdam was caught on four security cameras. The time his exit ticket was issued and fed into the barrier was encoded on magnetic strips. The moment he bought petrol with a credit card at the garage on the airport perimeter was recorded by Visa. But none of this information helped with the subsequent investigation into the car bomb explosion that killed him when he parked at his home in Haarlem.

CHAPTER 1

It took Richard Randall ten minutes to walk from his apartment in Pimlico to Victoria station. From Victoria, he caught the Gatwick Express, a fast train link to the airport terminal buildings that were about thirty miles from the centre of London. His departure gate was across Pier Six, which is something of a novelty because it is the largest air passenger bridge in the world. From there, he took in some great views of the aircraft.

The flight from Gatwick to Toulouse took two hours, and Randall then drove northwest in a hire car. Provence and the south coast he knew from childhood holidays, but the Midi-Pyrénées region was new to him. He had read a little about the area on the Internet while waiting in the British Airways lounge at Gatwick. The region was larger than Denmark or the Netherlands, and it had been created in the late twentieth century as a kind of administrative zone centred on Toulouse. The name chosen by politicians for the new region was descriptive, not historical: *Midi* means south, and *Pyrénées* refers to the mountains by Spain that mark the southern boundary.

Properties began to look more prosperous as he left Toulouse behind. Swimming pools and refurbished farmhouses confirmed what he had read in the flight magazine – the area attracted Europeans from the north who invested there and spent a few weeks of the year living in a reliably warm climate.

He enjoyed the drive, but he was not looking forward to the meeting with a young family trying to come to terms with an unexplained and tragic death. He knew they would expect him to bring news, and they might resent him if he went over the same ground as the Dutch police.

He had booked a room in a small, private hotel near the family home. The hotel was in a village called Valeilles. As he drove through the village looking for the hotel, he saw only a post office, a tiny school, a church with an overpopulated graveyard, and a village hall. It was mid-afternoon, and the houses were shuttered against the blazing sun. He saw no one walking.

He found the hotel easily, right as he started to climb the steep hill that led out of the village. He parked in the designated area to the left of an old, elegant, three-storey house. A mature lavender hedge separated the parking area from the colourful front garden. Dark-blue shutters contrasted agreeably with the white stone of the building. The shutters were closed on all the upstairs windows, which added to his earlier impression that everyone was resting in their bedrooms, waiting for the sun to sink. The reception area of the hotel smelt of furniture polish and cigar smoke. The wooden floor sounded solid, old, and original, and his footsteps echoed as he approached a dark oak counter behind which stood a middle-aged man with a handlebar moustache. Clearly, *he* was not resting, and he gave Randall a welcoming smile. His greeting was in French, but Randall was able to reply competently using what he had learned at school and practised on family holidays. He was handed his key with no check-in formalities and taken to a first-floor room at the front of the house. It had a huge double bed, ceiling-high wardrobes along one wall, and a desk and chair along another. All the furniture was elegant and made of solid wood that was built, Randall guessed, in the late nineteenth century. Nothing matched; the furniture seemed to be a collection of items bought randomly for quality and style. The bed was at right-angles to the windows. The tall windows reached from the height of Randall's knees to the ceiling, but any view was obstructed by the blue shutters he had observed upon arrival. He pushed them open and gazed out over the rooftops of the village, towards the church he had passed on the way in. He wondered about the history of the village and whether it had prospered in the past. He guessed there had been much suffering during the two world wars. Like many French towns and villages, it likely lost a high percentage of the male population during the First World War and felt the pain of German occupation in the next.

He was charmed by the hotel and the room. He immediately thought of Lisa and how nice it would be to spend a few romantic days with her in rural France. They had been to Paris and enjoyed the city, but he didn't consider that to be the real France. This was more typical – a kind of enchanting time warp with great scenery, great food, and great wine. He was very fond of her, but he knew it was risky for a police officer to have a journalist as a girlfriend. Of course, her interest was politicians, and they never discussed his work. Her conversation revolved mainly around political rumours and the scandals involving ministers and MPs. Few of her private, gossipy stories ever made a big splash, but Randall mused that if half of them were true, there were some very sexually active people in politics.

He hoped to get back to the hotel in time for dinner after visiting Rachel Craig. The menu he had seen by the front door looked tempting, traditional, and affordable. His only concern was that the chef would not cook the meat to his liking. It was an aspect of French culture he did not comprehend – it was as if they did not know the health risks of undercooked meat. For his part, he would always insist on his beef being well-done, or he would not eat it. *If necessary,* he thought to himself, *I will be extremely assertive with the chef.* He rehearsed the French words he would use to make his point, and he smiled to himself at the thought of asking to be taken to the kitchen to cook the meat himself while an arrogant chef flapped his arms and cursed his ignorant customer.

As soon as he had unpacked his bag, he telephoned the Craig home. Almost immediately, a young-sounding girl answered and handed the phone to her mother when he gave his name. Rachel Craig seemed bright and cheerful.

"You found your hotel without problems?"

"Yes, and the room is perfect. Thanks for recommending I stay here."

"I will pick you up in twenty minutes. It is easier for me to do that than give you detailed directions and risk you getting lost."

He quickly changed into more formal attire and waited. He used the time to reread the family profile compiled by the other interviewers who had questioned the family at different stages of the investigation. The conclusion he had reached back in London was that there was nothing to investigate except the possibility that there was something in the victim's life that no one had discovered yet. He needed to find something to explain why an expensive, professional operation had been funded by a person or organisation. He decided that a direct and structured line of questioning would take him no further, so he aimed to talk to the family and listen in lieu of his usual routine. He hoped to learn something about Craig that would break the deadlock of the investigation.

His department in Scotland Yard had taken over the case of the murder of Simon Craig from the Amsterdam police. Randall had just been promoted to chief inspector, and he was now the head of a new task group responsible for supporting foreign police forces in their investigations of serious crimes committed against British subjects who are living or travelling abroad. Sometimes, he was required to concentrate on the UK dimension of the victim's life and send a report to the lead investigators. Occasionally, though, as with the Craig case, he had to take over the inquiry because people living in the United Kingdom seemed to be the originators of the crime.

Randall had achieved reasonable success at each rank that he passed through during his rapid ascension. He had joined the police as a graduate, and although a university education was not essential, it was certainly beneficial. After all, promotion boards placed increasing emphasis on academic qualifications. They believed that a well-educated person was likely to be more politically correct in thought and deed and better able to adapt to the fast-changing requirements of modern policing.

He had done well at university. In addition to being a student, he was a footballer – a semi-professional athlete with a real chance of making the grade had he accepted the club offers before going to university. Fortunately, he could also hold his own as an academic. While climbing the ranks, he was fit and dressed smartly. He made a point of appearing as if he should be more senior than his actual rank by spending on quality clothes.

He was tall with broad shoulders. At 1.9 metres, he stood out in a crowd. With his large eyes, full lips, and olive-coloured face, he was, without a doubt, good looking. His colleagues considered him to be distant because he did not join in the locker-room banter or go for end-of-shift drinks at the local pub. Such actions were interpreted variously by his cohort as conceit, arrogance, or unfriendliness. In fact, it was just that he preferred the company of close friends and family. As he moved up through the lower ranks, the perception of him being a loner had been problematic. But now, as a chief inspector working in a small department, it mattered little. It amused him that fictional police officers were usually portrayed as unfit, permanently tired drunks with dysfunctional marital relationships and rude bosses. From what he had seen of his senior colleagues, it was quite possible to have a good career and a pleasant home life.

Rachel Craig picked him up at the hotel in a Toyota Land Cruiser. He could see her two daughters sitting in the back. The youngest girl waved and smiled while her sister opened the window and politely said, "Welcome to France chief inspector. Please get in the passenger seat beside Mummy." and started giggling. He guessed they had been rehearsing the welcome speech on the way to collect him. He introduced himself to the girls which set them giggling again. They arrived at the house ten minutes later and the children rushed off to change into their swimwear.

The farm house was built of the same white stone as the hotel but had dark green shutters that were fixed open. It faced south east and the sun was longer on the front. A colourful collection of pot plants decorated a narrow terrace beneath the downstairs windows. On the left of the house was a pigeonnier. He had noticed on the drive from Toulouse, many of these elegant lofts attached to properties. He pointed at it and asked Rachel Craig, "Were these functional or just decorative?"

"Apparently, they used the droppings as a manure supplement. But some of the designs are so sophisticated that I think they must also have been a status symbol. An owl lives in ours."

They entered the house and Rachel Craig put the kettle on. A dark brown Labrador dog rose from its bed and approached Randall warily.

"He's friendly. His name is Benny. He does not like the heat and sleeps most of the day. We have had him since he was a puppy. The kids love him. Amy writes to him sometimes and reads the letters to him, before she goes to bed. Tea or coffee of something cold?" Rachel Craig asked, changing the subject.

"Tea is fine. Thank you."

"I will make the tea and then we will sit in the shade by the pool and discuss Simon. The girls will be happy playing in the pool. They are planning to take you on a little walk when we finish. It should be cooler by then."

CHAPTER 2

Monthly board meetings of NESC took place in a large conference room on the fifth floor of the company's HQ. The walls were covered with pictures of steelworks and steelmaking machinery. The chairman believed that board members needed to be reminded of the scale and complexity of what they were in charge of. The huge conference table could accommodate thirty people; there were microphones, notepads, and pencils at each place setting. The room was wide enough to allow assistants, advisers, and interpreters to sit six feet behind their bosses, along the two long walls of the rectangular room. A sophisticated projector hung from the ceiling, enabling laptop presentations, videos, and live television to be beamed onto the white wall opposite the chairman. The distance between the chairman and the wall was so great that he could not see the images without getting closer. In order to accommodate such a shift, other people had to move and make space for him. He seemed to enjoy the disruption it caused, as evidenced by his refusal to have a second, nearer screen installed.

The chairman controlled meetings with charm and tolerance, and he allowed everybody to have their say. No one doubted his intellect or ability, but most thought he should be less lenient. Meetings sometimes ran several hours longer than scheduled, which meant that members had to guess the end time so they could stay on top of their other engagements. Every employee referred to him as *the chairman* in public, but in private, he was known as Old Stan.

The June meeting had hardly started when the subject came up. The chairman sounded frustrated as he questioned the human resources director.

"So no definite news from the police? Have they kept in touch?"

Ian Jackson looked up from his doodling and said, "Yes, they have handed the matter over to a chief inspector based at Scotland Yard. He belongs to one of their national squads. This squad handles serious crimes committed against Brits travelling or living overseas.

We are going to meet him when he gets back from seeing the family. He sounds keen and bright." He was consciously trying to sound upbeat because that is what the chairman wanted to hear.

The chairman repeated his statement of the month before and the month before that: "We must cooperate in full. It is in all our interests to know why this happened to an employee of this company. There may be some greater threat, or there may have been something going on behind our backs that we ought to know about. People don't just get murdered without reason, least of all by hitmen."

The other directors all nodded while the chief financial officer muttered under his breath something about the selfish old bastard being only interested in his own safety and the reputation of the company. The chairman heard enough to raise his head and ask, "John, you were saying?"

"Only that there is our own safety to consider and the reputation of the company," he replied, improvising cleverly, which drew smirks from his neighbours.

"Thank you, John. My thoughts precisely. Have we handled the family in a caring way, paid up on accident insurance and widow's pension?" The chairman queried as he looked again towards Jackson.

"Yes, all taken care of. The widow has received four times his annual salary in accident insurance, despite the uncertainty surrounding his death. His widow will also receive the normal death and service pension benefits. We placed strong pressure on the insurance company and gave them a choice: pay up or lose our business. We also wrote off his housing loan for an apartment in Battersea. It was covered by a life policy."

It was more of what the chairman wanted to hear. He had a thing about insurance companies and liked to see them beaten once in a while.

"Good. Thank you, Ian. Perhaps we can move on to something more positive: the plans for the opening ceremony in Poland. That's you Chris – but fairly brief, please. You've got twenty minutes."

The meeting went on for several more hours, mainly because Chris Holdwick gave a long and inappropriately detailed presentation on his plans for the opening ceremony of the new NESC steelworks in Poland. As the meeting broke up, Ian Jackson touched Tony Redder on the arm and gestured for him to follow. As sales and marketing director, Redder needed friends. Unlike all the other board members, his background did not involve steel. He was an outsider who was recruited from the alien world of retail. Jackson had certainly become something of a friend in recent weeks, but probably out of the need to have a confidant, not from admiration. They sat together in Jackson's office as he explained the reason for the conversation. The office was spacious, with a south facing window overlooking the Thames to the right of Lambeth Bridge. The furniture was plain white, including the desk, coffee table, and two leather armchairs. There were no pictures, academic certificates, or decorations of any kind. As they sat down in the armchairs, a young man entered with a tray that held two cups and a teapot.

"Tea for two," he said with a cheeky grin as he placed the tray on the coffee table and exited the room with a feminine spin of his hips. Jackson smiled.

"Don't jump to any conclusions, Tony, about that young man. You will be wrong."

"No comment."

"Actually, he is very popular with the ladies and also seems to like them. Things are changing. If you look at boy bands, for example, the feminine-looking ones are the ones the girls scream at. He is also an excellent PA," he added quickly.

"Perhaps there is a kind of role swap going on: men becoming more feminine in their behaviour and dress and women going the other way. Anyway, let's get down to business," said Redder.

"Sorry, Tony. I know we are going over old ground, but if this police officer wants to meet several more of us, I will steer him in your direction as Craig's boss. The important thing is that we give no hint of problems, just glowing tributes."

Redder sounded concerned. "It was easy with the Dutch because they were not really expecting anything – routine and polite background enquiries. What we don't know is whether Craig gave any hint to his family and friends, something that could be discovered by a more creative approach to the investigation."

Jackson thought for a while before replying, "You are right, but we don't know that this officer is any more interested than the Dutch. Certainly, there is nothing to suggest that somebody close to Craig had any idea what he was talking to us about. Thankfully, he was a very private guy and did not share his worries with his wife. She, at the same time, seems wrapped up in the children, France, and writing gardening books. She probably never listened to him, anyway."

Redder got up to leave.

"Perhaps. The links are so obscure that even we don't know much of the story for certain. Okay, see you in the morning at the strategy meeting, and let's hope Holdwick is not giving another presentation!"

* * *

The recycling committee met routinely every month, but they also held ad hoc meetings in between, when the need arose. Sometimes, the meetings were held in Brussels, at the headquarters of the European Steel Producers and Distributors Association; sometimes, they were held in more exotic places. It all depended on the wishes of the members. The ESPDA was a trade association formed to represent and promote the interests of its members. On the face of it, it was a perfectly respectable and legitimate organisation located in Brussels, close to the European parliament and important offices of the vast bureaucracy of the EU. What went on behind closed doors amounted to a price-fixing cartel. It was popularly known by those whose were involved in its secret and illegal activities as *the club*. Participants in club activities acted like members of a secret society. As senior directors of their companies, they were taking huge personal risks. They were breaking civil and criminal laws, and their employers would not be able to cover for them without admitting involvement. In the event of prosecution, the companies they worked for would claim no knowledge and say that their representative at club meetings was acting without their authority. There would be fines for the companies and some very annoyed shareholders, but the extent of the personal prosecutions would probably be limited to those directly involved. They would be left to hang out to dry.

The recycling committee was just one of a number of groups within the club aiming to fix quantities and prices. The name of the committee was a cover name – the members never discussed such mundane matters as recycling cars or old cans. Another important group within the club was the export committee. It talked to companies outside Europe, exchanged price information, and reached policy decisions in important steel-producing countries such as Japan, India, and Korea. Its members were great travellers, and they fed information to the other club committees.

The chairman of the recycling committee was a Dutchman called Theo Henstra. He was young to be so senior in his company, but luck, intelligence, and family connections had all played their part in his rise to such a high office before the age of forty-three. He spoke German, French, English, and Italian fluently … almost as fluently as his native tongue. He opened the meeting by asking the NESC representative for an update on Craig. Redder answered in a weary tone: "No developments except the case is now in the hands of the British police. They seem keen to pursue it for a few weeks."

"And will you be the new representative of NESC on this committee, Tony?" asked Henstra. "We would like it to be you."

"Yes, I will be. Craig was not as senior as you guys, but he was experienced. My CEO wanted me to keep my hands clean. Anyway, that has changed, and there is no qualified replacement working for me."

"Qualified or trustworthy?" asked Henstra.

"Both," answered Redder. "Both, if I am honest."

"Okay," said Henstra. "Understood. And you are most welcome. This is the first full meeting since Craig's death, but I have spoken to all of you privately." He picked up a piece of paper, glanced at it, and placed it back on the desk. "I have also spoken to the Dutch police, to a senior officer who happens to be a family friend. He was quite open in saying they have found nothing in Craig's past that might have provoked this terrible killing. I have a copy of the summary report of the investigation here with me if anyone wants to see it." He paused, looked around the table, and asked Redder, "And you know of nothing leaked by NESC that could cause the police to investigate closely the steel companies?"

"No," said Redder firmly

"Okay. The problem continues, but more in the background. And as time passes, the British police will lose interest. The Dutch police consider the matter dormant unless new evidence comes to light. Let us move on to the main agenda and the upcoming negotiations with Ford and GM."

Most car companies negotiated their supply contracts for steel and some other commodities once per year, starting the process in autumn and aiming to reach an agreement with sellers before the first of January. It was a bitter contest. Buyers had orders to save money year on year, and sellers had orders to improve margins by locking down price increases. For weeks and months, they struggled to reach a mutually acceptable compromise. The days of cosy and corrupt relationships had long since gone, and procurement teams avoided any kind of friendly contact during the negotiations. The aim of the recycling committee was to agree on how the companies represented around the table would bid. It was not just a matter of agreeing on prices, but also on bidding strategy. The car companies had factories in many locations throughout Europe, and each member of the recycling committee wanted a pre-agreed share of the business in locations close to their own factories. That way, they could minimise transport and storage costs. Over the years, the steel companies had become skilful at ensuring each member got a fair share of what they wanted and that prices were higher than they would have been with open competition.

With around fifteen million motor vehicles produced in Europe that required nearly seven million tonnes of steel, the prize for minimising or organising competition was enormous. Over drinks one evening, the members of the recycling committee had tried to estimate the value of their illegal activities. The slightly drunken and boastful conclusion they reached was that they saved their bosses and shareholders at least one billion euros per year. If anyone had asked them who the losers were, they would not have cared that ordinary people paid more for their cars than should have been the case. They thought their duty was to help their employers and shareholders, not the regular folks in the street.

CHAPTER 3

Randall was trying to reread the notes he had taken in France. He was sitting in the quiet of his office with his head thick with red wine following a birthday celebration dinner at an Italian restaurant. The celebration had been for his thirty-third birthday, and Lisa had insisted on taking him to dinner. Why she had chosen that particular restaurant he had no idea, but she was sure to note that it was authentic. Certainly, the noise level was Italian in nature: voices were raised much louder than necessary to hold a dinner conversation. Anyway, Lisa thought it a great place, and he had to admit the fish was good. He had learned from his weight-conscious days of playing football to avoid beer and stick to wine and plenty of water. This time, the water had failed to cope with the wine, three hours of sleep, and an early morning taxi home from the flat of a physically demanding and younger girlfriend.

By lunchtime, he was still not firing on all cylinders, so he decided to go for a walk in St James's Park. The weather was quintessentially English: sunshine and clouds with a strong, westerly breeze. The park was populated with a mixture of serious-looking office workers taking a break from their desks and tourists ambling along by the lake.

At school, he had loved literature and poetry. Putting creative thoughts on paper was to him what opera was to Morse or obscure modern music was to Banks. Thus, he sat by the lake and wrote in the notebook he kept for such moments:

The sun shines intermittently as large, white cumulus clouds scud across the sky and cast fast-moving shadows on the lake, grass, and grey-white Admiralty buildings in the distance. The brisk wind sets the leaves of the ancient horse chestnut trees oscillating like dancers with tied feet. The long, green skirts of the lakeside willows brush the surface of the water. The tops of the ripples on the famous, old lake distort the sunlight like prisms.

He had hundreds of such writings in various notebooks that he had compiled over many years. He had no idea what he would use them for. He enjoyed the moments when he was writing, though, and that was what mattered. When he was feeling down, writing was a form of therapy. He read his words again and smiled. *Not good, not bad,* he thought, *but who can judge?* He quite liked the bit about the willows, so he decided to show it to Lisa. After all, as a journalist, he figured she would have some training in descriptive writing.

New Scotland Yard is located in Westminster. It is within easy walking distance of the Houses of Parliament and the neighbouring main offices in Whitehall. Randall liked working there, and he enjoyed his lunchtime walks along Victoria Street to Westminster Abbey – or in the direction he had taken today, through St James's Park. Occasionally, and usually when it was raining, he visited the Army and Navy Store and wandered around the book and music sections.

On his way back to the office, he stopped for lunch in a quick-service cafe in the back streets, behind police headquarters. He sat at the only available seat on a high stool near a narrow ledge. He chose a chicken tikka sandwich and black coffee. He was facing a dull, grey-coloured wall, and he sipped the coffee while reading some notes he brought with him. He hated eating alone without something to read. Specifically, he hated looking lonely. In the kitchen, music was playing. One of the staff members sang along in a toneless voice to Robbie Williams's *Angels*. It was a song he really liked.

He thought back more than two years, to the one-day conference he had been to in Edinburg on the subject of professional killings. Representatives from across the world had attended, but the conference was dominated by the FBI and their case studies. He remembered the conclusions well: there are many examples of killings by professional teams motivated only by money. It is difficult – nearly impossible – to identify such teams by normal policing methods.

The recommendations from the conference were, predictably, intelligence sharing and the creation of an international task force. He doubted much had been done since the conference. He knew that it would not be until the public became truly alarmed by the number of cases that funding and resources would be made available. There had been two or three high-profile, professional killings in Britain in the last few years, and the newspapers were beginning to show an interest. He had heard talk in police circles of special training for senior officers, but no task force or special squad had been set up yet. He guessed from the files that the Dutch were in a similar position. Indeed, they had showed no special skills or knowledge in tackling the Craig case.

He finished his sandwich and headed back to the office, intending to travel to Penzance the following morning.

* * *

It had upset Susan Robson that she had lost so many of her clients' papers in the fire. There was nothing of great value, though, and most of the important documents could be replaced. Also, she doubted whether anyone would really suffer as a result. Still, it upset her. It would delay business and make her look like an incompetent solicitor. The cause of the fire was thought to be an electrical fault in the roof's wiring. Indirectly, it was her fault for not taking more precautions to safeguard her business. She always advised her clients to have their properties surveyed, yet she had hurried through her purchase without practising what she preached. It was her first setback since moving away from city life. She had given up a promising career in a major London practise to ensure that she could be independent and control her own destiny. She also wanted get a change of scenery after separating from her husband. The divorce was just a few weeks away, and the move to Cornwall was designed to help close that happy (and then unhappy) chapter of her life.

She loved the rugged coastline and remoteness of Cornwall. During the weekends, she and her two boys drove the few miles from Penzance to St Ives and strolled through the lanes to the harbour. Or they went to Sennen Cove and walked along the sandy beach. Or they parked the car at Cape Cornwall and climbed to the headland to watch the waves crash on the rocks below. The boys seemed to enjoy such walks as much as she did, and wherever they went, they knew they could expect a decent lunch on the way home. It was an extravagance she felt was justified because they would chat to her and each other in a mature and relaxed way in those settings. At home, she was on duty; she would prepare and serve, and they would distract themselves with computers, television, and their own rooms. When they were out to lunch, they were focused and well-mannered, and they enjoyed the opportunity to choose their meals.

In general, she was pleased with the move to Penzance, but sometimes she missed the excitement of London. Still, she certainly felt that the family was more secure in Penzance than London. The boys were happy at a local, private school where they prepared for exams, played sports, and grew up fast. She knew that it would only be two years before Mark went to university and another two after that before John went. She felt the hard work of parenting was behind her, and that she could concentrate a little more on herself. She had a quiet but adequate legal practice in Penzance that handled the affairs of farmers, fishermen, and local businessmen. The house she bought in Penzance was far larger than anything she could have afforded in or around London. Close to the main street with a large, sea-facing terrace, it was a fantastic purchase.

Her home made her very happy. She could not imagine anything more suitable for herself or her children. She liked the town, which had once been a fishing village but grown to become one of the main shopping centres for people living in west Cornwall. She did not feel too cut-off from London because the railway from Paddington had been constructed as far west as Penzance and operated with regular services that linked the major towns and cities of Devon and Cornwall to the capital. An occasional treat for her and the boys entailed taking the ferry to the Scilly Isles. On calm days, the five-hour return trip was a real pleasure.

The school organised enough sporting and social events to keep the boys from feeling as if they were missing out on bright lights, pubs, and clubs. The school helped them manage their expectations, and it encouraged the boys to think that the first step was to get to university to have some fun well away from parents.

For Rachel, the remaining question was whether she wanted a man in her life again. She doubted it. *Anyway,* she mused, *Penzance is probably not the best place to bump into the right guy.* She knew she was still attractive to mature men, though. She kept in good shape; she had a pleasant, rounded face; she had strong, feminine lips; and she had rich, dark brown eyes. The big question for her was whether she was attracted by men any more.

Her relationship with Simon Craig had been a disaster. Three months of fascination, lust, and obsession had been followed by three months of misery. He was the wrong man at the wrong time – actually, he was probably the wrong man at any time. Her excuse might have been that her husband had just walked out for another woman, but a man like Craig was not the emotional solution. She had known as much at the time, but she could not control her desire. Age, experience, and responsibility did not seem to help her avoid the temptation of Craig … or the miserable consequences. The speed with which he had dumped her and moved on to the beautiful Svetlana had shocked her. Having met Svetlana, though, she understood how attractive and irresistible she would have been to him. That was some consolation for her injured pride.

The Dutch police visited her because Craig had left a will that she had drawn up. During their affair, she was amazed to find out one evening that he had not even thought about writing a will. She had advised him to do it immediately so that there would be no delays or disputes in the event of his death. Finally, he listened and let her act as his solicitor.

The Dutch had only asked her routine questions. They seemed committed to the idea that he had only written the will because he was expecting to die. They were assuming that he had received a threat or warning and felt it necessary to get his wishes down on paper. They wanted to know her impression of his reasons and attitude at the time he asked for her help writing the will. She assured them he was reluctant. However, because of her wise advice, he had written the simple, one-page document. She convinced them that he hadn't shed any tears or suggested it would be needed in the near future.

The one physical reminder of that relationship was the package of papers he sent her for safekeeping. He instructed her to send the papers to the appropriate authorities if he asked her to, or if he died. He trusted her to know what to do because of her legal training. As soon as she received them – against his instructions – she read them and recognised their importance and potential value. The content made her angry. The papers told the story of highly paid, professional people from very large companies who consistently and knowingly broke international law. It seemed they believed themselves to be among the elite, those who did not need to work within the law. They referred to themselves as *the club*. What was worse, the notes and reports indicated that bureaucrats working in EU organisations had actually helped the club by organising meetings in some developing countries and pretending the club was part of an official trade delegation. Craig's notes also revealed that some EU officials had asked for money from the club to cover the personal risks they were taking with their careers and pensions. Craig named some key officials who had received bribes and comfort payments.

She had lain awake several nights weighing her options. Her final decision was to do nothing unless he instructed her to do so. And then a violent, premeditated, and expensive murder ended his life. Her instincts told her that his death and the scandal recorded in the package of papers were linked. Fortunately, long before the fire, she had taken the documents home and stored them in her private safe. As soon as she heard of his death on the news, her main fear was that Simon Craig might have told someone that he sent her some important papers. She feared that the police or some criminals would come looking for them. The fire provided the perfect excuse for losing the papers. After a few weeks and no incidents, she started to think constructively about how to use the information to her advantage.

* * *

It seemed strange to Richard Randall that an Englishmen would have located his family in France when his job was in Holland. But the climate, the house, the location, the garden, and the swimming pool were good reasons why anybody would put up with the inconvenience and expense of travelling to and fro each weekend. As they sat by the pool, Rachel Craig explained that he travelled all over Europe most weeks, so it made little difference to the family where he lived Monday through Thursday. She had her own interests, and had written two successful books on gardening in different climates. She claimed to be well on with a third about growing vegetables in southern Europe.

Randall and Rachel Craig sat on a shaded, raised terrace looking out over the large, mature, and well-maintained garden. The swimming pool was to the left of where they sat, and the children could be seen playing. There was no need for Rachel to move. She had served tea and homemade fruit cake, and she seemed relaxed and ready to talk.

"He had great plans for this house and was saving to have the work done next year. With the payouts I have received since his death, we can now afford to do everything he talked about and more," she said with irony in her voice. She hesitated, sipped her tea, and carried on: "He said a few times after the children were born that he was proud that, if he died young, the family would be secure. He was thinking of a car or a plane crash with all the travelling he did. NESC were very good and supportive with people flying out here to make sure we didn't have any extra worries during the first few weeks. They were almost too attentive at times." She spoke with a flat, unemotional voice as the children played in the pool noisily. She was a little older than Richard, and she was some twelve years younger than her husband when he died. She looked well and obviously cared about her appearance. She was wearing knee-length cream shorts and a well-ironed, dark blue T-shirt.

"How have the children coped?" he asked

"Very badly for the first two or three weeks because they were very close. His absence during the week made him a sort of mythical hero to them. They would start looking forward to seeing him on about Wednesday, and they would grow very excited by Friday evening. He was kind to them, but they knew who was boss. Children like that certainty in a relationship, someone to respect and admire."

He nodded, remembering that some of his teachers had gained the same sort of respect and then never seemed to have discipline problems.

"The first weekend was awful for them; they did not fully comprehend what happened until that first Friday. I had explained everything to them from the first day because I thought the greatest danger was mystifying his death. It was hard but essential. I took advice from a child psychologist attached to their school, and he supported my approach."

Richard steered the conversation towards a subject in the reports that he had noted with particular interest.

"But he was not Sophie's natural father. Did that make any difference to the way she reacted?"

"It probably made it worse. She never knew her real father – he did a runner as soon as I announced I was pregnant. Simon came along some years later and was a terrific success as far as she was concerned. She knew what it was like not to have a dad around the place, and that made her appreciate him all the more."

"What happened to her natural father?" he asked, wishing to continue the theme.

"It was a student relationship. We lived together in the final year, and stupidly, I allowed myself to get pregnant. I believed it was the real thing. He felt betrayed, cornered, trapped. I don't blame him now, but at the time, I was devastated. He disappeared to America to do postgrad studies and became a successful career academic. His parents were very generous, and they still are. They have plenty of money. As they saw it, their genius son would have been stifled by family responsibilities. But they are decent people and salved their consciences." Once again, she spoke in matter-of-fact tones. The events in her life were stripped of bitterness or any other emotion.

"Do you hear from him, the father?" he asked, making a mental note to have him checked out more carefully than the Dutch had managed.

"No, only his parents. It's all rather Victorian, really," she said as she laughed.

It struck Richard that everything she was saying was related to the children and the past.

"What about you? How are you handling this devastating event?" he asked

"Getting through the worst, I think," she said hesitantly. "I have to keep in control and minimise the distress to the children. If I crack, they crack. In the end, I have been told, I will pay a price for not giving in for a few days and having a good cry. We shall see. I am writing a diary each day about these events that includes how I feel and what thoughts I have. I will reread it in a year or so to see whether it is worth publishing. It could help somebody else get through such a situation. Anyway, writing has helped me."

"Is this a good place to bring up children, for you to gradually try and move on in your life?" asked Randall.

Rachel looked down at her hands and hesitated before answering.

19

"That is a good question to which I do not yet know the answer. The children are settled in school and their close friends are very kind and supportive. In general, French children are less aggressive and more sensitive than English children. Perhaps it is different in Paris or Lyon but in this region, it seems to be the case," she continued thoughtfully. "The boys are particularly charming and usually very close to their mothers and grandparents. But there is a problem of demographics. There are too many young people leaving these farming areas for the cities. Villages like this are under-populated and the numbers are still declining as the old generation of farmers die. However, people moving here from other parts of Europe are helping to change that and there is a quite large and relatively young expatriate community in and around the village. Fortunately, the French authorities are very reluctant to close schools and so the kids enjoy small class sizes and lots of attention from some excellent teachers."

"Unlike England." Randall suggested.

She smiled for the first time and concluded.

"Unlike poor England. Anyway, sorry to be long-winded and to answer your question fully, it is a good place for the children and hopefully they will leave here for University and make their own choices. At this stage, I do not see myself anywhere else."

"Tell me more about Simon please," asked Randall. "Not the saintly father of two beautiful children but the real man."

"That's tough but if you think it will help, I will try to be honest," she said in a gloomy voice. "The trouble is that when someone dies people prefer to remember only the pluses."

"You mean that everyone around was singing his praises and being pious even though you had some reservations based on your close personal and private relationship?"

"In a way. You see it is not only the person and the memories you are mourning but your own situation. Under the surface I hold some resentment that I have been left to cope on my own again. It is made even worse, because it could be partly his fault."

"Rachel, you are being very open. Tell me about him please because it may give me something new to consider alongside all the bland interview reports I have been given by the Dutch."

She hesitated and then began.

"He had a successful career. He did not make the very top but got close to it. He was good looking with eyes that could virtually hypnotise women. He was charming when he wanted to be; he could turn it on like so many salesmen. He had the X factor that women love."

"Do you think he charmed a few ladies when you were married?" asked Randall.

"Oh yes. Right to the end, I think. The company has recruited many ambitious, young, female graduates over the last few years, and from what Simon told me, they were very competitive – they'd do anything to get ahead of their rivals."

"But why are you so sure he exploited the situation?"

"Because I knew him. Because he was always sending and receiving texts. Because he was so self-obsessed"

"What do you mean by *self-obsessed?*" asked Randall.

"Fussing about clothes, preening himself, asking if he looked good, slim, and handsome. If we went to a barbecue or party and there was a pretty woman there, he would start experimenting with his charm to see whether she was attracted to him. It was sickening, and he would boast to me afterwards if one swallowed his bait. So if he did that with me around, what would he have been like at work?"

"Did you ever confront him?"

Again she hesitated before saying, "A bit, but not seriously. I was shit-scared of losing him because he was a good and loving father and provided for us well. You see, Richard, I am a whore deep down."

Richard was dumbstruck, and in some ways, he wished the conversation and ended sooner. Still, though, he needed more answers. "Did you fear he might leave you and the kids?"

"No, not really. Not for a few years, anyway. Perhaps when they were teenagers. I think we were like his foundation on which he could build another life or two without the whole building collapsing."

"Do you think he had someone special, someone he really trusted outside his family?"

"Not sure, but probably there was another me. Apparently, according to the books I read as a teenager, there often is. One loyal, loving wife is not enough of a foundation for this type of man."

"Wow," said Randall, "I have never explored this subject before, and I am shocked. I am also very sorry to put you through this ordeal."

"It is not an ordeal. I have confronted these demons alone and for a long time. It is good to discuss them with someone not close to the family."

"One last question, please," said Randall as he frowned, trying to remember the phrase she had used earlier. "You said that NESC were almost too attentive at times. What did you mean?"

"My turn to be surprised. I thought you missed that. Perhaps you should have been a lawyer," she said with a laugh.

"I nearly was," said Randall. "Please explain."

"They were looking for something. They wanted to know if I knew where Simon kept private papers. I showed them his filing cabinet and opened the safe. I let them look around the house. After a few more questions they seemed satisfied. Sophie told me they also asked her whether she knew where her father hid private things. That annoyed me."

"Who were they, specifically?"

"A guy called Ronald Barker and one of his less sophisticated henchman. Simon hated Barker, and I could see why. All public school accent and false charm – a real creep. Simon told me that the best way to wind him up was to call him Ronnie."

"I have not met him yet, but thanks for the warning. It sounds like they were not sure whether this *something* existed. Otherwise, they would have been more persistent," said Randall thoughtfully. "Probably just checking."

"But what could this *something* be?" asked Rachel.

"Sounds like company documents that they wanted back, but I have no idea what they might have contained. I feel we are getting somewhere, though. Thank you for being so open with me."

"Here come the children," said Rachel with a smile.

Sophie, the eldest daughter, towel around her shoulders, approached Richard tentatively. She was about eleven with curly, fair hair. She was clearly on her way to becoming a teenage stunner. Richard smiled warmly when she asked, "Do you like our house?"

"Yes, very much. It is a beautiful place. I always came to France on holiday with my parents, and I love the countryside, the food, and the warmer weather."

"I don't remember much about England, but I didn't like Holland. Would you like to see our woods? I will get changed and take you there."

"And me," said the younger girl before she rushed into the house after her sister.

Rachel Craig smiled and stated, "Be sure to tell them why you are here. Talk openly about their father if they ask any questions. There are no secrets."

He knew she was right, but he still felt uncomfortable as they climbed a hill behind the house and headed towards a large group of trees. The children called the woods their secret place, and they showed him the paths and fallen trees with pride in their young voices. They named the woodland plants in French and English.

"This was Daddy's favourite place when he was alive," stated Sophie.

"You must miss him, Sophie," he said as a sympathetic statement rather than a question.

"Yes, but they told Mummy that he would not have known a thing, would not have suffered. It is no good to feel sad, he would not have liked that," she said firmly.

He wondered whether her resolve was healthy and natural. Her next sentence convinced him that it was not: "When I am older, I am going to find out why this happened."

"That's my job," he argued. "Your father would have wanted you to get on with your life and not think of something so negative."

"I have to know why. I can't stand not knowing why," she said, starting to cry.

"Don't cry, Sophie," said Amy in a tiny, concerned voice.

* * *

He drove back to the hotel, confused by his own emotions. The children had really got to him, and though their mother had not sought sympathy, he felt very sympathetic towards her. Whether

Craig was a womanising rogue or not, she had been living with the fear and suspicion for years.

He thought about himself and his future. He wondered whether he would ever have children, and he wondered how he would cope with bringing them up.

At the hotel, he ordered a large whisky and water at the bar before going to his room. He knew whisky and wine were a bad mix, but he decided to take the risk.

"I really need this drink," he said to the man behind the bar who smiled knowingly. He was the same man that had welcomed him and shown him his room. Randall wondered whether he also served as the chef.

"What time would you like dinner, Mr Randall? Will it just be you?"

"Yes, just me. Eight o'clock, please."

"I can recommend the beef. The chef will cook it to perfection."

* * *

Later, having changed back into his more casual clothes, he went to dinner. There were only about ten tables in the dining room that doubled as a breakfast room and restaurant. It was eight o'clock, and every table was taken except the one reserved for him. He was the only single occupant of a table. It was small: just one chair and one setting. He assumed it was brought from another room because it seemed out of place. Obviously, they did not want him occupying one of the main tables that were for four or six diners. The menu was in French without an English translation, but he coped. He ordered Roquefort and leek quiche to start and grilled medallions of beef tenderloin in a wine and onion sauce for his main course. His request for the meat to be well-done was met with a nod and a sympathetic look from the waiter. Randall decided to emphasise the point by repeating that the meat needed to be cooked through, not just dark on the outside. The waiter nodded, and a few moments later, he returned with the chef who confirmed the order with Randall. He seemed satisfied that he understood Randall's request and said he would do as instructed. Randall ordered a glass of local wine. The red house wine was the only wine available by the glass. Randall sat waiting for dinner, and he used the time to summarise the main points of the conversation with the family. His official notebook had the complete record, but he wanted to reduce his notes to a single page of salient themes he could ponder. As he skimmed through the detailed notes, he remembered a few words spoken by the youngest daughter, Amy, on the way back from the woods. He had not taken a note of it at the time because he hadn't paid much attention. After all, he was still choked up from Sophie's earlier comments about her father.

He recalled Amy's words by visualising her face: "Daddy is going to come to live with us soon. All the time," she said with a serious look.

Sophie snapped back cruelly, "No, Daddy is dead, Amy. You know that. He will not be able to live with us now."

Amy replied quietly, still not entirely defeated by her sister's logic, "Yes, I forgot. But he said he would."

"She's only five," Sophie said as an excuse for her sister's words.

He made some notes and put a box around the words. *Is that true? What was Craig planning to do? Could he afford to leave a well-paid job with NESC and still rebuild the house?*

The food was excellent, and to celebrate obtaining perfectly cooked beef, he ordered a second glass of red wine. Later, after coffee, he asked the waiter to thank the chef for a superb meal that complied with his request. The waiter rushed off, and the chef appeared with a grin to shake Randall's hand. In fast but clear French, he said, "My pleasure. We get many English visitors, and I like to know exactly what they want when they say well-done. It may surprise you, but I also like my meat cooked through (but without a hint of scorching on the outside)."

Randall then headed for his room, feeling happy with himself and liking the hotel even more. The meal and the charm of the chef were something to tell Lisa about.

He phoned Rachel Craig. He had thought of doing it earlier, but he decided that the restaurant was not the place given the background noise of cutlery and dinner conversations. Rachel answered the phone, and he recounted rather apologetically Amy's statement. She laughed a little and said that her husband often had deep and earnest adult conversations with their children, which he did not always repeat to her unless one of them said something funny. She was certain that he had no hope of retiring from NESC for six years, before he was fifty. Only then could he move permanently to France. She said that the NESC pension fund allowed retirement from fifty onwards, and he had always planned to leave as soon as possible. She suspected that it was wishful thinking on the part of Amy – that *soon* really meant *a few years.*

In a strange way, he felt disappointed. He had hoped he would unearth a small mystery to explore as a result of the conversation, but Rachel Craig's answers sounded reasonable and honest. Before ending the conversation, he told her about the chef and how much he had enjoyed the meal. She confirmed that he was considered by the locals to be a very good chef. She also said that the restaurant was usually full.

He did not completely reject Amy's words, though, because he figured there had to be something in Craig's life to explain his murder. He applied his mind to thinking of ways Craig could have funded a life of leisure in France. He wrote a list: *save, capital gain, win, inherit, defraud, extort, steal.*

He thought back to the files. From memory, there were a few thousand pounds in the bank, some shares, and some worthless share options. There were certainly not enough to retire on. His wife's book royalties were two or three thousand pounds, and the advance on her third book was only five hundred pounds. Those facts did not rule out the possibility that he expected a windfall in the future, but there was no indication where it would come from. He put a ring around the words *extort* and *defraud,* and then he put his list on the bedside table. The two words, he imagined, might explain the violent and expensive end to Craig's life. At any rate, it was something to think about on the flight home.

Before going to bed, he scribbled some lines in his private notebook. He wanted to capture the mood and emotion of the afternoon:

The sun shines, mocking the darkness of her thoughts.
The shadows lengthen as the story unfolds.
They embrace and seem to welcome the gloom in her mind.

The joyous noise of children playing grows faint, drowned out by the message screaming through her words.
She looks shocked at the thoughts she has voiced.
Sadness clouds her eyes. Realisation. Conclusions reached.
No doubts now. Bad man destroyed her family, her hopes, and her illusions.

CHAPTER 4

Svetlana was sitting on the balcony when Susan Robson phoned her. She had been smoking and gazing at the Thames. The sun was setting, but even at ten o'clock in the evening, there was a midsummer brightness in the sky. The call from the Penzance was a welcome distraction.

"Hello, Svetlana, are you able to talk right now?"

"Of course. How is delightful Penzance? How are the boys?"

"All is good. How are you coping?" asked Susan, sounding genuinely concerned.

"Through the worst, I think, but it's not good if I am on my own for too long."

"Yes, I know the problem. I am heading to London tomorrow for two or three days. Can we meet up for dinner?"

"Love to. How about Tuesday around seven?" Svetlana asked.

"Great, I will book somewhere nice and text you the restaurant name and address when I arrive."

"Okay. Do you think we can start to move things forward now, Susan?"

"Yes, I will suggest some ideas when we meet."

When they ended the conversation, Svetlana felt much happier. She wanted to get on with their plans. She wondered where her devious mind came from, and she immediately thought of her father. She knew he had been through tough times, and he had survived and prospered.

Her father was from Russia. He was sent to Cracow in Soviet times as a city administrator. She had no idea what a city administrator did in those days because he would not talk about his communist past often. Svetlana suspected he was ashamed. She remembered sitting and drinking coffee with him in the main square in Cracow; it was a few weeks before she would be leaving for England. An old man approached their table, pointing at her father, and began shouting.

Her father ignored him. A small crowd gathered, though, and the old man got louder and braver. He stood, yelled his family name, and asked her father whether he remembered. Eventually, he neared her father to spit at him. Her father stayed motionless for a few seconds, and then he took Svetlana's hand and led her away quietly.

She asked her father what the man was talking about. His answer was blunt: he had been given the job of reallocating housing, which resulted in some people moving to smaller apartments to allow larger families to have more space. Some people bribed him not to move them or to find something larger or better for them. He concluded his story by saying that the system revealed winners and losers, and some losers still hated him.

In the early 1990s, her father found himself a good job in a bank and became more and more prosperous. Svetlana was fond of him, but she was also careful not to challenge him. He was a proud man with very traditional views about the family. Her mother was a tough and determined Polish lady who dominated the household, controlled the family budget, and organised everything from meals to holidays to boyfriends.

Three years in London had taught Svetlana many things. Often, she compared herself with successful English girls in NESC. She soon learned that she was as good and as intelligent as most of them. When she first arrived, she felt inferior, naive, and ill-educated. Over time, though, she made friends with other Poles, and most said they had felt the same for the first few months. The other important thing she learned was that men found her attractive. This surprised her because she had never thought of herself as beautiful. Inevitably, her low self-esteem got her into a relationship she should have avoided. But after everything, Svetlana found herself reflecting on those early days with Craig and knew she did not regret loving him.

* * *

Randall got up early the next morning. He wanted to make a journey north before heading back to Toulouse and catching his flight home. As a teenager, his father had taken him to the museum village of Oradour-sur-Glane. And when he checked a map in the hire car, he was hopeful that he could fit in a second visit. At any rate, it was no more than ninety minutes from his hotel, and he decided to go. He remembered it as a sad, haunting place: a village where over six hundred men, women, and children were massacred by a German Waffen SS company in the summer of 1944. His father told him that, after the end of the war, the French president at the time had declared the village a permanent memorial, one that should not be rebuilt. Randall recollected grimly the visit to the village church where the women and children were murdered while locked inside. The walls bore the bullet marks of machine guns. The visit was an extremely emotional experience for Randall, which is what his father had intended. And many years later, he was hoping the sight of the homes, vehicles, furniture, cycles, and prams left as they were when abandoned on that fateful June day would help him keep his life in perspective.

* * *

Ronald Barker was not enjoying his holiday even though everything about it was perfect. For the fourth year running, his wife had stayed behind to tell friends and neighbours that he had gone to a conference in America. He remembered how shocked she was when she first found out that he liked young boys. She had hurled insults at him for days, but then she calmed down as if she understood (or at least tolerated) his behaviour. After that, he was allowed two weeks in Thailand every year as long as he maintained the lifestyle she had grown to expect. Besides, she didn't want to spend old age alone or be forced to leave their wonderful home.

He had not risen to the very top of NESC – always the bridesmaid, a good number two. But he was loyal, reliable, and educated at one of England's top private schools before attending Cambridge. Predictably, he was highly articulate and well read, and he was also a good cricketer in his day and still fair at squash. He was known as a nine-handicap golfer who served on the membership committee of his Surrey club. Born twenty years too late, his style was out of fashion. In his opinion, the yobs – clever but crude people from state schools and modern universities – were taking over big companies. Still, he could work with them … and not just in the interest of his pension. After all, he had internalised the merits of loyalty.

But now he was worried that his loyalty had taken him too far into risky territory. The death of Craig had shaken him more than any other event in his life. He knew there was a link between his loyal actions – so eagerly carried out at the time – and the dreadful explosion. He was sure the link was too obscure to be found out, but he was concerned that one of his contacts could be so ruthless. He found it troublesome that he did not know which of his associates had reacted so violently, and he worried that, if other Craigs came out of the woodwork in the future, they would be dealt with comparably. Preservation of one's company and one's reputation was important, but he wondered how far his contacts might go. He hoped the death of Craig would be a sufficient deterrent for anyone else contemplating the same sort of blackmail.

Lying by the pool, exhausted by his nocturnal activities, and depressed by his own depravity, he imagined the slippery slope that he and his colleagues might be sliding down. With half-closed eyes, he saw images of covered heads, cameras flashing, and television reports of their demise. He could imagine jokes at the golf club, his wife's final condemnation, and a picture of his house in local newspapers. His depression grew worse. He called for a brandy from a passing waiter, and as it stimulated him, he switched his mind to positive thoughts about the night ahead.

* * *

It was over lunch on Monday, back in London, that Richard Randall became more committed to the idea that Amy's words had spurred in his mind. He vowed to put more pressure on people who might be hiding part of the story. The trigger for his new position was a startled look, a misplaced question, a laugh of dismissal, and obvious discomfort. The lunch was with Ian Jackson of NESC. The startled look came from Jackson when Richard mentioned his conversation with Craig's daughter. The misplaced question was about the girl's age, and the laugh of dismissal was in response to the answer: five years old. In Richard's opinion, Jackson should have confirmed or dismissed the notion of Craig leaving NESC instead of enquiring about the source of the story. The laugh heightened Richard's interest because it was one of relief. And Richard watched Jackson carefully over the remainder of the lunch as he asked a long series of questions about pension funds and early retirement. He made it clear via his questions that the little girl's statement was in his mind. Jackson struggled to retain complete control of his body language, but his words were perfectly judged.

They shook hands in the restaurant doorway, and Jackson confirmed that he would send Richard a list of the people with whom Craig had worked closely over the last three years.

Jackson hesitated as he turned to hail a taxi and asked, "Are you going to interview them all?"

"Probably. And please get me all the people he has worked, whether or not they're still employed by NESC. The Dutch should have done this, but they seemed happy to speak only to you senior guys." Randall knew his last statement implied there was something to be found out if the right people were asked. He was happy to leave that message with Jackson.

* * *

Back at Scotland Yard, he assigned two officers to research NESC and its directors. He told them to ignore all information published by NESC and concentrate on local, regional, national, and international newspaper reports. Also, he instructed them to talk to city analysts specialising in metal industries and the publishers of trade journals. He then sat at his desk and wrote down a first attempt at explaining the murder based on intuition, guesswork, and imagination. His preliminary conclusion was that Craig was blackmailing someone, expecting a payoff and the chance to retire in France. He decided to work with his hypothesis for the remaining nine days. He vowed to push hard for leads to support the hypothesis, which would enable him to extend the investigation. In the event of failure, he would file the report and hope that new evidence would appear one day to prompt him to reopen the case, perhaps years later. It was a do-or-die approach that might be criticised by another investigating officer, but he did not want to follow the same steps that got the Dutch nowhere.

* * *

Jackson and Redder met in a pub near the NESC headquarters. It was a mews pub overlooking Vincent Square. Jackson had reflected on his lunch with Randall, and he concluded that he had handled it. Still, he wanted to tell Redder about it. They sat outside at a pavement table in an atmosphere full of diesel fumes from passing cars. It was a typical summer evening in London: noisy and smelly and full of commuters, shoppers, and tourists. London came alive when the sun shone. People stood outside pubs and crowded the areas where drinks were served. Some smoked, relieved to be able to enjoy a cigarette in the dry and warm weather. Smoking had long since been banned from pubs, and the remaining addicts suffered most in winter.

"A good thing about warm days in London is the girls," joked Jackson. "I've liked short skirts since the sixties, but it's the top half that gets a better showing these days."

"Yes, there are a lot of stories about you in the office. Seems you are a bit of a lad," replied Redder. "Retailing is the sort of industry you should be in. Full of women."

Jackson laughed, sipped his beer, and shifted his voice to a more professional tone. "Might give it a try if steel carries on the way things are going. God knows how we will ever make serious money. I hear the fund managers want dramatic changes as soon as the new chairman is in place." Redder nodded and Jackson changed the subject: "My lunch with the policeman went okay. He is a genuinely bright guy. Read law at Bristol. Don't understand why he joined the police with his background. Looks as if he's got some funny blood, half Indian or something, I would say."

"I hope our head of personnel is not racist," muttered Redder.

"No, just an observation, just setting the scene," explained Jackson while staring at the backside of a tall, slim girl on the opposite side of the street. Redder watched his eyes follow the girl until she disappeared from sight, and he speculated about Jackson's private life. His name was linked with two or three secretaries, an accountant, and a legal assistant. Judging by his interest in the passing girls, though, they were not enough to keep him occupied.

"No worries, then?" asked Redder.

"Not really. He did pick up something from one of Craig's daughters about him retiring to France soon," Jackson replied in a slightly cautious tone.

Redder became concerned and queried, "Did he read much into her comments?"

"He was interested, no doubt, but the girl is only five. We all know that *soon* can mean anything at that age. He did rather flog the subject of pensions and early retirements, though. And he asked some quite detailed questions," Jackson continued tentatively as he thought back on the lunch with Randall. "He wants to meet some of Craig's old colleagues, and I faxed him a list this afternoon. He implied that the Dutch had not done a complete job."

Redder began to wonder whether the lunch really had gone well – and whether Randall was getting his teeth into something. He knew it would take a clever guy to work out why Craig was expecting to have the money to retire. And he knew it would take more than a genius to piece together the whole jigsaw. He mused, *Even if the murder could be explained, what then? There would be suspicion, but no one in NESC knows who ordered the killing.*

The murderers themselves were described in the papers as professional killers who were unlikely to be caught. Like it or not – and he definitely did not like it – a thorough job had been done on Craig. Five steel companies knew why it had been done, but he didn't know which one had been desperate enough to order a killing. NESC would have paid him off in return for the documents and his silence. Craig's blackmail was simple: he would testify against the steel companies with the huge number of documents he had collected. Indeed, he had evidence of countless illegal meetings that had been going on for ten years. Craig told them that the evidence was with his solicitor. And it seemed that Craig did fear for his safety because he told Redder that his solicitor was instructed to send the documents to the authorities if he died.

Their first judgement had been that the amount he asked for was a small price to pay for his silence. All Craig wanted was enough money to live on and remodel his house. The second and more difficult judgement was whether he would come back for more. It was a risky judgement, but no more risky than refusing his demands and waiting to see what he did. Upon reflection, Redder regretted his and Jackson's decision to involve Ronald Barker. It seemed right at the time because the security department of NESC reported to Barker, and Craig was certainly a threat to security. Barker had insisted on notifying the other steel companies of the decision to pay-off Craig. A few days later, Craig was dead. Redder and Jackson waited nervously for a few weeks after Craig's death, expecting the documents with his solicitor to surface. But Barker was relaxed and tried to convince them that there was no chance of that happening. Curiously, he never disclosed to them the reasons for his confidence.

* * *

Randall looked through the list of Craig's colleagues. Most still worked for NESC; three had retired in their mid-fifties, and two had joined other companies. As requested, Jackson had provided office, mobile, and home telephone numbers. Randall telephoned everyone on the list, including two people on holiday who duly called back after he left messages on their mobiles. He prompted them to talk freely about Craig. He offered a few direct questions – just enough to keep the conversations focused. From these calls, he drew up a short list of people he wanted to meet face to face. He selected for interview those who had been close to Craig and were talkative on the telephone. He was gambling on learning something from their unguarded comments. Time was running out, and he had to take shortcuts.

It was late in the afternoon on the day after his lunch with Jackson that he completed his calls. Almost immediately after he finished, his mobile rang. The caller seemed surprised to be speaking to him, but he introduced himself quickly: "Oh good! Yes, my name is Ball. I understand from a friend that you have been talking to colleagues of poor Simon Craig. I worked for him for years and thought I would contact you in case you tried to ring me but couldn't get through. I just got back from the cricket match."

It was interesting to Randall that Ball was not on his list, and he made a mental note to talk to Jackson.

"What was the close-of-play score?" asked Randall. He was genuinely interested.

"Poor day for England again. All out for two twenty odd," replied Ball

"Another inquest in the papers tomorrow, I suppose,' said Randall before asking him a more relevant question that contained two lies.

35

"Yes, I did try to ring you. Thanks for calling. NESC told me you knew him well."

Ball sounded pleased when he said, "Travelled with him a lot. He was okay to work for. Always under pressure. Not enough orders, too many orders, wrong orders, too low prices, etc. Usual problems for a sales director – you can't win in that job."

"No, I suppose not," Randall said without conviction.

Ball reinforced his point: "No, it is a tough industry. Not easy to make money, and the board members need someone to blame so they don't have to look at themselves."

Randall thought Ball might be useful and asked, "Can we meet, Mr Ball?"

"Yes, I have plenty of time on my hands now that I am retired. What about lunch tomorrow at my club? I will text you the address in a minute."

Randall groaned inwardly with thoughts of lamb and overcooked vegetables coupled with silly, overdone accents. But he accepted the offer, and they agreed on a quarter to one. As soon as Ball hung up, Randall phoned Ian Jackson at NESC.

"The name of a chap called *Ball* has come up in conversation as a close colleague of Craig, but he was not on your list."

Jackson paused, repeated the name, and volunteered to check him out and phone back. Within ten minutes, he called back, full of apologies. "Yes, sorry, we missed him. Don't know why. He was made redundant last year; we had to get rid of him at the first opportunity. He was the old style of salesman – all public school accent and gin and tonics. Became a pain. Lost his licence, drank too much at the wrong times, and insulted a customer at the dinner table."

"Thanks for coming back so quickly," said Randall," I know the type." As he hung up, he smiled at the thought of lunch with an alleged drunk. *It could be a long afternoon,* he mused.

CHAPTER 5

Olga, Svetlana's mother, had been worrying about her daughter for weeks. She knew part of the story, but not all of it. She knew a dear friend of Svetlana's had died and that she was devastated. Svetlana said she could not go to the funeral. Olga assumed that the dead person had been a married man and she had been his mistress, like a character in a Victorian novel.

Olga had seen Svetlana's vulnerability first-hand as a teenager (and later as a university student in Cracow). Too often, back then, she had moaned to her mother that boys did not like her or that her friends always attracted the nice boys. Olga knew the reasons why. She was too clever and too pretty. Nice boys were nervous around her and feared rejection. Bad boys tried their luck with her in their usual direct and conceited manner, but that didn't do much for Svetlana. The result was that she was largely ignored by her male peers. She reached a point where she switched off from everyone, studied hard, and became a model student who received excellent marks and endless praise from tutors and senior academics.

Olga also knew she was extremely proud to get a job in England, but she was very lonely for the first few months. And then, suddenly, everything was perfect: the job, the country, her life. Olga realised that everything became good when a particular man took over her daughter's life and she fell in love for the first time.

Their last conversation on Sunday evening was a new worry for Olga. Svetlana seemed more like her old self and said she was looking forward to having dinner with a lawyer friend. She said that the two of them were very strong and would make some people suffer for their arrogance. Olga had no idea what she meant, but she feared Svetlana was going to get into some trouble.

It had been bad enough watching her husband in his younger days digging holes for himself, trying to beat the system. But his motivation was money to support his family, not revenge. She was worried about Svetlana's fondness for her uncle, Peter. Olga thought he was a wicked man and a bad influence. He was her brother, and she knew he could be ruthless and evil. He had run his department in the secret police in Cracow like a thug, and he surrounded himself with cruel and mindless morons. Since retirement, he had been providing private security for rich people. She suspected his reputation had earned him some very dirty (but well-paid) tasks. He often boasted to her about the money he was earning, and she doubted such large sums would be paid for acting as a bodyguard, merely.

Olga prayed that Svetlana had more intelligence and common sense than her father and uncle, but there were signs she was not as sensible as her mother had hoped.

* * *

Ricardo Denso considered it a job well done. He liked living and working in Switzerland. *It's civilised,* he thought, *compared with Italy.* A well-done job meant he would be secure in his role as head of company security. Although he was in his mid-fifties, Denso liked to think he was just reaching his prime. He could afford expensive clothes for the first time in his life, and he had ordered a top-of-the-line Bentley sports saloon, which he thought would look perfect in a city of wealth such as Zurich. He had a beautiful house on Dolderstrasse that looked out over Lake Zurich. The Dolderbahn funicular was a short walk away. It took him down into the town if he didn't want to drink and drive or high into the hills above the city if he wanted to walk and enjoy the view.

He was a short man with broad shoulders and a round, podgy face. He was a little overweight, he had small eyes, and he had a long noise. Overall, it could be said that he was not a handsome man, but his one redeeming feature was an amazing smile that, when turned on, revealed nearly perfect teeth. His smile could quickly overcome negative first impressions, and it often charmed new acquaintances when combined with his soft-voiced eloquence. His father had worked in a car factory in Turin, fathered five children by the first and only woman he had ever loved, and devoted all his spare time to his wife and family. In Denso's opinion, he was the most decent and loyal man a wife could ever hope for. Denso phoned his parents twice per week and never ceased to be amazed by the enthusiastic way they described their humdrum existence. It brought him joy to think of them. Often, he told himself to visit soon and catch up on family news over a glass of Italian wine.

He met with the chief executive officer quite often, usually when checking for electronic surveillance equipment in the latter's office, car, and home. At times, they talked about personal security for the top men. Occasionally, he attended board meetings and reported on cases of serious theft or fraud that his team had discovered. But that special meeting a few weeks prior had been different and very private. They had gone for a walk by the lake. It was obvious to Denso as they set out in the spring sunshine that the man was worried and would take no risks of being overheard.

"There is an idiot in Britain seriously threatening our company and several others, including his own," The CEO said. "I will give you his details, and you must take it from there. The Brits are tidying up paperwork, and they think we should do the same. I fear they are underestimating the risks; they are not doing enough because they think like bureaucrats. You and I, Denso, must think like gangsters and eliminate this risk. We must stop other people from threatening us."

Denso needed no further instructions, and through a network of intermediaries, he set up an expensive and effective operation. There was no risk to his employers, nothing to trace back to them or him. He had done similar things before in another career back in Italy. It was easier in Switzerland, he had discovered, because people were more professional and secretive. For Denso, it had meant a cash bonus that was nicely hidden in a numbered account. *A few more opportunities like this,* he thought, *and I can contemplate a very comfortable retirement.* Already, he had started to invest for the future, but nothing too grand that would attract attention. First, there was the old farmhouse on Elba, and then there was some land around the house. They were small deals that a successful businessman should be able to afford. The next year, he would do some remodelling using local labour paid partly with cash. It was a good way to lose some money in the local economy and ensure a loyal workforce. Ten years later he planned on having a magnificent property in his favourite place. It would evolve with no show of wealth. But he would be on a beautiful island with a marvellous climate. Security forces would watch visitors come and go; they would protect him quietly. And there was easy access by ferry to the mainland and bright lights if he needed some excitement.

Denso thought about the way NESC had tried to handle Craig. The fire in Cornwall had been a last-minute move by them. That was the British way of tidying up the paperwork. Barker had assured his boss that all that was necessary had been done to eliminate any records. But the fire was a random action with no certainty of success. His boss had wanted to go one step further and eliminate the man.

The British did not know who had ordered the killing from those they had warned of the risk. They were totally horrified, and they probably wished they had kept quiet. But Barker had alerted the big five and warned them to check their files, burn their diaries and travel records, and stand by while NESC bought off their man. Pompous Barker, so typically English, had assumed that everyone would accept his assurances that enough was being done. Not Denso's boss, though – he was not going to risk his company on the word of the British. They were famous for leaks, after all. And besides, blackmailers often came back for more. Easy money is addictive. The event taught them all a lesson. There were a dozen or so men spread around the big steel companies who knew as much and had been as involved as Craig. They needed such a warning to deter them from getting greedy or vindictive. They would be worried by what happened to Craig; they would put two and two together and take heed.

Barker had telephoned all his contacts in Europe a few weeks after the Haarlem bombing: "We had best put our arms around these other chaps and show we appreciate what they do. I am sure they are worried and feel vulnerable after recent events, and we need them loyal and motivated."

"Typical of the British," Denso's boss had said, "full of wisdom based on lessons they should never have needed to learn. Stating the bloody obvious, preaching to bloody Johnny foreigner again. I worked in that country for ten years. God, they are infuriating. They think they are so bloody superior. One good thing came out of it, though: I learned to swear like they do!"

Denso had laughed. He did not know much about them except that English girls had a reputation he wanted to put to the test before he was too old.

* * *

The lunch with Ball was not what Randall had expected. Ball was waiting alone at the bar and drinking orange juice. The club looked as if it had seen better times, and there was a tired look to the furniture and decoration.

"A drink, Chief Inspector?" he asked after shaking hands.

"Same as you, please. Since we are lunching together, how about first names? Mine is Richard," he said. He didn't want his rank to be bandied about.

"Yes, good. I'm Andrew. Scruffy place, isn't it? You will be pleased to know we are eating two doors down the road at a much better restaurant. Can't stand roasted meat and two veg at this time of day, especially if the veg is overcooked. The only reason I come here is morning coffee and the good selection of newspapers in the lounge." Richard smiled and thought, *So much for predictions.*

"How are you enjoying retirement?" he asked.

"Oh great. Recommend it to anyone over fifty-five with a chance of a good pension. Each year gets tougher as you get older. Of course, you know I was given the push. I deliberately became a pain so that they would make me redundant ... with a pension. I wanted out so I played the old-fashioned drunk. It was about the time I collected enough speeding points to be banned. And I would have struggled without the car."

In a few sentences, Ball had painted a very different picture from Jackson's. He looked fit, healthy, and alert. He was tall with grey hair, and he had a straight back that made him look like a retired colonel.

"So you enjoyed the cricket?" asked Randall, wanting to keep the small talk going until they reached the relative privacy of a table.

"Enjoyed the atmosphere and the weather. The batting by England was crap, but it didn't spoil the day."

Ball continued talking about cricket, the weather, and football in the relaxed style of a salesman. He was obviously skilled at finding common ground with a complete stranger. He continued, "There was a young chap called Richard Randall who played in the GM conference a few years ago. Midfielder, highly rated." He looked at Randall with intrigue in his eyes.

"Yes, I played for a few years before joining the police. I'm very surprised you remember."

"Easy. I watch Sutton or Kingston depending on who is it at home or who has the best fixture. Both fairly local. I prefer good amateur or semi-professional football. Real people, not spoilt superstars."

They headed for the restaurant, and when they arrived, it was obvious he was a regular. He was greeted with smiles and handshakes. Over lunch, the conversation quickly shifted to Simon Craig.

"I can't give you evidence nor even a partial explanation, but some background may help," said Ball over his main course. "For many years, Simon was disappearing two or three times a month to meetings held in obscure places throughout Europe."

"Surely that is normal for a sales director?"

"Yes and no. Travel is normal, but he was alone, and no specific entries were logged in his diary. Plus, there were no reports of his visits or meetings, no briefings before he went. In large companies, all these things are normal procedure. If senior people like Craig visit a customer, the responsible salesman goes as well to answer detailed questions and write the notes. Of course, occasionally, there are secret meetings with customers. It can happen if they are being taken over or want their supplier to invest in them. It can also happen if they are in financial difficulty and want help. But that is rare, not something that happens several times every month."

This made sense to Randall. A sales director at a big company would not spend his time selling, especially not on his own. Ball echoed his thoughts: "If we assume he was not out there alone trying to drum up new business, then his mystery trips need explaining. I dug around a few months before leaving the company because I was intrigued by Craig's absences and had nothing to lose at that point if I aroused suspicion. I discovered that NESC had deleted all records of his flight and hotel bookings."

"Interesting. You have some ideas about what he may have been doing?"

"Several possibilities. He could have been making money on the side, selling below the market price and getting backhanders from the happy customers. The only loser would be his employer. I rule this one out because it seems the company also wanted secrecy and must have expected to gain something by supporting his activities."

As Ball explained a whole range of other possibilities, Randall began to realise how murky big business and contract negotiation could be. There was no clear answer, but there were plenty of ideas for further investigation. Of course, Randall could not investigate the company or Ball's possibilities immediately, but he satisfied himself that the motive for killing Craig was a threat to reveal a corporate secret. The blackmail theory held good; he was convinced that NESC| was being blackmailed. The content of Craig's threat to his employers was not as important. It was their behaviour since the threat (and their role in his death) that interested Randall.

When he returned to his office, Richard reflected on how his instincts led him to like Andrew Ball. Of course, he was flattered to be remembered as a footballer, but Ball had a pleasant, easy manner about him, too. There was another quality he could not put his finger on – self-assurance for certain, but it was more than that. He seemed at peace with himself, as if he had achieved his ambition and had nothing to prove to himself or anyone else. Richard doubted that that sense of fulfilment came from a career in NESC. Religion, sport, family, or an earlier career were all possibilities. Richard judged it unnecessary to probe over lunch, but he decided that, if they were to meet again, he would explore the man's past out of personal interest.

When they did talk again some weeks later, Ball's special qualities showed again. Finally, over dinner in London after Ball's return from Egypt, Richard learned enough about the man to satisfy his curiosity and confirm his judgement that Ball had unusual abilities and self-possession.

* * *

Hans Weber turned off the television, bored with golf. He walked over to the sitting room window that occupied the entire wall, opened it, and stepped onto the balcony. He looked down at Dubai Marina and the surrounding construction projects. They were outrageous, ostentatious, and ambitious. Work went on day and night with poorly paid foreign labour working long shifts in the appalling heat. In Weber's opinion, Dubai was an enigma. It was a playground for the wealthy, an international business hub, and a building site.

The ratio of local people to foreigners was unlike anywhere else he knew. Emiratis made up less than 20 per cent of the population. Foreign businesses operating in the free zones meant there was a large community of expatriate middle managers and their families. High-rise blocks with comfortable apartments, swimming pools, and gyms housed the majority of Europeans and Americans. High salaries, tax-free incomes, accommodation allowances, free schooling, and gratis health care meant many people of moderate ability and achievement had status and disposable incomes they could not have dreamed off in their native countries. The rewards for being willing to sacrifice home comforts were high. How they handled the novelty of apparent wealth varied, but with banks willing to lend large amounts at low interest, the car showrooms of the more expensive brands were usually busy at weekends as eager buyers tried to buy happiness. As they paced the showrooms and questioned grovelling salesmen from India or North Africa, they imagined the envy of their friends and siblings back home at the thought of picking up a Mercedes or BMW or Range Rover.

Weber's apartment was on the twenty-seventh floor of The Address Hotel. It was an apartment in a luxury hotel that had been built recently. He looked left, towards Jebel Ali and the cranes of the fast-expanding port. Away in the distance, through the haze, he could barely see the tower of a rope-making factory sticking out of the desert. The tower was close to his beloved Jebel Ali Golf Club, which was one of the first golf clubs in Dubai. He spent two or three hours every day during autumn, winter, and spring there. But the current temperature was too high, and he was getting restless.

For three or more months, the temperatures hovered around 45 degrees Celsius or worse, and he was thus confined to air-conditioned spaces such as his apartment, his car, and shopping malls. He stepped back inside before the heat became overpowering and slid the door shut.

"Why do we stay here in summer, Irina?" he asked his wife.

"Because you are too mean and lazy to go somewhere else, my love," she replied with a laugh.

"Perhaps we should go and see your wonderful family."

"You hate Ukraine. And my family."

"*Hate* is a strong word, and it is not true. I like Ukraine very much in summer, especially the girls."

"You are a dirty, old man."

"If I was not, you would still be working in the bookstore for fifty dollars per week and hanging around gyms in the evening looking for the perfect man."

"Thank you for those kind words," she said with a snort.

The thirty-year age difference was a constant reason to tease each other, but the relationship worked well. Plus, their ceaseless banter amused many of their friends.

"Okay, we go," he said firmly. "I know you are desperate to show off to the bunch of losers you call family."

"Thanks, Hans. They are family and should be respected. We Ukrainians stick close to our relatives."

"Got the message. We will rent one of those wooden cabins on the lake at that place with the fake Spanish galleon."

"Yes, I know where you mean. I will book two weeks starting Sunday," she said, trying to hide her excitement.

"Book the flights to Vienna through Emirates and then Austrian Airlines to your lovely Dnepro. Business class."

"Wow, you are being generous. Sure you don't want me at the back to save money?"

"No, I want you to sit next to me so that I can talk to you and annoy you while you are trying to watch the movie."

Dnepro was his abbreviation for the city of Dnepropetrovsk. With no direct flights from Dubai, they could go via Kiev, Istanbul, or Vienna. Weber preferred the Vienna option with a stopover in an airport hotel and a civilised, mid-morning departure time the next day.

Weber was sixty years old, and he had grey hair and a wrinkled face. He kept himself slim and fit, though. He had to, given how much older he was than his wife.

Despite the testy banter, he loved Irina. He thought she was the most beautiful girl he had ever met. She was tall and slim, and she had long, fair hair and pale blue, Slavic eyes. He met her in a bookshop in Kiev while he was there on business. She was serving at the till, but the bookshop was empty. In short order, they started talking. The next day, after a sleepless night thinking about her, he went back to the shop and invited her to dinner. He enjoyed her wonderful company, and instead of trying to get her to come back to his hotel, he invited her to visit him in Brussels. He promised to book her a room in a five-star hotel and pay her airfare. She feigned mild interest, and they exchanged telephone numbers and e-mail addresses before saying goodnight.

He returned to Brussels and waited. And then, two weeks after their dinner, she e-mailed him and explained that she would love to meet him in Brussels and could take five days holiday (two of which would be taken up with travelling). In what he soon learned was typical, she asked him to transfer to her bank account two thousand dollars to cover her visa costs, airfare, and some spending money. She provided her bank account details in the e-mail, obviously confident he would agree. He sent the money without hesitation and confirmed that he had booked her a suite in the Stanhope in central Brussels.

He met her at the airport, and she hugged him in the arrivals hall like a long-lost friend. He enjoyed showing her the city and taking her to the best restaurants. He found her company exhilarating, and she showed her pleasure by constantly chatting about the places they visited and the things they saw. At every landmark, she gave him her camera and posed for a photograph. Over the three days, he took dozens of shots with her camera. Of course, he told her he wanted to sleep with her; she declined his offer, though, saying that she needed to be convinced he wanted to look after her properly and build a relationship.

Over the following three months, they made short visits to London, Paris, Madrid, and Rome. Each time, he sent her money in advance and booked two rooms in the best hotels. To have the freedom to make the trips, she gave up her job in the bookshop after he sent her the equivalent of two years' salary. During each visit, he hoped she would share her bed with him, but she declined until they got to Rome. He remained calm and patient, however, enjoying her energetic company.

As soon as they arrived in Rome, she announced over a glass of champagne that he had to pass one last suitability test. She called it the sexual compatibility test. For three nights, he was put through his paces. And over breakfast, on their last day in Rome, she declared that she was ready to live with him and marry him as soon as possible.

Five years later, he was a pensioner with plenty of free time and money. He had retired from a long career in the European Commission. His generous pension plus investment income meant he could enjoy a very comfortable lifestyle with Irina. In every job he had in the Commission, he managed to find ways to use his position to earn a little extra. In fact, little extras had become big extras over the last few years of his career. His investment portfolio included apartments in London, Paris, Florence, Lugarno, and Dublin.

His last and most lucrative post in the European Commission had been in the Directorate General for Competition (DG IV). He quickly learned the paradox of DG IV: it existed to strengthen competition under the largely protectionist umbrella of the European Commission. Thus, being too vigilant in the application of competition law (or too puritanical in the interpretation of the law) could work against the interests of the EU. After all, it could be argued that, if the Chinese were dumping cheap products on the EU market, it wouldn't be a bad idea to stop them by going over there and having a little chat. Perhaps a more sophisticated pricing model could be developed; perhaps they could learn how to increase profit and reduce volume. And perhaps they could agree on an acceptable market share and volume target that would leave space for EU producers on a country-by-country basis.

The alternative was to start legal proceedings to have import duties imposed on specific products. Unfortunately, the process of nailing duties on products was slow, tortuous, and potentially damaging to international relations. There were examples of imported products being banned in China as retaliation against duties being imposed by other countries.

Weber had thrived in the paradoxical environment. Big companies would consult him, ask him to arrange secret and illegal meetings, and request that he turn a blind eye to wrongdoing. He was rewarded by companies for not imposing his authority when he became aware of blatant abuses of competition law. Of course, those who did not seek his help – or those were too naive to understand there was an alternative solution to their problems – felt the full force of his authority and the law. Through the uncooperative ones, he built a good reputation as a tough enforcer even though most of the serious breaches of competition law were never pursued.

Despite his success at bending the rules, he was starting to feel the past closing in on him. An old friend still working in the directorate phoned to tell him that the chief of a big Danish company had told the newly appointed head of DG IV that he needed to look closely at the work of Weber. It turned out that the Dane and the new head of DG IV had been to university together and were occasional drinking partners. Weber knew the Dane in question because he had had a serious run-in with him over suspected price-fixing of printing paper. He had been clumsy and hasty in suggesting to the Dane that he could make the problem go away for a fee. By then, he was only weeks away from retirement and looking to maximise his income before he left.

Weber was also haunted by one other event: the death of Craig. He knew Craig well, and he had been very involved with the club. He was deeply shocked that white-collar crime like price-fixing could lead to such extreme criminality. Ultimately, he was becoming frightened. When he thought about the number of products other than steel covered by price-fixing arrangements and the many people involved, he feared the worst. He feared that, one day, word would get out, the dam would burst. He was worried a huge scandal would destroy the reputation of many people, including himself. He imagined the investigations, the show trials, and the long prison sentences as politicians tried to cleanse the EU of those responsible. It would be presented to the public as an aberration that had been orchestrated by a generation of dinosaurs. In Weber's nightmares, he was the scapegoat, paraded through the streets as the last personification of an otherwise-extinct generation of self-seeking bureaucrats.

CHAPTER 6

Back at the office, Randall checked the Internet timetables and selected the seven o'clock from Paddington to arrive later in the morning in Penzance for what he expected to be a wasted trip. The notes the Amsterdam police took during their interview with Susan Robson suggested she knew little about her client. Dinner with Lisa would be fun, but the dawn start to his day meant he would have to persuade her to make it an early night for once. He had never been able to exist on four or five hours sleep, but Lisa always talked about clubs and dancing after the meal. *Overactive something. Overactive everything,* he thought and smiled to himself. He got a strange look from a WPC passing his open door.

He arrived early at Paddington by taxi, and he waited for his platform number to be displayed on the departures board. He was almost always early for appointments, trains, and flights. At times, he envied those who took a more relaxed approach to time, but he continually allowed for unexpected events such as traffic accidents. When he boarded, he found the first-class carriage was empty except for a middle-aged lady struggling with her luggage. He helped her and received a warm smile that suggested she considered such gallantry a surprise. She asked him where he was going, and when he said Penzance, she smiled and said that her husband came from Penzance, but they lived in Exeter.

"Nice place, but not for me. He would go back tomorrow, but I find it too dull in winter and too crowded in summer."

"My first visit. And only for a few hours," responded Randall.

"First and last, probably. You will see everything in two hours."

She stared gloomily out the window as the train pulled away from the platform. They did not speak again until he helped with her luggage at Exeter St. David's station. She thanked him and wished him luck. As they pulled away, he saw an overweight and moody-looking man grab her luggage and charge towards the exit without a smile, hug, or a kiss. *So much for marriage,* he thought and began to reflect on his own situation.

It was a difficult evening with Lisa. At least for him – not so for Lisa who was bouncing with excitement. She exclaimed, "Great news! I'm going to work in Washington for one year on our USA edition."

"Congratulations. I will miss you."

"Don't be daft. We've had some fun, and I'll be able to pop home for the occasional weekend," she stated. Her indifference hurt him, and the whole evening was spent talking about her plans, her ambitions, and the arrangements she was making for the move.

After going to bed beside her (without intimacy, which neither of them seemed interested in), he slept poorly. He kept trying to convince himself that everything would be okay, that absence would make the heart grow fonder. But he also knew the other saying: out of sight, out of mind. He believed the latter would turn out to be true in Lisa's case. A single, successful, pretty girl on the loose in a strange city would soon find a male companion to show her the best restaurants. He would charm her into his arms.

He felt depressed as he contemplated his future over a First Great Western complimentary coffee. His brain told him that he had had enough of that sort of relationship. Because he was in his early thirties and a senior officer, he figured it was time for something more stable. It was perhaps a boring conclusion, but it was probably necessary. His heart was not convinced, but his brain added a career dimension. He feared being labelled a playboy if he did not settle down soon. He knew such a perception could cause problems with or delay his next promotion, so his brain told him not to risk it, to take time and look for stability and quality. It also told him that a good or bad choice could make a huge difference in terms of his image and career. His heart, on the other hand, had a different opinion: he loved the girl and would be devastated if he lost her due to his professional ambitions. The conflict between heart and brain was something to reflect on, he decided, but for the moment, he was agreeing with his heart and cursing his brain.

The train was on time, and with twenty minutes to spare before he met with Susan Robson, he decided to wander around. The railway station was at the end of the line, so there were no tracks continuing west. It was possible for Randall to walk out the back of the station and reach the town centre in minutes, but he chose Wharf Road, which took him along the harbour to Quayside and the embarkation point for the isles of Scilly Ferry. After the stuffy compartment, he enjoyed the salt- and fish-infused air. Memories of family holidays in those easy years before adolescence rushed into his mind.

Cornwall had been the family's holiday destination until Randall started at senior school and had to learn French. After that, his father decided to switch to France. And for several years, they spent the summer enjoying the better weather and food of southern France.

Leaving the sea behind him, he found his way through some quiet lanes to Market Jew Street where Robson had her office. It was the original shopping centre of Penzance. It was charming but not thriving because, he guessed, serious spenders went to the retail park he had seen from the train, a few miles to the east.

He quickly found Susan Robson's office with the help of the instructions she had given him over the phone. It occupied the first floor of a three-storey building. Below was a charity shop; her office was on the first floor. Surprisingly, she seemed pleased to see him. He apologised for needing to go over old ground, and he explained that he had to review the investigation carried out by the Dutch.

"No need to apologise," she said in very definite terms. "I have thought a lot about Simon Craig and those missing papers."

"Missing papers?"

"I told the Dutch police. Don't you know about the fire?"

Over the next ten minutes, she told a story of how the papers had arrived with a letter from Craig, how she had obeyed the instructions, how she had lost everything in a fire at her office.

"You have no idea what the package may have contained?"

"No. In retrospect, I think I should have telephoned him and established what it was he was asking me to hold," she answered. She was lying.

"Did anyone else, other than the Dutch police, contact you about Craig?"

"Only someone from his pension fund," she answered. "Routine questions about whether I was still his solicitor."

"Do pension funds often do that?"

"Never in my experience, but they said it was a new policy of theirs to ensure they had up-to-date information in the event of an employee's death."

"But they could have asked Craig. And how did they know to phone you?" he asked, feeling irritated in the face of her calm acceptance of their enquiry.

"They said that Craig had registered a will with them, that he was abroad at that time, and that they only needed to check my post code and telephone number. They said he had notified them that I was his solicitor."

"When was this?"

"About two weeks before he died."

Randall frowned: "Good timing," he muttered.

"What do you mean? Oh I see. You think there is a connection?"

"How do you know the call was genuine?" he asked casually, trying not to make her feel stupid.

"Yes, you are right. I was stupid; I took it at face value. I did not query the call or question the caller."

"You had no reason at that time. The information you gave was not confidential. It may not be connected." He gave his warmest, most reassuring smile.

"Thanks, but we both know I should have insisted on phoning back." She began to wring her hands and said, "Added to all this, I am concerned about the fire. The more I think about it, the more paranoid I become."

"Why?"

"Coincidences. A day before the fire, my secretary found a man wandering through our offices when she came back from lunch. I was in court, my partner and his secretary were out, and our articled clerk was taking a defence statement at the local prison. This guy was able to walk in off the street. It was careless of us, but he had a good story: he claimed to be a town surveyor checking the fabric of the building. It was a routine health and safety check."

"You say it was a story?"

"Yes. After the fire, I phoned various departments of the town council and county council, and no one knew anything about the visit. They recommended I talk to the police."

"Did you report it?"

"Yes. The local police did investigate (probably quite seriously given the fact that there was a fire), but the answer was what I expected. There was no visit from a legitimate surveyor. In fact, the official inspection is not due for another three months."

"Okay, thanks. This may or may not be important. I will meet with the Penzance police before I go back to London this afternoon. They know I am here because we observe protocol and inform them of visits to their territory," he added.

As if on cue, his mobile rang. Susan heard the following words: "No, I'm fine. Yes, it was on time. No, thanks. As I said yesterday, I'm happy to walk. Well yes, I would like to call in and check a couple of points with you concerning the fire in the main street at the solicitor's office. Yes, that would be helpful, save time. See you in about twenty minutes."

He turned back to Susan Robson and said, "Sorry about that, but they are keen to help. They are going to dig out the file on the fire while I walk to the police station."

"Do you know where it is? Do you need directions?" asked Robson.

"I have a street map with the police station marked, but rather than looking like a tourist, please recommend the best and most interesting route. I am not in a hurry."

He walked slowly along the route Robson proposed, making a slight detour to admire some buildings he spotted in North Parade. The further from the centre he got, the more poorly stocked the shops were. The window displays were old-fashioned and usually tired looking. It reminded him again of family holidays and the excitement of spending long-saved pocket money in similar shops.

The police station in Penalverne Drive was larger and more modern than what Randall had expected. There was something approaching a guard of honour in the entrance hall. It was almost as if the canteen had been emptied to make the place look busy. He guessed that was precisely what had happened. It was much different than a London police station; there, a visit from a senior Scotland Yard officer would be treated with cool indifference.

He briefed Detective Inspector Richmond on his meeting with Susan Robson, accepted a cup of tea, and raised the question of the fire investigation.

"Was it a local fire officer who investigated the cause?"

"No. According to our file, the insurance company insisted on a full forensic investigation, so two experts from Plymouth were called in at their expense."

"What were the main findings?" asked Randall.

"Accidental due to an electrical fault in the roof space. Old wiring was damaged by mice or rats, probably. The roof space was used for storage, so the fire spread very quickly. Blazing material fell from the roof and ceiling onto boxes of files and old furniture in the store room above the office."

Some polite conversation, a walk around the police station, and a cheese and pickle baguette rounded his visit. The desk sergeant was a Londoner, and he remembered Randall as a good footballer. He told his colleagues, and that seemed to interest his partners at lunch more than police matters.

Richmond talked about the good and bad of working in Penzance, and he concluded that they were probably safer and less challenged than most other forces. Other officers agreed, and Randall got the impression that they were a happy group who mixed well socially and professionally. Even if complacent, he assumed they did an adequate job to avoid closer scrutiny from their Devon and Cornwall Police superiors.

Randall walked back to Penzance station despite the protests of his new friends who wanted to provide a car and driver. He then caught the three o'clock train to Plymouth. A senior fire officer met him at the station as arranged by mobile phone, and they chose a bench in the station hall. During the next hour, Randall learned all he needed to know about the problems of detecting arson.

The train to London was far more crowded than earlier in the day, and the ringing of telephones coupled with the loud and facile conversations irritated him. Still, he tried to review in his mind the main points of his discussions that day. The fire officer had confirmed what he suspected: professional arson is very difficult to detect. The pathological arsonist mostly uses crude methods to start a fire, but the professional uses sophisticated materials that can start a fire *and* be destroyed completely by the heat. The most interesting aspects of the fire were the motive and who gave the instructions. To take such extreme action suggested that someone suspected or knew that Craig had sent important papers to Susan Robson.

His mobile phone vibrated in his pocket, and he could see from the display that it was Lisa. She spoke quickly as if she had been rehearsing her lines.

"I treated you appallingly last night – all self, self, and more self. I do care about us."

"Good. So do I." he said.

"But I am so excited about the new job," she added quickly, spoiling everything again.

"I am very pleased; it is a great opportunity. Why don't you meet me at Paddington, I will be there at fifteen past eight, off the Plymouth train. We can celebrate properly."

She agreed to meet him at the station.

* * *

Susan and Svetlana arranged via SMS to meet in the Prince Regent Pub in Marylebone High Street. It was an old haunt of Susan's, but it didn't have any sentimental connections to her husband or Craig. She was staying at The Churchill, which was a short walk away. She considered staying with an old friend, but she decided that they would end up talking about the past and digging up too many old memories that were best left buried. Therefore, she spoilt herself with spa treatments, good food, and expensive wine. It had taken her sometime to recover her self-esteem after separating from her husband and the Craig debacle. She wanted her trip to London to be a statement of her newfound self-confidence and independence.

Susan got to the bar of the Prince Regent first and ordered a gin and tonic. Svetlana arrived a few minutes late, apologised, and gave Susan a big hug followed by a beaming smile.

"Great to see you, Susan. You look relaxed and somehow different from when I last saw you. Younger as well."

"For those complements, I will love you forever, Sveta. My beauty treatments were obviously worth their money. Now have a drink and unwind a bit yourself."

They chatted about their jobs, Susan's children, and the latest celebrity scandals before making the short walk to the restaurant chosen by Susan. She had booked a table before leaving Penzance knowing the place was popular. Svetlana was impressed with her choice and loved the Victorian gothic fire station that had been converted into a very upmarket eating place.

"This gets great reviews, Susan. I don't think anyone can get a table here without booking days in advance."

"Yes, I phoned from Penzance three days ago, and the only table I could get was for early evening."

The restaurant was famous for the attentiveness of its waiters, and as soon as the girls entered, they felt like special guests in a family home. Inevitably, heads turned as Svetlana was led to their table. Susan felt good about herself and enjoyed the reflected glory of being seen with someone so stunning. To her left, she noticed a girl exchanging angry words with her companion. His loaded fork had not moved above his chin since his eyes had first focused on Svetlana's legs. Susan smiled and speculated how their evening might unfold unless he quickly said the right things to reassure and calm his companion.

They ordered their first courses. Because it was a truly classic Italian trattoria, Susan ordered Amarone from the extensive wine list. The waiter complemented Susan on the choice, probably because it was one of their most expensive bottles of Italian wine on the list. But Susan knew what she was doing – she was determined to make it a special evening in celebration of their partnership.

"I enjoyed our weekend in Oxford, Susan. It was a great idea, and it really helped me start to recover from the loss of Simon."

"Yes, it was nice. It was also good to get to know each other and find common interests," replied Susan as she put down her wine glass and leaned forward to look Svetlana in the eye. Svetlana smiled in response.

"We are a strange couple. When I visited you in Penzance, I had no idea you were Simon's ex-girlfriend … the one before me." She hesitated, frowned, and sipped some wine.

"Look, I know we talked about some of this in Oxford, but I was such a mess then. I can't recollect much of what we talked about. What I do remember is that it was good and therapeutic, and I was extremely grateful to you for contacting me after his death. I also recall very well our joint commitment to stir the pot and make some trouble for some very arrogant people. We can discuss that later, but let's cover some of the old ground so that we move forward with no misconceptions about each other's motives and expectations."

"Very well put, Sveta. You are quite right to want to clarify things before we discuss next steps. I will summarise our discussions so far, and if you suddenly remember things or want me to move on, just interrupt."

"Great, Susan, thanks for your patience."

"I really took a liking to you when you visited Penzance. You are great company and a deep thinker. For a number of reasons, I worked out that the man buying the apartment was Simon. The man you described to me sounded like Simon, and you took a call from someone who showed up as *Simon* on the screen of your mobile. There's something I did not tell you in Oxford because I did not want you to be upset about it, but the number you put on the DHL label when you sent Simon's package was your number. I dialled that number to let Simon (or his PA or whoever sent it) know the package had arrived safely. When I entered the number, your name came up from my contact list. Then I had no doubt that your Simon was Simon Craig, my ex-lover."

"That was careless of me," interrupted Svetlana. "If it had really mattered to keep it a secret from you, then I screwed up at least twice."

"Well look on the bright side: we would not be here now if I had not found out. Anyway, I was very impressed by what you told me in Penzance about your take on modern Poland, the Nazi occupation, and the times when the country was part of the Soviet Union. You talked passionately about how the people of Poland had suffered in the twentieth century under the leadership of morons and criminals. But what seemed to worry you most is the behaviour of low-level state officials and bureaucrats when the leadership gave them the green light to victimise, bully, and exploit sections of society. You referred to times in Poland's history when cruel and ill-educated people were given power and uniforms before being let loose. Allowed to break the law and not be punished, to spread fear and suspicion through society, to isolate and demonise certain segments of society, to encourage ordinary people to join the game."

"Susan, stop. Did I really say all that over our dinner in Penzance? I know we had too much wine, but I should remember such a great speech."

"Yes, Svetlana. You summarised by saying, 'That is what happens when the lunatics take over the asylum.' We were slightly drunk, and we repeated those words several times in loud voices, much to the annoyance of the table next to us."

"Well I am very proud if I was that lucid and passionate after a bottle of red wine. Very proud. But these are commonly held views; I was not exactly breaking new ground."

"True, but you also talked about corruption and how it can easily become the norm for everyone in authority."

"Yes, a friend of mine went to university in Ukraine, but no matter how good her work was, she had to bribe her tutors to get the marks recorded. A popular joke in Ukraine asks, 'What does a police officer most want for his birthday? The whole day with a speed gun.' I know Ukraine is an extreme example, but the stories people tell are utterly disgusting. You get the impression that, if there is an honest person in Ukraine, it is just because the person hasn't found the opportunity to be wicked." Svetlana spoke the final words with deep feeling.

"Okay, let's summarise. I got to like you in Penzance. I very much liked your opinions about people in authority and corruption. I knew of your relationship with Simon. Simon died, and I felt very sorry for you. The mistress is usually alone and must keep her head down. You did not seem the type to turn up at a funeral and announce yourself. I let the dust settle and contacted you. The next part of the story is set in Oxford with you in pretty poor shape."

"You explained to me in Oxford the significance of Simon's papers. *That* I remember. You also admitted that part of the reason for meeting me was to see if I was a potential ally in a complex battle you wanted to fight. We need to go over this again, but I know I agreed to be involved, and I can think of no reason to change my mind. Convince me again – as you must have done in Oxford – and we will be a team."

"Thanks, I will try. As you know, I trained as a lawyer. In my opinion, if the educated professional classes in Europe start to think and act as though they are above the law, we are heading for serious trouble. We saw it happen in banking. On top of this, if the highly educated senior officials of government departments aid and abet (or turn a blind eye, as they probably did with banking), then we will become no better than Ukraine." Susan stopped, drew a breath, sipped her wine, and carried on: "Corruption and blackmail inevitably become part of the picture. Simon's papers name corrupt officials and describe what they did. The technically correct action for me as a lawyer and good citizen would be to take the evidence to the competition authorities, but I am sure the whole matter would be swept under the carpet."

Svetlana nodded in agreement and said, "And the evidence, without Simon as a witness, would not be taken seriously."

"For sure. Too many senior officials involved, and if the whole story came out, the credibility of the directorate would be destroyed. My objective is to strengthen the evidence, show steel is the tip of the iceberg, and prove that many other producers are playing the same game with their precious merchandise. I want to turn at least one senior official from DG IV to our side and tell his story. I want at least five Simon Craigs from different industries to turn to our side and beg to tell their story before they become criminals. I want the whole scandal to start in an American newspaper so there can be no cover-up." Susan stopped talking, leaned back in her chair, looked at Svetlana, and grinned. "Let's relax now and order some desserts and a suitably sweet white wine to go with them." She then gestured for a waiter.

They sat and discussed the food and the people at other tables. The couple Susan noticed earlier had left, but they seemed to be on friendly terms. Presumably, the man had made his peace or eaten humble pie.

Over coffee, Svetlana affirmed her commitment in the Russian style by banging the table with her wine glass. She drew attention from neighbours, checked herself, and then announced in a quiet voice, "We must have a really smart plan and put some trusted people between us and any front line action. Cheers, Susan."

CHAPTER 7

Lisa was looking forward to an evening with Richard, and she was pleased to take a taxi to meet him. She always considered Paddington the most romantic of the big London railway stations. The interior of the station had been greatly modernised and was populated with shops and fast-food outlets, but the shell of the building was largely unchanged from the original design by Isambard Kingdom Brunel, the mighty Victorian engineer.

As she walked from the taxi drop-off point and entered the main building, she imagined the tragic stories and relationships that must have ended on the platforms during the two great wars. She then noticed the little statue of Paddington Bear. Her dad had bought her a Paddington Bear from the small souvenir shop when she was about six years old. She still had the bear and its label: "Please look after this bear." But she did not have her dad anymore. He had gone too soon, like those servicemen who caught trains from Paddington to nowhere.

Lisa had studied modern history at university. In her opinion, her best work was on the period that spanned from 1890 to1920. She was fascinated by the First World War and the changes that took place in society during and after those fateful years.

Lisa had read that Paddington station had received wounded soldiers returning from the trenches of the battlefields. They had been laid out on stretchers along the platforms as they were offloaded from the trains. From there, they went to London hospitals. There was hopeful and hopeless waiting as volunteers handed out tea, cigarettes, and a few cheerful words.

She never ceased to be amazed by the decisions of politicians that led to the mindless waste of that war. As a historian and political journalist, she had grown to dislike most politicians and their power-seeking, attention-seeking ways. She once described to Richard, half-jokingly, their behaviour as so many seedy characters masturbating in public in the name of democracy. She considered the First World War to be the ultimate car crash, and the political leaders and dinosaur military leaders were the only ones to blame.

Lisa knew she had been cruel to Richard – or at least inconsiderate. There was no doubt in her mind that she loved Richard, and she saw no reason why their relationship could not survive the separation. She was flattered by his disappointment at the news. He had been shattered for a few minutes before regaining his composure, putting on a brave face, and saying all the right things to congratulate her. But she sensed Richard had another problem with her news that concerned the meaning and direction of their relationship. She guessed that being a single man would very soon play against him in his career. It was difficult for her to accept in the twenty-first century, but she acknowledged that journalists were a breed apart, and journalism was one of few careers that did not necessitate conformity.

He had not proposed to her in the two years they had been together. She suspected he had not made a move because, early in their relationship, she made it clear that marriage before thirty was not in her life plan and that she wanted children as late as possible. It seemed that, rather than face rejection, he had ignored the subject and left the ring in the jeweller's window.

The arrivals board updated, and she moved closer to platform eight, where the Plymouth train was expected in ten minutes. *More time to think,* she mused. Her instincts told her that they had reached a critical point in their relationship, that the discussion over dinner could become very negative if she was not sensitive to his needs and plans. *Perhaps,* she thought, *engagement would be a good compromise between his desire to be more settled and my desire to wait. Many pluses and not too many negatives ... assuming the terms are properly defined.* The critical term for her was that she could move to Washington. In her mind, marriage could wait for at least one year. She smiled to herself as she decided that she would propose to him that evening, as soon as they had their first glass of champagne. She pulled out her mobile and rang their favourite restaurant. She confirmed their table booking and ordered a bottle of the house champagne to be put on ice.

* * *

The next morning, Randall got to the office early to review the research on NESC. There were plenty of press cuttings and reports by financial analysts. NESC was a publicly quoted company, so there was commentary and opinions on the performance of the company and the people running it. The two officers assigned to the task sat opposite him. Wendy Thomas took the lead:

"We have found three themes that run through everything we have read, and all three could be important negatives, but we believe the third one we will come to is the most significant."

She had a firm, concise, formal style of speaking. She spoke as if she were giving evidence. Her stern, unsmiling face was consistent with her voice. *Not much charm,* thought Randall, *but she seems very competent.*

"The first is about safety in the steelworks. They have had some very bad press. Too many avoidable accidents. The internal enquiries were handled badly according to the reports. A number of fines by the health and safety authorities. The second is about their financial situation. High borrowing and low profits that lead to questions about whether they can survive. The third is slightly more obscure and relates to rumours of NESC and other steel companies being involved in serious breaches of competition law."

"Price-fixing cartels?" Randall interrupted.

"Yes. Sophisticated and long-running cartels."

"Do we know where the rumour came from?"

"Yes. A personal assistant of one of the senior directors of a French steel company went to the newspapers with a story about her boss. They had had an affair that ended when he dumped her for another mistress. So it was a case of hell, fury, and a woman scorned. She claimed to know all the details of something known in steel industry circles as *the club*. She named the companies involved, including NESC. She had dates, meeting places, copies of travel documents, and meeting notes she had typed for him. She took it to a French newspaper and got some coverage. As a result, the matter was referred to the Competition Inspectorate. It is their job to stamp out anti-competitive practices within the EU or by EU companies operating elsewhere. Nothing was heard after that, and we can only assume they investigated her claims and found nothing."

Randall was desperately trying to remember a lecture he had attended at university as he spoke: "We covered competition law at university, but very briefly. I doubt I spent more than two hours on the subject. But from memory, I think it can involve criminal prosecutions. I think they told us that things known as hard-core cartels are considered the most serious form of anti-competitive behaviour."

"Yes, sir, that is true. We checked on the Internet, and individuals can get long prison sentences and unlimited fines for being involved. The types of cartels they hit hardest are ones that involve price-fixing, market sharing, and production quota-setting."

"But aren't there are also penalties for the companies who send their employees to these meetings?" asked Randall

"Up to 10 per cent of worldwide turnover."

"So for NESC, we could be talking several hundreds of millions?"

"Yes. But it gets worse: customers can make damages claims if they believe they have suffered from higher prices as a result of the cartel. The damages are limitless and are determined by the courts. Imagine if NESC ended up in court in the United States with a huge damages claim to defend. There would be little sympathy because anti-trust laws are strict and strongly imposed by judges there."

Keiron Walker spoke for the first time: "And there is the issue of loss of reputation for the company and its board members. The problem seems to be that, while the EU and our own Office of Fair Trading are trying to crack down, they are not bringing many cases to a conclusion. The difficulties are obtaining good evidence, the time it takes to prepare the case, the time it takes to hear the inevitable appeal, and the process required to collect the fine. Usually, it all takes years. So *under investigation* is a far cry from *brought to justice*."

Randall thanked the officers and ended the meeting. He sat back and reflected on the new information. He needed to talk to Ball again – he knew something strange was going on, if not the details. Whatever Craig had been doing, it seemed to have the support of NESC. And if not the support, according to Ball, they had been prepared to cover his tracks and hide his role. Another conversation with Ball seemed like a logical step to try to get the man to speculate further on what Craig's role might have been.

He was also aware that he was neglecting another line of enquiry; he needed to know more about Craig's sex life. Craig's wife had given him a pretty clear picture of the type of man she had married. He needed to follow-up and find out whether there was another important relationship. It was clear from the files that no one had looked into his sex life. He wondered, *Perhaps an angry husband decided to get rid of him. Perhaps the case was simply one of jealousy and revenge.* He doubted it, but finding out whether there was another significant woman was also a logical step to take. He thought another strange feature of the Dutch investigation was that there were no interviews of Craig's male friends. Randall assumed Craig would have one or two close friends or drinking partners, but as far as he could see, no one had made contact with them. It was another subject to discuss with Ball.

* * *

Ball's home number was answered by a machine with a message stating that he was out of the country. The message said that he could be contacted via another number, and Randall dialled that one.

"Helen Daniels speaking. How can I help?" said a young, friendly voice.

"My name is Richard Randall, and I am hoping to contact Andrew Ball."

"Hello, Mr Randall. Mr Ball is away for a few weeks on a special assignment."

"A special assignment? For whom?"

"Oh I'm sorry Mr Randall, you have come through on my direct line. You probably don't know that this is NESC. Mr Ball has kindly agreed to help us with a special project in Egypt."

"How exciting for him," said Richard unenthusiastically. "May I ask what you do at NESC?"

"Normally, Mr Randall, we don't talk so openly on the telephone, but Mr Jackson said you might ring. I am Mr Jackson's PA. He asked me to brief you if you called. He knows you met Mr Ball and might wish to follow-up. Would you like to speak to Mr Jackson?"

Headed off at the pass, thought Randall as he politely declined to speak to Jackson. There was no doubt Ball was on some highly paid expatriate package to add to his redundancy payout and company pension. The fact that he had accepted the job, packed his bags, and left the country in only two days suggested he had been keen to oblige. He called Wendy Thomas and asked her to check for Andrew Ball on recent flight lists. *I'm not just going to take the word of the NESC people,* he thought. She returned his call in twenty minutes: "No Andrew Ball travelled to Egypt or any other destination in North Africa from any UK airport."

He phoned his new friend, Helen at NESC, and asked to be put through to Jackson. After a few polite words of introduction and having stated that there were no new developments, he raised the question of Ball's whereabouts.

"Helen very kindly offered to put me through earlier, but I was already late for a meeting," he said to Jackson.

"No problem. What did you make of Ball?"

"He certainly was not what I expected. Much more professional," he began and then added, "sober."

"No, quite right. I did some checking after you first mentioned him, and it seems he was acting the fool because he wanted to leave with a redundancy package. Quite a talented bloke by all accounts, but he was totally fed up with his job. It happens all too often with people in their late fifties, early sixties. Such a waste for the company." Randall admired the skilful build up to the punchline.

"We needed some help in Cairo. A project out there has gone off the rails. Stocks of finished goods laying everywhere, and no one is selling it fast enough. Just the sort of thing to suit his talents. And the money we offered for a six-month contract was good."

"He must have been keen to help because he seems to have left quickly. When did he fly out?"

Jackson laughed and replied, "He bloody well drove. Just got his licence back and wanted to give his new MR3 a good outing."

"So you have to wait a while before you get your man to Cairo. I thought it was urgent?" Randall asked, suspecting that Jackson was happy that Ball was out of his reach and that there was nothing urgent to be done in Cairo.

"Well beggars can't be choosers, I suppose. Seems crazy to me, but he has promised to start work in eight to ten days."

"Long and tiring drive, though – even in a BMW."

"Easier than you might think, apparently. Ball planned to drive to Naples and then take a ferry to Tripoli via Catania and Valetta, and then he'll be close to Cairo by road."

"Sounds quite an attractive option if you have the time," commented Randall. "Obviously a keen traveller."

"Yes, he said he had travelled the world in his career and never seen anything. He wanted to do it differently this time. It was really a condition he imposed, but we were not unhappy to pay his costs. It probably won't be much more than the price of a business class ticket."

"Good. Well let's hope he enjoys himself," said Richard.

"Anything you wanted from him that I might be able to help with?" asked Jackson in his usual, smooth style.

"No, daft really," lied Randall. "Andrew had an old school friend who was my football coach ten years ago. We are still in touch, and I promised to let Andrew have his address."

"E-mail it to Helen, and she will pass it on gladly," offered Jackson, not believing a word of Randall's story.

After he hung up, Randall sat back in his chair to take stock of the case. After a few minutes, his mind started to drift in the general direction of Lisa. Specifically, he was mulling over their dinner the night before. He had never been a great fan of champagne, but he enjoyed it sometimes as an aperitif. The night prior, he had nearly choked on the bloody stuff when Lisa calmly proposed to him. He was on his second glass, starting to relax after the trip to Penzance, and she said, "Richard, I have been thinking." This worried him because she usually called him Rich. "Perhaps we should put our relationship on a semi-formal footing."

"Meaning?"

"I think we should get engaged."

He was speechless for a few moments, and then he smiled broadly, grabbed her hand off the table, and put it to his lips.

"Brilliant idea, but I should be the one doing the proposing."

"Come on, Rich, this is the twenty-first century. Women should have equal rights, including to propose."

"Okay. I accept gratefully. Now we must celebrate and finish this bottle."

"Great. However, there is a term attached to my proposal, and that is that I go to Washington and spend a year proving myself before we get married."

"It's a deal," said Randall.

A noise outside his door brought him back to the present. He knew he had to choose an engagement ring, something really special. *I can afford it,* he told himself, *because my income far exceeds my outgoings for the first time in my life.*

He thought about his mum and how her parents had been horrified when she told them she had met and Englishman at University and they wanted to marry. Randall's Indian grandparents had nothing against the English and enjoyed living in London but they still had some kind of hang-up about mixed race marriages and particularly the religious implications. Randall's grandparents had only met twice before their wedding day and had no choice but to make the best of an arranged marriage typical of their culture. In fact it seemed to have worked well for them, and as they got older they gave the impression of becoming closer and closer. Although they accepted their daughter should make her own choice of husband, they did not want her to marry outside their faith. Putting the wishes of her parents aside, Randall's mother had gone ahead and married an Englishman. The Grandparents did not speak to her for several years but when son Richard was born, they had relented, forgiven and doted over the baby.

He had once asked his dad whether he had ever been confronted by racial abuse or innuendo concerning marrying an Indian. His father had replied that his mother was so beautiful and petite that everyone just admired her and envied him. Randall doubted that was the whole truth considering attitudes in Britain thirty-five years earlier, but it was an admirable and dignified answer.

His father had read medicine at university before becoming a hardworking and prosperous general practitioner in Hampstead, which was a few miles north-west of central London. He loved cricket and spent his spare time in the summer watching county matches at Lords or the Oval and test matches on television. Richard suspected his father had been a little disappointed when football rather than cricket became his son's preferred sport.

Thinking of his father reminded him that he should visit his parents at the weekend and break the news of his engagement to Lisa. He knew they would be happy because they had met her many times and fussed over her as if she were already part of the family. Their only disappointment would be the wedding. However modern their outlook, his parents would not understand her moving to Washington and leaving him behind. They would expect the wedding arrangements to start immediately. Nevertheless, he looked forward to breaking the news, and he hoped Lisa would go with him and explain the Washington angle from her point of view. He figured she could probably convince them it would be a good career step. Careers and ambition they understood, but they also believed in togetherness and family. Their minds would agree with Lisa, but their hearts would not.

He was very happy, but he did not expect plain sailing with Lisa. The year away would be tough for him, and he feared a time of highs and lows. With the lows would come periods of depression that would cling to him like autumn fog before something positive from her would swing his mood away upward. And then his energy would return, and the world would again seem bright and joyous.

CHAPTER 8

A few kilometres south of Limoges in west-central France, Andrew Ball called Rachel Craig using his newly acquired SIM card. He pretended to be on holiday and told Rachel that he would passing near their home on the way to Biarritz. He was confident of an invitation to the house even though he had only met her two or three times. She seemed delighted to hear from him, and without hesitation, she offered dinner and a bed for the night. He smiled to himself as he put the mobile back in his shirt pocket. NESC had no idea that he had already deviated from the travel plan discussed with Jackson. And just in case they had a means of tracking his credit card usage and bank withdrawals, he brought plenty of cash with him. For the next few days, he planned to avoid leaving any obvious trail.

He thought back to his meeting with Jackson. *Pathetic that such a senior man could be so transparent. The offer was ridiculous. The terms so flexible, the money so generous.* Contrary to what Jackson may have intended, it had hardened his resolve to find out more about the reasons for Craig's death. NESC believed they were covering the risk that he had seen enough when working for Craig to piece together the whole picture. They wanted him out of the way for a few weeks until Randall gave up on the case.

Jackson had hardly hidden his anxiety regarding Ball's lunch with Randall. For his part, he invented a version he knew Jackson would like: "We talked a lot about football and cricket, and when he pushed me, I suggested that Craig may have been taking backhanders from customers. I raised some suspicions, but nothing very specific." He believed telling Jackson a half-truth would be more acceptable than reporting nothing. Jackson sounded pleased, and Ball wondered whether Jackson would adopt the same theme with Randall and with his NESC colleagues. Everybody would be happier if Craig's murder could be partially justified or rationalised as revenge by fellow criminals. It angered Ball that he may have triggered something that

Jackson could develop – probably as a whispering campaign – in order to blacken Craig's name.

Ball was starting to regret that he had not been more direct and honest with Randall, but he knew that Randall would never be able to build a case against NESC. Ball was certain that NESC would not have had any direct involvement in the car bomb. The murder was Randall's interest and responsibility, and when Randall finally admitted to himself and his superiors that there was no evidence to identify or convict the bombers, the case would be filed. Ball, however, had his own agenda. And he had no intention of giving up until he knew what had caused people to hire expensive hitmen to take care of an apparently unimportant colleague.

* * *

Rachel Craig was looking forward to seeing Andrew again. He was a decent guy in her mind, one of the few people her husband had really liked and respected. Simon once said that Andrew was strangely vague about his life before NESC. She remembered him saying that Andrew seemed not only better educated, but also more rounded, more confident, worldlier than one would expect from a person who had joined the company from a government department. A number of times, Simon had been amazed at Andrew's knowledge of places. Simon had speculated as to how someone who said he had spent twenty boring years in the Ministry of Agriculture could be so at ease in some of the more obscure cities of Eastern Europe. Simon had also been devastated when Ball started to play up. He had guessed Ball wanted early retirement, but he felt let down by him. Out of interest, Rachel considered probing him a little over dinner and trying to understand why he had not simply asked Simon to arrange redundancy. After all, he was his boss.

The motorway ended just north of Cahors. A sign stated that, in three more months, the new section to Toulouse would open. For the moment, though, Ball had to endure a slow crawl along country roads that meandered around the city of Cahors before heading through vineyards in the direction of Agen. He drove quickly on the open road, slowing only to pass through the small villages. Everything was quiet. In one village, the tabac was open. Several people were standing outside and talking. In another, there was no more sign of life than a dog sleeping in the shade of a white, stone building and a tractor returning from the fields. Tall, plain trees lined the roads, and their thick leaves caused the sun to strobe – one fraction of a second, the sun dazzling him, the next, he was shaded. The last fifty kilometres of bends and hills enabled Ball to enjoy the BMW. Constant gear changes made it a perfect experience. *A real contrast to the boredom of the motorway,* he thought.

He arrived exhilarated and ready to charm the family with some well-chosen gifts. He made a big fuss of the girls, handing out English-language magazines and novels thoughtfully purchased on the ferry. He was an instant hit, and to confirm their new devotion, they insisted he sit between them at the dinner table. He knew from his own experience as a parent that the way to a mother's heart was through her children.

"It's Anglo-French cooking here, but the wine is genuine," said Rachel with a laugh as the children directed Ball to his chair. "And thanks for thinking of us and calling by. We all speak good French, but it is nice to be able to relax into English occasionally and hear about things in England."

"My pleasure. This is a wonderful place to start my holiday, and I am so pleased to finally meet the girls."

The girls giggled and wriggled their chairs a little closer to him.

* * *

Ricardo Denso looked at the e-mailed transcript of the short conversation. He was sitting in his office in Zurich. It looked ordinary enough: an English friend calling on his way through France. Clearly, she had been pleased to hear from him and knew him well enough to invite him to stay. But Ricardo Denso was ever vigilant; he took nothing at face value. Often, he wasted time and money, but more often, his caution paid off. He was intrigued that the incoming call had been made from a French mobile number. It was possible that a holidaymaker would buy a SIM card upon arrival in France, but that probably meant he had removed his normal SIM card and was out of contact with colleagues, friends, and family. Of course, he could have bought a new mobile in France and kept his usual one active.

Perhaps he even had a phone with two SIM cards. Denso did not have the answers, but he was unhappy.

He called the Bordeaux-based security company he had employed to tap Rachel Craig's telephone. He wanted to know whether Ball had bought or rented a mobile in the last couple of days. He knew the name of the visitor from the transcript because Andrew Ball had had to introduce himself. But it was the behaviour of Mr Ball that interested Ricardo Denso. *Easy stuff,* thought Denso, so he asked for an answer within two hours. He also asked that a call list be available every morning for as long as Ball's number remained active.

* * *

"It's a wonderful place, Rachel. Simon was a real bore about France, this house, and the children. I understand why now." The children had gone to bed, and it was quiet on the terrace. With no street lights for miles, the stars were bright against the black sky.

"Yes, it is. At first, after Simon's death, it lost its magic. We wondered whether we could cope with staying here given all the memories. I am pleased we did. The first piece of advice I would give anyone in a similar situation would be to embrace the emotions, don't try to escape by a change of scenery. That's doubly true if children are involved. They need the security of their school and the support of school friends."

They sat up late into the evening discussing the possible and probable causes of Simon's death. Some of it was speculation. By midnight, after several cups of coffee, glasses of wine, and precautionary swigs of Evian, they were no further forward.

The next day offered a fantastic morning. The sky was clear, but it felt chilly until the sun started to rise over the foothills. And then the heat brought a sense of anticipation of another summer day. Andrew Ball was showered and dressed by half past seven. Rachel took the children to school soon after. As they left, there was much hugging and many promises of a rapid return. The children were driven away smiling and waving. Andrew sighed. He believed that an enduring image had locked itself away in his mind. He knew that, in the future, if he thought of Simon or Rachel or that house in France, he would imagine the children waving through the car window. A strange melancholy spread over him, but he did not know why. *Maybe I just miss family life,* he thought, *the energy children bring to a house and garden. There's the constant awareness a parent is forced to have when young children are around.* Of course, there's stress, but there's also fun and humour and sorrow and fear. Take all that away, and nothing in the future can compare. Ball buttered some toast, poured hot water on some coffee granules, and took his breakfast onto the terrace. He found shade, and he sat and ate and drank and thought.

During their discussions the night before, they concluded that Randall would not get much further with the case. They agreed that it was important to be realistic, that catching the killers was not of particular importance to Rachel. She said that she felt a constant unease, though, due to not knowing the reason he had been killed. In black moments, she imagined Simon had been involved in serious crime and punished by fellow criminals. His image and memory was tarnished because someone had paid to have him killed. That plausible fact seemed to associate him with criminal activities.

"I would like to know the truth for my own peace of mind," she said, "and to be able to tell the children a balanced story when they grow up. At the moment, I feel a bit like someone who received a telegram that read, 'Missing. Believed killed in action.' It doesn't provide closure. Something is left nagging away."

When she returned from dropping the children off, Ball had finished his breakfast and was putting his overnight case in the car.

"Andrew, can I ask you a personal question before you go?"

"Of course," said Ball. "Try me."

"What did you actually do before joining NESC? Andrew did not believe your CV. He thought your background was probably more interesting than twenty years in the Ministry of Agriculture."

"Why did he think that?"

"He said you seemed to know your way around one or two Eastern European cities you visited together. And on one occasion, he was sure you understood a notice in a railway station even though it was written in Cyrillic."

"Very observant of him," said Ball with a laugh. "I obviously blew my cover. But seriously, I was sponsored by the Army to study Russian at university. After I graduated and was commissioned as a junior officer, I was selected to work in military intelligence. It was the height of the Cold War, and Russian speakers were a rare commodity. It just so happened that I liked the language and achieved a high level of fluency."

"So how did you end up a salesman in NESC?" asked Rachel, intrigued by his story.

"NESC back then was one of many state-owned companies. A few of us were placed in these government-run companies because it gave us a perfect cover story. We were able to travel on business trips to foreign countries, attend conferences, and join delegations to almost anywhere … including parts of the Soviet Union. There was another problem around that time: too much information about our intelligence activities was being leaked to the Russians. By becoming detached from the intelligence organisations and working in companies like NESC, we hoped we would disappear off the Russian radar. Once we were placed in companies, our links back to our old intelligence departments were only through a newly created and independent third-party organisation based in a university that appeared to do innocent research."

"Oh so you were a spy?" asked Rachel with an astonished look on her face.

"Gathering intelligence was very important during those times and, it came from many different sources, including from agents in the field. The military always thought the cold war would end only after an armed confrontation. But here and in America, there were enlightened politicians, influenced mainly by academics, who thought the end of the Soviet Union would be caused by economic factors."

"*Enlightened politician* sounds like a contradiction," said Rachel with a laugh.

"Perhaps," replied Ball, "but I met a few thoughtful guys who were influential behind the scenes on defence and intelligence committees. The trouble with politicians is that they often play at being the man in the street, but most of them are very well educated and certainly not from the street. Attitudes are not helped by the atmosphere around the House of Commons. It's a cross between a private school six form and an elite club. Many MPs develop and then project an image that fits well in that club but looks facile to the general public."

"Sorry, Andrew, I should not have interrupted. Please go on."

"Anyway, our job was to gather information about the effectiveness or efficiency of different parts of the Soviet economy. In my case, their metals industry. It was a huge and important part of their economy, but it was highly inefficient and behind the West in a technological sense. Competence in producing metals determines, to a large extent, the sophistication of what they can make from them."

"So you mean their ability to make modern weapons?" suggested Rachel.

"Yes, but also their ability to keep the population happy with affordable cars, televisions, and washing machines. Really, all the things we take for granted now that were new to the working man in Western Europe before the late 1950s."

"Were the people of the Soviet Union aware of the improvements our society had enjoyed since the end of the war?"

"Generally, yes. We believe so. And that was certainly the case by the early 1980s."

"I guess you would say that those who saw a kind of socio-economic end to the Soviet Union were right?" suggested Rachel.

"Yes, and I am proud of the way the intelligence work we did on the economy finally persuaded even the most belligerent hawks to wait for the system to self-destruct."

"From what you say, you must have been a higher ranking intelligence officer than you were an employee in NESC. Did that bother you?"

"No," replied Ball. "For my cover story, I needed to be a simple, travelling salesman, not a boss."

"How many people in NESC knew about your background?"

"Only the chairman at the time I was appointed. He is long dead, but he was entirely trusted to keep a secret. A false CV was written, and that became my official personal history as far as anyone was concerned."

"Is any of what you just told me an official secret?" asked Rachel.

"The general background is not. My involvement should remain a secret. Technically, I should never admit to being involved in any specific intelligence activities," replied Ball.

"Okay, I will respect that. Simon always thought there was more to you than meets the eye, and he was obviously right about you and your special qualities. I am sure he would have loved to hear the true story."

"Thanks, Rachel. And if you ever need any help, just e-mail – I will ring you immediately."

Andrew Ball left the house just after eleven o'clock in the morning, and he headed for the road that would take him south, to Toulouse. He was not going to Biarritz on the Atlantic coast as he had told Rachel; rather, he was headed east to Italy via Marseille and Monaco on the Mediterranean. He would stop in Genoa for the night. It would be about five hundred miles from Toulouse, on good roads with nice mountain and coastal scenery along the Riviera coast. And then it would be south again to the port of Naples. He decided to buy a new SIM card for his mobile as soon as he crossed the border into Italy. He could then let Jackson know exactly where he was and tell him that he was making good progress on his way to Cairo. He would even give him his Italian number and promise to keep it active all the way to Cairo. He smiled to himself. He was being paid well to enjoy himself.

The day after Ball crossed into Italy, Denso became puzzled. It seemed that Ball had bought a SIM card in France in his own name. That much the security company could find out. The number had been used once to call Rachel Craig and nothing more. The SIM was no longer in use or even connected to a mobile phone. He scratched his nose in annoyance. He needed to know more about the Englishman just in case he posed a threat. In short, he wanted to understand the connection between Ball and the Craigs.

He decided to call Barker and check whether Ball had been his colleague at NESC. After calling the NESC number, he was put through to Barker's assistant. She answered, "Mr Barker's office." She spoke with a polished, home-counties accent. Denso would not have known whether it was posh, but it was a version of English he understood.

"Good morning. This is Ricardo Denso of Swiss Metals hoping to speak to Mr Barker."

"Is he expecting your call, Mr Denso?"

"Probably not," he replied. He was starting to get irritated, but he continued in a civil tone: "I am sure he will want to speak to me."

"Okay, Mr Denso. He is in a meeting at the moment that ends in about an hour. I will tell him you called. Please leave me your number, and he will call you back if he thinks it necessary."

"He has my number, but I will give it to you, too. That way there are no excuses. Believe me, it is necessary for him to call me back. And it must be today." He was getting frustrated, and his volatile personality was becoming aggressive. He banged down the phone, lit a cigarette, and uttered a long stream of Anglo-Italian swear words.

He agreed with his boss – the English had a good array of colourful swear words. He strung at least eight of them together before reverting to Italian.

* * *

Ronald Barker left the meeting cursing political correctness and the modern world in general. He had attended yet another meeting on gender and race equality in the workplace. He got back to his office after an urgent restroom stop, and his assistant, the loyal and attentive Doreen, handed him a list of callers. He saw Denso's name and cringed. Of all the people he had dealt with over the years, he was the most creepy and frightening of them all. He asked himself why a head of the security department would expect someone in his position to return a call. NESC had its own security people, and the head of that department reported to him. He picked up the phone, rang David Lawrence, and asked, "David, do you know a man called Denso? He works at Swiss Metals."

"Of course, Mr Barker. Not a pleasant character."

"You have met him?"

"Yes. Two or three times at conferences."

"Please call him and ask why he is trying to speak to me."

"I will. Sorry you have been bothered with somebody who should have known to call me first."

"No problem, David. Please call him, find out what he wants, and talk to me. Give him nothing and tell him nothing without my clearance."

"Okay, Mr Barker. Understood."

Barker hung up and hoped he could forget Denso for an hour or two to enjoy a gin and tonic and lunch in the board members' dining room. *To hell with correctness,* he thought. In his mind, there was no point working hard at school and university and getting to the top in a career if everyone would be treated equally. NESC was one of the few companies that still had a special dining room for board members. *Thank God I'm still allowed such privileges.* The idea of carrying a tray in a single-status canteen was as appealing to Barker as a dose of the clap. He was on his third glass of wine when David Lawrence called his mobile.

"I spoke to Denso. He was not happy talking to the monkey, as he put it, but the bottom line is that he wants to know if we have an employee or ex-employee called Andrew Ball."

"What did you tell him?" asked Barker, trying not to slur his speech.

"No idea, I said. I told him I would check our records and call him back tomorrow."

"Very good. Let him stew and do nothing."

"Okay. Thanks. And sorry to disturb your lunch," said Lawrence without a hint of sarcasm.

Barker knew his lunchtime drinking was becoming excessive, and he vowed to cut down once he was sure the Craig case was of no interest to the police.

* * *

Randall returned to his office after a very constructive meeting with his boss. He had sent Chief Superintendent Sawyer a written update the previous day. Randall was impressed that Sawyer had read it and did not want to go through it with him. Instead, he stated, "Craig did not understand that if he blackmailed NESC, he was actually blackmailing every steel company in this price-fixing ring."

"You agree that blackmail is the most likely reason for his death and that he underestimated the risks?"

"Yes, Richard. We should assume NESC tipped-off all their friends. And one of the companies was not satisfied with NESC's proposal to buy Craig's silence."

"May I ask if you are surprised that big companies such as these are involved in illegal activities like this?"

"No. To them, it is like driving over the speed limit. It's against the law, but we all do it and hope we don't get caught. What is more, unlike speeding, the financial rewards of anti-competitive behaviour can be huge. Billions of pounds, dollars, or euros. That is why the fines are becoming very significant and the numbers of investigations by the authorities are increasing."

"Where do you think I should focus my attention?" asked Randall.

"Try and get some written evidence of this cartel. I will take it to the right people. There will not be an exciting murder trial, but there will be heavy fines and criminal proceedings against the individuals involved. Possibly against their bosses, too, if they can be shown to have sanctioned such activities. The newspapers will have a field day, especially with the Craig murder in the background."

"It seems the evidence went up in smoke."

Sawyer shook his head and said, "I do not believe there was only one copy. No one with such important documents relies on only one."

"Yes," agreed Randall, "I think that's what NESC thought. For a time, they were looking. Certainly, they searched the house in France."

"*Cherchez la femme*, Richard," he said with a smile and continued: "He was a ladies' man. He probably had at least one regular girlfriend. Find her. I expect she knows more than his wife. By the way, Richard, I very much admire the way you got Mrs Craig to open up to you. It gives us a new lead."

"Thank you, sir," answered Richard. He was pleased with himself.

"It is important. We have plenty of thick-skinned policemen on the force. Your report of the conversation shows you to be thoughtful and sensitive. Good work."

Later, Randall phoned Wendy Thomas from his office and asked her to join him and bring Keiron Walker. They were tied up with another case and asked for twenty minutes to wrap up their work. He had forgotten that he had put Wendy in charge of interviewing eighteen rugby players who had returned from a tour of Canada without the nineteenth member of their group. His body was discovered in the River Rouge in Toronto about a week after they left. They had no choice at the time but to report him missing and catch their flight home. The Canadian police, now dealing with a murder enquiry, wanted all the players to be interviewed. The dead man had been stabbed to death, and his body was thrown in the river. Responsibility for conducting the first wave of interviews was given to Randall's department.

Exactly twenty minutes later, Wendy Thomas knocked and entered Randall's office. She was followed by Keiron Walker. Unfortunately, Walker looked too much like a young constable. He was tall and strong, and he had military-length hair. He looked rather old-fashioned in a navy blue blazer, grey trousers, and black shoes. His tie was a modest, dark red one. Randall knew that he could not walk into a pub without people becoming wary.

Randall opened the discussion by saying, "I have just come from a very helpful case review with Mr Sawyer. I have to confess, I think I have missed a trick or two so far in the investigation. When we interviewed Craig's colleagues, we were trying to find out whether they knew of anything he was involved in that could explain his death."

"And that is how the Dutch approached the problem," said Wendy. "It is logical. So what can we do differently?"

"Mr Sawyer wants us to *cherchez la femme*. We need to find out whether he had a serious girlfriend, and if so, we need to talk to her. Sawyer believes she may know more than his wife or be safeguarding some documents."

"It is an interesting idea," said Walker. "Craig seemed to have three segments to his life: France, Holland, and London. The Dutch segment consisted of an office and an apartment in Haarlem where he stayed Sunday night after he got back from France. It seems he took care of his Dutch duties on a Monday, and then he travelled elsewhere. Usually, he travelled back to Schiphol Airport on a Friday afternoon to connect with his flight to Toulouse. The French segment we understand. The London segment may be where we should concentrate."

"Why was he based in Holland when most of his staff were in London and most of his customers were anywhere but Holland?" asked Randall.

Wendy Thomas offered an explanation: "From reading the press cuttings, NESC merged with a large Dutch company. It seems Dutch people were sent to different parts of NESC, and people from NESC were sent to Holland. I guess it was political and something to do with sharing each other's cultures."

"Can we find out how often he was in London without going through NESC?" asked Randall.

"I can get that information from the airlines," said Wendy, "but I think we need to find shortcuts. Let us suppose we find he was in London two nights per week on average. So what? We need to know whom he met, slept with, and shared information. With respect, sir, if we are too methodical, too linear, we will run out of time. We need one or two people to gossip to us." She then hesitated for a moment and added, "Sorry, sir, I did not mean to be impertinent."

"It was a brilliant input, Wendy. Thanks. No need to apologise; you are dead right."

"Let's run through the NESC junior staff we interviewed last time and see if we can remember any gossipy people," proposed Walker.

They settled on three people who had worked for Craig in London. Wendy agreed to be responsible for two girls who had joined as graduate trainees the previous year, and Walker was left to meet a confident salesman who had seemed very sure about his prospects in the company once Craig was dead.

"Our tactic should be for you to try and meet them after work in a pub and get them talking about Craig. No formal interview, no notebooks."

"What reason do we give for the second interview without giving too much away?" asked Walker.

"I think we can say that our investigations have found something in his personal life that could explain what happened. We can say that we are no longer looking at the professional side of his life. It's a sort of half-truth that hints at a private scandal," suggested Richard.

"Sounds good," said Wendy. "That should get them speculating."

"Okay, thanks. Please go and call these guys. Try and fix some meetings."

Randall reflected on their discussion and smiled about the comment concerning linear thinking. Wendy was right, and fortunately, she had the courage to say it. Something was bugging him, though; there was something in the back of his mind, but he could not identify the issue.

CHAPTER 9

Susan Robson decided to telephone Randall. She was a little nervous, but she needed to know whether he was making any progress with the case and whether he had found other copies of the Craig documents. She was worried that Randall might be more committed to the case than the Dutch had been. Fortunately for her, she had some information to feed him to justify the call. And she had even more to offer if she thought she needed to send him on a wild goose chase. It really depended on where Randall was concentrating his efforts – and whether he was starting to look closely at the history of Craig's private life. She did not want Randall finding out about her affair with Craig because, during the interview, she had spoken only of a distant, formal, and professional relationship with the man. The success of her plans depended upon Randall believing that the only copies of Craig's documents were destroyed in the fire.

Randall seemed pleased to hear from her when she introduced herself. *A real charmer,* she thought. She plucked up the courage to explain why she believed that Craig had chosen a solicitor practising hundreds of miles from London.

"When he appointed me, he clearly stated that he had chosen me because I am not a provincial solicitor in terms of my background."

"Where did you practise before? And what elements of law did you specialise in?" asked Randall.

"London. One of the big firms. Company law was my specialisation, and towards the end, I was doing quite a bit of competition consultancy. You know, advising companies how not to fall foul of the Office of Fair Trading and the directorate in Brussels. That kind of thing."

"Interesting. Thanks for telling me all of this. It could be very relevant to what we think was in that envelope."

"You mean, you think the documents may have contained evidence of company wrongdoing? You think he chose me because I would know what they meant and who to send them to?"

"Exactly. Seems logical."

"How are your investigations going?" she asked, trying to sound casual.

"Not well. We think he would have kept other copies of the documents, not just the ones in that envelope he sent you. We have no idea where to look. Perhaps he had a friend he trusted, but we do not have a name yet. Anything else you have thought of?" Randall asked, suspecting that, given her tone, she might have something else to say.

She thought quickly and decided it was the right time to deploy diversionary tactics. "Yes, I remember something. It may be complete nonsense, but I'm sure you can decide best."

"Go on. I'm intrigued."

"A few months after Craig contacted me, I got a call from a lady in London who said a friend had recommended me to her. Out of interest, I asked who, but she quickly changed the subject. She said she made an offer on an apartment in London and wanted me to handle the legal side. I did the work for her, and the purchase went through without any problems. It was an expensive apartment in the development called St George Wharf in Vauxhall, London. She bought it in her name."

"Yes, I know it well. Very nice," said Randall. "But what was unusual about her or the purchase."

"Nothing. She came to my office here in Penzance to sign the documents. She liked it so much that she stayed a couple of days. I showed her around because she is Polish and had not visited many places outside London. She is a very attractive girl with blond hair – plus, she's in great shape. In pubs or restaurants or just walking down the street, she got noticed. She seemed full of life, and she was great fun to be with." She then stopped, apologised, and began again: "Sorry, I am being longwinded. Nearly at the end."

"No problem," said Randall, "I sense there is a punchline."

"Yes. I think she was Craig's mistress. It occurred to me last night when taking a shower."

"Why do you think that?"

"We went out to dinner on her last night here, and we both drank too much wine. She told me she was having an affair with a married man who had a family in France. Evidently, it was hard because she never saw him at weekends."

"Interesting," said Randall. "Did she mention his name?"

"No, but I saw the name *Simon* on her mobile when she took an incoming call in the restaurant. It may just be a coincidence, but I doubt it."

"Can you give me the name and address of your client?" asked Randall.

"As you know, I technically cannot. But because this is a murder enquiry, you could easily get a court order forcing me to disclose it. So to save time and money, I will give you the address and her name."

"Thanks. We will be discreet. Please give me her mobile number, and I promise not to say how I got it." She agreed, he wrote it down, and he ended the conversation by reminding her to call if she thought of anything else.

After the call, he sat for a while thinking about her words. He wondered whether he should stop Thomas and Walker from meeting the potential NESC gossips they had selected. He decided to let them go ahead with the hope that they could find more information about Craig's other mistresses ... if there were others. In all probability, the attractive, Polish girl described by Rachel Robson would provide some answers, but he did not want to close off other avenues of enquiry. Thus, in the meantime, he phoned an ex-colleague based in Kennington and asked him to send a uniformed constable to the management offices of St George Wharf. He asked that the constable find out who owned apartment 734 in Drakes House and establish whether the owner lived there or rented it out.

* * *

Simon Craig had been very active in the months leading up to his death, but not because he expected to die. He was not putting his house in order like a terminally ill patient. On the contrary, he was bringing his personal affairs to a kind of climax, a point when he could start all over again by building an entirely new lifestyle. Of course, he accepted that many people had expectations of him. And he knew that he had responsibilities, including Rachel, the children, Svetlana, and Susan. However, his plan was to throw off the baggage of his past and start all over again in a new country with serious money in the bank. He would walk away leaving Rachel comfortable. Svetlana was already taken care of, and as far as he was concerned, Susan could look after herself in the time warp called Penzance.

Craig had had a problem with women dating back to when he first had easy access to female company. That was during his first summer job, at age sixteen. He worked for two months in a large department store where the women outnumbered the men considerably. He attended a boys-only school, and his first sexual interest was a boy in his class called David. He was obsessed with David for several months, but nothing came of it. David had rejected his first advance, and Craig did not want the misery of another refusal (or the risk of being mocked by others). At the time, he had found it strange that, after rejecting Craig, David remained close to him and seemed devoted. A few years later – with some experience of the strange ways of women – he realised that David's initial refusal was probably an invitation to try harder. He often wondered what would have happened if David had agreed to experiment.

He quickly discovered during that summer, while surrounded by female sales staff, that he was no longer interested in boys. The girls were mostly from humble backgrounds, and they had left school at the earliest opportunity to earn money and have fun. Craig, on the other hand, came from a wealthy family and had every intention of having fun *and* going to university.

He was slightly below average height, but he was slim and straight backed. He wore his wavy hair long. His fair hair, clear skin, and small hands gave him a slightly feminine appearance, which he exaggerated by choosing pastel, tight shirts and pullovers. His most outstanding feature was a pair of dark blue eyes that sparkled when he smiled. Those eyes (and the skill with which he used them) bewitched many people over the following years.

His first physical encounter with the opposite sex was with a school teacher who was also working during the summer holidays. She was seven years his senior, and she seduced him one afternoon when they were alone in a stockroom, supposedly reorganising shoe boxes that had been spread across the floor after a busy Saturday morning. She organised his clothes, his hands, and other parts of his antimony while her tongue aroused him.

Of course, he thought it was love. He did not sleep for nights thinking about the girl. He tried to meet her before work, after work, and in the canteen during coffee, lunch, and tea breaks, but she ignored him. For a few desperate days his mind dwelled solely on the memory of her touch. The spell was finally broken when he saw her two weeks later, walking hand in hand in the park with a man about her age. She stopped and introduced Craig to Joe, her fiancé. Craig was confused and bitter, but he had the good sense to accept the message and move on. And he never stopped moving on, much to the chagrin of many women who came after the teacher.

After leaving university with a second-class honours degree, he took a gap year. With his final exams behind him, he spent the summer touring the Greek islands. He found work as a waiter in most resorts, and he saved enough money to fund a winter trip to Australia. By mid-October, the tourists had left the islands. The bars and restaurants closed as the weather turned cold and windy, and he made his way back to Athens and the International airport.

He arrived in Sydney in early November after stopping in Hong Kong and Singapore. Immediately, he fell in love with the city and grew to admire the local people for their pride in their city and their enthusiasm for everything Australian.

He made little attempt to keep in contact with his parents and two younger sisters. They were devoted to him and wanted regular news of his travels, but he was too selfish to consider them and wanted to dodge any questions from his parents about career plans. His father strongly disapproved of his travels and apparent lack of ambition; they argued every time they spoke to each other. His father was an architect, a partner in a successful firm in Guildford in Surrey. He was a serious man who loved his family and provided a good home and education for his children. His behaviour was predictable. Every Friday, he took the family to an Indian restaurant – always the same restaurant with the same table by the window. Holidays were always in rented cottages.

He did not mix much with people outside of work, and he never went to the pub. He enjoyed watching sport on television, but he never talked about playing after leaving school. He had married the first woman he went out with, and he was happy with his choice. It seemed she was happy to be his wife. To Simon Craig his father's actions were beneath contempt. He could not understand how his father and mother could be so dull. For all his life, he felt as if he had to fight some hereditary disorder he called *complacency disease*. Thus, he never settled and kept challenging himself to ensure the disease did not take a grip.

He quickly found a job in a bar in Sydney, and after a month in a cheap boarding house, he was invited to join some other people in a house share. One of the other barmen was heading back to Germany, and he was honour-bound to find an acceptable replacement before he left. Craig was delighted. He was sharing an accommodation with two guys and a girl in the coastal suburb of the Northern Beaches.

It was not central Sydney, but it had its own charm and subculture. Plus, there was plenty of casual work for barmen and waiters in the area. The men he lived with were Chinese, and they were both very private individuals. They spoke poor English and quickly became bored with trying. The girl was an Australian from Perth. Craig found her to be the most enchanting girl he had ever met. Her personality and spirit were diametrically opposed to Craig's cynicism. She was short and slim with fair hair in a pageboy cut. Her tanned complexion complemented her pale blue eyes, which were large and exaggerated by her small nose and elongated face. She blinked a lot as if to protect them from unwanted attention. They shone and sparkled when she was happy, and Craig learned to read her moods between the blinks. She mostly wore shorts and bright T-shirts on days off, and she didn't seem to care whether her outfits matched or clashed. She never ironed her casual clothes, and her overall appearance was dishevelled yet clean.

For six months Cindy organised Craig's life. She took him to concerts and the theatre, and she even taught him to surf. They spent all they earned and enjoyed being together night and day. He had no plans beyond a few days, and he never discussed his career or returning to England.

They drifted through the Australian summer blissfully unaware of the consequences of their carefree existence. At one point, Craig thought it might be his destiny to enjoy life and love without responsibility. He liked being a barman and the simplicity of that lifestyle. Working, spending the money he earned, and making love without any intellectual input seemed perfect.

He was prepared to believe he was in love, but as he was swept along towards her vision of the future, doubts started to surface in his mind. He began to have reservations about the direction she was taking him. And she never hesitated long enough to ask his opinion or question what she was doing. Basically, she had a plan for her future, and he was part of it.

After much nagging, she persuaded him to visit her parents in Perth. The visit was a mind-numbing experience for Craig, and his doubts became stronger. Cindy's father worked for the city council and noted proudly that he was responsible for the administration of planning consents. Her mother was a talkative, friendly woman who welcomed Craig with the worrying news that Cindy had told her everything about him.

"Welcome to our family, Simon. We have never seen Cindy so happy," she exclaimed over dinner on the first night. She was a teacher in a junior school and spoke to Craig in a booming voice that would have carried to the back of any classroom.

Cindy had two younger brothers who were both personal trainers at a local gym. They lived at home and seemed very close. The older brother was called Michael, and the younger one was named Patrick.

"Don't shout, Mum. You are not at school, and one extra person does not make a class," said Patrick as he shot a friendly smile at his mother.

"The boys will stay with friends tonight. You can have their room, Simon. Cindy will sleep in her room, as usual," she announced without lowering her voice. The look on her face was so innocent that Craig doubted she even contemplated the fact that they might sleep together in Sydney.

"Thank you, Mum. I will lock my door," said Cindy with an irony completely lost on her mother. "Tomorrow, I will show Simon the city, and we will have lunch somewhere out. Our flight is not until eight, so we will come back for tea with you and dad and take our bags," continued Cindy as she winked at Simon.

"Of course your dad and I would like to spend more time with you, but we understand that you want to show Simon the city without us tagging along."

"Yes, Mum, I can imagine how you would behave. You would go into teacher mode and give him a history lesson while dad acted as the tour guide, dragging us from place to place. We want to relax. If we miss anything, we will see it next time."

"Young love!" sneered Michael, rolling his eyes as he grinned at his brother.

The brothers left shortly after dinner. They showed little enthusiasm for leaving home for even one night. The breadth of the family's interest in the world began and ended in Perth. To them, Craig was a foreign novelty act who belonged to Cindy – but he was of little significance to them. If she was happy, they were happy, but they did not ask him about England, his family, or his ambitions. Cindy seemed totally at ease with her parents, and she oozed love for her father. He said nothing to Craig save some pleasantries about the weather and cricket, but when he spoke to Cindy, his tone softened. His affection for his daughter was obvious.

Over a whisky nightcap, Craig fell into deep despair when Cindy's father looked longingly at his wife and declared that she was the first woman he ever went out with, and he had never looked at another woman since that first date. Craig hoped the groan he tried to suppress was not audible, and he quickly sipped some whisky to hide his face. The words reminded him of his equally contented parents back in England. It worried him that Cindy had never commented on her parent's lifestyle, never hinted that she thought it staid and boring. He feared that she thought it was something to aspire to.

Cindy showed him her bedroom proudly. It was large enough for a bed, desk, and wardrobe, but little else. The bed was covered in soft toys, and the walls were plastered with boy band posters.

He lay in bed that night without the thought of trying Cindy's door. The walls of the house were so thin that he suspected her parents would hear even the tearing of a condom packet. Her pride in her bedroom had depressed him, too, because it illustrated the contented mind-set he so despised. As he began to fall asleep, he wondered what Cindy had done with the soft toys when she went to bed, which one she was cuddling instead of him.

* * *

It was about a week after the trip to Perth that Cindy announced she was pregnant. As Craig felt the noose tightening around his neck, she talked excitedly about marriage and the child. And that was when he understood the purpose of the trip. There was no doubt she already knew she was pregnant, which made it an introductory trip for the future husband and father.

The problem Cindy faced was that she did not really know Craig; she had never spent enough time thinking about the kind of man he was. She assumed he would be delighted when she broke the news of her pregnancy; she assumed he would gush about wedding plans and baby names. Craig, though, was deeply depressed and thinking through his options. He pretended to be happy, but he knew it was time to act in his own self-interest.

He waited for the initial excitement to die down, and then he took her to her favourite restaurant to try to confront the issue in a friendly way. He started by telling her that, before he could do anything, he had to find a serious job and decide on a career. He explained that it was too early to be think about marriage, too early to consider children. He tried to reason with her, but she had no doubts about marriage and the child. In her view, having a child would force him to grow up and tackle issues such as his career and their home.

He was not willing to contemplate settling down, and as a matter of fact, Cindy had started to irritate him before she became pregnant. He decided he had no option but to leave Australia. He secretly booked a one-way ticket to London. And when the day came, he packed his bags while she was at work. With a slightly heavy heart, he wrote a note, left it on her pillow, and headed for the airport. By the time she read the note, he was in the air, sighing with relief.

He had given Cindy his parent's address, and some months later, he received a letter from her. The letter stated that she had given birth to a healthy boy, Colin, on the second of November. The address she gave was her parents' residence, so he assumed she went back to Perth to live with them. He sent her a congratulatory letter and asked her to keep in touch. In the following twenty-one years, she never asked for money, but she kept him informed of the boy's progress through school and university. The last letter from Cindy informed Craig that their son had died in a car crash on his way to work. He was twenty-one years old and training to be an architect. She enclosed a graduation photograph taken earlier that year. Craig stared at it for hours with tears in his eyes. His son was a male replica of Cindy, the Cindy he had known when she was that age. He was sad that he had never met his son.

CHAPTER 10

Wendy Thomas and Keiron Walker reported back to Randall on their meetings with the NESC staff. Walker spoke first: "I met Tony Bishop, one of Craig's salesmen, in a pub. He bought into the idea that Craig's private life could be important to the investigation. He was not a great admirer of Craig. He said he was very secretive and rarely took time to communicate with his team. Bishop likes team players. He said Craig was not because he took little trouble to connect with his staff except to give formal instructions. I sense that Bishop likes team hugs and lots of cosy chats with the boss."

"I know the type," said Randall, "but why did he think Craig's personal life was important?"

"He said he had been out a few times with a Polish girl working in the public relations department at NESC. Her name is Svetlana Kovalik. At the time, she had just joined the company, and he thought she needed a friend to show her around London. From the way he spoke about her, it seems he fancied her. Anyway, suddenly, she was not interested in him. He didn't know why. A few months later, he was in a restaurant in Knightsbridge with a client. Two tables away and in deep conversation, he saw Craig and the lovely Svetlana."

"Interesting. We now have two references to this Polish girl. One was made by Susan Robson, and now we have this one," observed Randall. "People have professional relationships and personal relationships, friendships and love affairs. Other than jealousy, why do you think he linked this apparent friendship to Craig's death?"

"I asked him, but his reply was rather childish. He said that she might have a big brother who didn't like her going out with an older, married man like Craig," replied Walker with a grin.

"So based on that sighting in a restaurant, Bishop decided they were an item. Tenuous, but probably true. I guess he willingly jumped to the conclusion to explain her rejection of him. Okay, Wendy, tell us about your friends."

"The first girl I met is called Heather Simpson. We also met in a pub, and she downed two pints of lager in the time I got through a white wine and soda. Quite a girl. She is loud, talkative, swears in every sentence, and speaks negatively about her colleagues. She seems to have a huge chip on her shoulder. She is, without doubt, the perfect gossip … after a few pints of her beloved lager."

"Anything interesting from her?" asked Randall.

"She admired Craig. She said he was a good boss who let people get on with their jobs. Her venom was directed at Jackson, who she described as the greatest shagger of all time. She listed his known conquests in NESC, and she suggested there were probably many others. It seems a number of her friends were used and abused by the great Mr Jackson. Nothing else interesting," she concluded.

"Was our Polish friend on the list of Jackson's conquests?"

"No, she wasn't mentioned."

"Okay, what about the second girl?" prompted Randall.

"She is called Deborah Small. She's a quiet girl who does not visit pubs and would only talk to me on the way to the railway station. We walked along the Embankment and across Vauxhall Bridge, which gave me enough time to learn that she knew little about Craig's private life. She said he kept to himself. She gossiped about some of her friends being willing to drop their pants for other bosses with the hope of making faster progress in their careers, but she did not think Craig was interested. In her opinion, he was too occupied with his family in France. She did say she figured he was a wonderful and loving husband and parent, which suggests she had a bit of a crush on him."

"Little did she know!" commented Walker.

"Well we have quite a sordid picture of life in NESC. The bit about Jackson is particularly interesting, though hardly our business. Still, it will certainly colour my thinking if I meet him again. Should we ever find he has obstructed the investigation, I will take pleasure in trying to turn it into a pervert the course of justice case," grumbled Randall. "Moving on. We must find out more about this Svetlana. I do not want to interview her until we confirm she still owns the apartment Robson told me about. I do not believe she had the money to buy the apartment, and the most obvious source is a lover – probably Craig.

The interesting thing is that Craig appeared to have very little money or investments. It's very strange."

Randall took a short lunch break in the canteen, a place he thought he should be seen two or three times each week. The food was tolerable, but the noise of plates being cleared and stacked, the animated conversations of people, and the rubbing of chair legs on the tiled floor made it an uncomfortable place for him. He would rather eat and contemplate in quiet than eat and talk amid that clamour. Back in his office, Randall found an e-mail from his colleague in Kennington:

"Hi, Richard. The information is as follows:

The apartment in question belongs to an offshore property company registered in Ras al-Khaimah in the United Arab Emirates. No names of directors have been supplied. The property is managed by a local company called Landlord Consultancy and Property Services. There have been tenants living there for four months. An Indian couple. The concierge of Drakes House said a very attractive, young lady lived there for a while during the winter, but he has not seen her since the Indian couple moved in. He did not know her name, but he thought she looked foreign."

I'm sorry, Richard, but that is all we could find out.

Regards, Sam"

It was not the news he had expected. To make progress, it seemed he had to do four things. The first was to check with the land registry to ensure that the original purchase matched Susan Robson's story. At the same time, he could confirm with the registry that another transfer of ownership had happened involving an offshore company. The second was to meet Svetlana after he had all the facts. He could discuss the purchase and sale of the apartment with her and ask how she was able to afford it. The third (and most difficult) was to ask her about her personal and financial relationship with Craig without implicating Susan Robson, which would be a breach of confidentiality. And the final thing he needed to establish was whether Craig had left Svetlana any secret documents.

The *something* that had been bugging him the previous day finally broke to the surface, which cleared his mind. He grabbed the file sent to him by the Dutch and scanned the pages quickly. Nothing. They had searched the apartment Craig had rented in Haarlem, but no one had established where he lived when visiting London. *Perhaps,* thought Randall, *he stayed in hotels, perhaps he had an apartment, or perhaps he stayed with Svetlana or another friend.* Randall cursed the Dutch for not checking that angle, but he decided to park the subject until he concluded his meeting with Svetlana.

He called the number Susan Robson had given him and introduced himself. He explained that he was responsible for the investigation into Simon Craig's death. Her reply surprised him: "I wondered when someone would get around to me. I did not believe we were so discreet that our relationship would not be discovered. I'm guessing we were seen together – walking hand in hand in Hyde Park or climbing into a taxi outside a theatre. Is that not how people are discovered in films?"

"Actually, you were seen in a restaurant, but that is irrelevant to our investigation."

"What is relevant, then?" she asked.

"I would like to meet and discuss several issues with you, please. Your knowledge could help our investigation."

"Do I have any choice?"

"Yes, you do. It is entirely your decision whether to cooperate."

"Okay. You are being very straightforward, and I appreciate that. These have been tough times, but I am just about ready to tell my story. I will finish here at six and go to your office around half past six. I will phone you when I am in the lobby; you can organise my security clearance."

"Sounds like you know our systems," said Craig with a laugh.

"No, but I can guess. NESC is just the same. Unfortunately, it is the way of the world since terrorism became our biggest fear."

"I appreciate your cooperation and look forward to meeting you at around half past six. I will ask a female colleague to be present and take notes. I am sure you understand that this is a procedural necessity to protect both our interests," he said bluntly and hung up.

He already liked the sound of her. She had a strong accent, but she had spoken good, modern English. Plus, she seemed decisive and willing to help. The fact she had volunteered to head to his office suggested she had no fear. He looked around his office and mused, *she will be my first visitor from the outside.* The office was the regulation size for his rank. His desk was in front of a shatterproof, double-glazed window that could not be opened. Apart from his desk, there was a low table, a sofa, two easy chairs in the right-hand corner of the room, and a bookshelf to the left of the door. He had done nothing to personalise the room. There were no pictures or certificates on the walls, no books in the bookshelf other than police manuals. It was dull and uninspiring. It was his first private office, and although he was proud of it and relieved to have some personal space, he did not want to show his pleasure to colleagues during the first week or two by adorning it with a private collection of photographs or paintings.

* * *

Cindy found the letter from Craig on her pillow the first evening after he left:

> *"Dearest Cindy,*
>
> *We had a great time together, and I really enjoyed your company. I'll never forget the wonderful way you introduced me to Sydney and the fun we had.*
>
> *For a time, I really loved you. Every moment with you was special. But gradually, that feeling started to fade, and by the time we went to visit your parents, I was already planning to return to England and start a career.*
>
> *The biggest shock for me was your pregnancy ... and that you were pleased. We never discussed marriage,*

but you automatically assumed that marriage and the child was the inevitable next step for us. Right now, as I leave Australia and you behind, I think you were unfair to me. In fact, I think you were selfish and rather childish.

I cannot advise you on whether to have the child or have an abortion. Your heart will decide. I am sure your family will also help you make the right decision.

Good luck and please let me know what you decide. Keep in touch – you have my parents' address.

Love, Simon'

Cindy cried for two days, spoke to no one, and kept the devastating news to herself. On the third day, she called her mother. They met in Sydney, and her mother stayed for a week to give what comfort she could to her daughter. Cindy's feelings were mixed. Her memories of the good times with Craig made her cry; she missed him badly. But most of all, her own stupidity, naivety, and selfishness made her cry. She read his letter many times over during those traumatic days, and she found herself agreeing with him. She admitted to herself that she had tried to trap him.

Cindy moved back to Perth with the full support of her family. Her father kicked his two sons out of the house to make room for Cindy and the baby. Her father became a proud grandfather, and he provided for Cindy and the child as he had for his own children. Baby Colin was much loved and grew up to be a level-headed young man with a passion for sailing and architecture. His interest in the design of buildings started at school when the class studied European history. He copied drawings from books of Greek temples, Roman palaces, and the great cathedrals of Northern Europe. He looked like his mother, had the unlimited optimism of her father, and the loner's instincts of his father. He was comfortable in his own company and did not need to be part of social groups. He had a few friends at the sailing club, some student friends, and a girlfriend he had known since his school days. He did not need to study too hard, and he was capable of focusing on exam preparation at the right time to ensure he got good grades. It was characteristic he had inherited from his father: Simon Craig also breezed through school and university without stretching himself for more than a few weeks each year.

As her son grew older, Cindy developed an interest in photography. She read all she could on the subject, and then she took a college course. She had an eye for unusual interpretations of everyday happenings. After taking her son to school, she toured Perth on foot or by public transport looking for opportunities to expand her portfolio. She entered photographic competitions. She framed some of her pictures, and she displayed her work in art galleries. She met interior designers and persuaded several to offer her pictures to clients. Some of her more commercial pictures sold well in local souvenir shops. In time, she started to make money and believe in herself.

By the time Colin went to university, she was getting noticed in photographic circles. She was taken seriously when she came second in a national photographic competition sponsored by a TV channel. The top five pictures were shown on television and displayed in the entrance to the company's headquarters. A photographic magazine bought the rights to reproduce the winning pictures and publish them in its monthly issue. Whatever the judges thought, the opinion among professionals and the general public was that her picture should have won. One journalist commented that her picture captured a moment that could have happened at any time in any place. In the journalist's opinion that made it interesting on an international level.

As if to prove a point, a company specialising in processing and distributing reproduction art signed a contract with Cindy to make one thousand copies for the UK market. They would be sold in department stores and shops that sold home furnishings. They took an option on up to five thousand additional copies. They paid Cindy handsomely, and she was able to travel while continuing her pursuit of unusual interpretations. Cities were her preferred subjects, and she travelled to Europe and the United States in search of inspiration from the everyday activities of ordinary people.

She never thought seriously about trying to see Craig when she visited London. In her opinion, too much time had passed; she imagined that they would act like strangers trying to make polite conversation while contemplating their past. She had grown up and found her own way through life with his child. She suspected he was happy to forget their time together, happy to avoid exhibiting guilt, regret, or curiosity. She had never married. Instead, she put her energy into bringing up her child and cultivating her photography craft. She had long since convinced herself that she and Colin were better off without a man in the equation. She also figured that her success stemmed from a single-mindedness that few men would understand or tolerate.

She was in Athens when her father phoned. He was almost unable to speak through his tears, but he finally managed to relate the death of her son. Immediately, she rushed home to arrange the funeral. The flight to Perth was the longest, saddest, and loneliest experience of her life. All she wanted to do was sit with her family and grieve at home, but she had to act as normal as she followed the airport procedures. And then she sat for hours in a cramped aircraft, staring at the seat in front of her and remembering his life. Once home, she found her parents and Colin's girlfriend utterly defeated, unable to cope, consumed by grief. For the first time, she had to be the strong member of the family and take control. She wanted to sit and cry and remember him, but that was not an option while surrounded by shocked and listless people. It was probably that responsibility that got her through the blackest days.

CHAPTER 11

True to her word, Svetlana arrived at New Scotland Yard at exactly 6:30 p.m. In the meantime, she was asked to leave her passport at the desk by the street entrance and pass through a scanner. When Randall reached the ground floor, she was standing by the lift. She was accompanied by a police officer who waited to hand her over to Randall. As he got out of the lift, he saw at least four pairs of eyes trained on Svetlana in what can only be described as *ogling mode*. Randall tried to look unsurprised and casual as they introduced themselves and shook hands, but it was not easy in the face of such a beautiful woman.

As they got in the lift, she said, "Mr Randall, why did you come down to meet me when you could have sent a more junior officer?"

"I never thought of sending anybody. You kindly agreed to meet me here, and it seemed the natural and polite thing to do."

"Interesting. My colleagues in NESC would have sent a PA if one was still working at this time or bullied someone junior. Anything to avoid being polite and natural."

"No comment," said Randall drily

"So you have met some of them?"

"Yes. I understand what you are saying, but we are not in business – we are public servants and must keep our egos in check."

"Very good, Mr Randal, very good. You understand well the type of people I work with," she said with intensity. The *V*s she spoke sounded a bit like *W*s.

When they arrived at his office, Wendy Thomas was already waiting. She was sitting on the sofa. It could accommodate two people, and there were two armchairs on either side of a low table. On the table was sparkling and still water, three glasses, some coffee cups, and two insulated pots (one containing coffee, the other filled with hot water). Teabags were arranged in a small, porcelain tray with several options including breakfast, peppermint, and camomile teas.

When Svetlana walked into the office, Wendy's eyes widened visibly as she jumped up to introduce herself. *Oh my God,* thought Wendy, *this woman looks too good to be true. I pity any meek man who wants to woo her. He will be so nervous he'll never find the right things to say.* Randall noticed that Wendy was temporarily overawed. He also noticed that Svetlana was careful to put her at ease with a friendly remark: "I hope you have not been waiting long. The next time, I will arrive earlier to allow for security procedures."

Randall offered tea and coffee. Svetlana chose camomile, Wendy stuck with water, and Randall decided on coffee. Wendy felt uncomfortable with Randall pouring and serving. As the junior officer, whether female or male, it should have been her responsibility. But she guessed that Randall wanted to be the host in his own office and not portray Wendy as a serving girl. She was impressed, just as she had been when Randall went downstairs to collect the visitor in her stead. She was growing to like her boss. At first, he had seemed too distant, intellectual, and democratic to be a good senior police officer. For the first few days, she wondered how such an ineffectual person could reach high rank at such a young age. But she was starting to notice his strengths, including his ability to build loyalty and trust among the people who worked for him.

"Thank you for agreeing to see me and visiting us here, Ms Kovalik," Randall began.

"Please, let's use first names, Richard. I think this is going to be a tough session for me. I will tell you about Craig and our relationship, but it will be painful at times. I will be talking about my personal life; formality will feel out of place."

"Agreed," said Randall. "Let me start by sharing with you, Svetlana, our recent thoughts about the case to set the scene for this meeting. Firstly, we do not expect to find the killers. The crime happened on foreign soil many weeks ago, and the killers were almost certainly paid assassins. Perhaps, one day, new information will help identify them, but right now the trail is dead. The Dutch did their best at the time."

"In fact," added Wendy, "from reading their file, they put in a great deal of effort in the first few days, but the bomb probably exploded after the killer or killers already left Europe."

"So it was a very sophisticated murder. And that means it was expensive, I assume," said Svetlana before Randall continued.

"Yes, and this is the point we are interested in. The question is *why?* And if we can answer that, we may be able to bring a conspiracy to commit murder case against somebody or an organisation. Conspiracy is almost as serious as actual murder in some circumstances. There has to be an explanation in his private life or in his professional life. In Simon Craig's case, the two lives appear almost inseparable – except, perhaps, for the family in France."

"That is a very shrewd assessment, Richard. I never met his family, but from the way he talked, they were in a special compartment in his mind, and the contents of that compartment were certainly not something to be discussed with me," Svetlana added with bitterness.

"Another aspect we are looking at is the possibility that Craig was involved in some criminal activity, or at least aware of something. And maybe that became a problem to someone. We will pursue this line because certain facts support the idea. I cannot tell you what those facts are, but you may be able to help put a few more pieces in the jigsaw."

"I will try, but I may not know as much as you think. Anyway, I will help because I think you will find Simon was a foolish adventurer and dreamer, but he did not deserve that violent death. He was definitely involved in a number of dubious activities, though, and I will tell you what I know. Who is to say that there are not others at risk for the same activities?"

"Yes, that concerns us. Please tell us what you feel comfortable with, starting from when you first met him. I am interested in the image he portrayed," said Randall wanting her to lead the discussion on her own terms.

"I met him for the first time in Holland. My job was to design the NESC stand for a large exhibition in Dusseldorf. The budget and design approval was his responsibility, so I met him in his office near Amsterdam. He was pleased with my work and invited me to lunch in a wonderful canal-side restaurant. The interior looked unchanged from the eighteenth century. He was charming and very pleasant company. The restaurant was special to him, and he was known there. The owner fussed and fawned over him. I was impressed with Andrew's charm and self-confidence, but I knew he was married. I had no intention of leading him on. He had something of a reputation as a ladies' man. The trouble is that good-looking and successful men are assumed to be chasing women, but it's often the women chasing them.

"At any rate, it was not my intention to pursue him. Lunch was good, and we parted with a formal handshake. I forgot about him for a time, but I boasted to my friends about the lunch. About a week later, I got a text message from him saying that he would be in London the following Tuesday. He wanted to finalise the plans for the exhibition. He said the only window in his schedule was in the evening, so he asked about dinner. Complete bullshit, of course, but like a lamb to the slaughter, I agreed."

Wendy laughed and commented, "Giving the dinner a professional context made it difficult to refuse."

Svetlana continued with a sigh and a nod at Wendy. "He asked me a few questions about Poland and whether I enjoyed England. I noticed he was not really listening to my replies. I wanted to impress him with thoughtful and intelligent reflections on Poland and my new life in England, but he was always concentrating on the menu or the wine list. His main topic of conversation that evening was his role in NESC. He was the first senior guy from the company I had met socially. I was interested to know more about life near the top, and he had plenty of stories to tell. Simon came across as a humorous cynic. It sounds like a contradiction, but he could tell a humorous story about a colleague without a hint of criticism, yet I somehow formed a negative impression of the guy he was describing. In retrospect, I don't think I ever heard him say anything genuinely positive about the company or the people who ran it. The lasting impression I got from that dinner was that Simon thought he was cleverer than any of his bosses and that he was going to be extremely successful despite them and his job at NESC."

"Wow Svetlana, that is pretty blunt. But it's very helpful. So far, he's not coming across as a very nice guy," remarked Randall.

"Nice enough for me to fall for him … despite his huge ego and cynicism. It took a few more dinners, shows, and romantic walks, but after a few weeks, I really missed him when he was not in London. I lived for his texts and phone calls. I checked my phone every few minutes and worried when I did not hear from him for more than a day. Perhaps I was enjoying the excitement of being in love rather than the love itself. I was quite lonely anyway, so I probably got involved more easily than a person surrounded by family and friends."

"Where did he live when in London, Svetlana?" asked Randall.

"He had an apartment in Battersea. The company gave him a housing loan before he moved to Holland, and they let him keep it because it was expected he would move back to London. After the initial excitement of the merger and the ridiculous moving around of people in the name of culture swapping, it was assumed people would return to their home country."

"What happened to it after his death?"

"Good question. I had a set of keys, and I left a few pieces of clothing and some books and CDs there. Towards the end, he usually stayed at my place. When I went there after his death, everything had been removed except the furniture. Clothes, books, and papers – everything easily removed – was gone. I thought it strange, but I guess the apartment was part of his estate and became the property of his wife."

"Not sure," said Randall, "there's nothing in my files about this apartment. Another question, please – and I hope you will not find it too direct: did you ever have any business or financial dealings with Simon Craig?"

"You seem well informed, Richard. I think you would not have asked this question if you did not know the answer. Yes, he was very generous to me, but behind the generosity were selfish motives. I will explain. He had been selling NESC products all over the world for many years. At least 30 per cent of what he sold went to Asia, Africa, and the Middle East. To give that meaning, he was responsible for sales of about two million tonnes of steel each year to these places. Imagine if you could make a dollar per tonne on two million tonnes. In fact, through many intermediaries, Andrew was making, on average, five dollars per tonne, or ten million dollars per year. He was very rich."

Wendy gave a whistle of amazement, and Randall stared at Svetlana before expressing his surprise. "You have really shocked me, Svetlana. And to use an English expression, you have set the cat among the pigeons. We had a very different understanding of his wealth and earnings. But please tell me how you got involved."

"Simple. He wanted to give me a gift, so he offered me money to buy an apartment in a good location on the River Thames. Of course, I accepted. To avoid any questions about how I obtained the money, he got an elite private bank in the Channel Islands to lend it to me."

"Where is the apartment exactly?" asked Randal, even though he already knew the answer.

"St George Wharf. Very nice location. A few weeks after the purchase, he paid off the loan, so I had my gift. The records in the United Kingdom still say it was financed by a secured loan, and technically, the bank still has that security. But such banks thrive on handshakes, client trust, and codes of honour. So no debt on paper in the Channel Islands means no debt, even if it is on record here."

"Do you live there now?" Randall asked Svetlana.

"No. I sold it."

"Why did you sell it so quickly? Did you not like it?"

She hesitated. For the first time, she seemed reluctant to answer the question, but finally she said, "I am the owner of an offshore company. I sold it to that company. My offshore company got equity from one of Craig's overseas investment companies, so I had free cash to buy another apartment. I now live in that second apartment, also in St George Wharf."

"So one way or another, you own two expensive apartments courtesy of Simon Craig. And presumably, you earn a rental income from one of them, right?"

"Yes. He could afford to be generous, but as I said just now, there were selfish motives. In other words, there was a catch. He needed me as a messenger. I was Simon's contact, and then, through my uncle in Poland, I arranged messages to be delivered to key people on behalf of Simon. I am not going to tell you anything about the messages because it would not be in my interest."

"Yes, Svetlana, I understand. But can you tell me the general purpose of the messages?"

"As his business empire expanded, he got into real estate investment. To make big money and reduce risks, he needed to influence planning decisions or he needed inside information on land about to be designated for private or industrial construction. That sort of thing. At times, people were bribed; other times, people were threatened. My uncle specialised in persuading people to cooperate.

He had been a senior officer in a particularly unpleasant department of the secret police in Poland. He has two or three ugly friends as helpers."

"So at some point, you must have told Simon about your uncle," Wendy stated.

"Yes, early on. He came to England, and Simon and I had dinner with him. He told some colourful stories about his career that Simon seemed to like. They went off together after dinner on a wild vodka drinking session, and I went home. I can only imagine the stories my uncle Peter would have told after a few vodkas on top of beer and wine. The next day, Simon had a bad hangover, but he was enthusiastic about my uncle and said he could be very useful. It was the start of a close relationship, and I think my uncle made Simon more bold and ruthless. Anyway, he was always on special tasks for Simon, and I believe the results were spectacular."

"Did he ever mention competition law, price-fixing, cartels, or anything like that?"

"Only in passing. Several times, he came back from meetings with the big steel companies and talked of *the club*. It seems they were into all kinds of tricky dealings to avoid fighting it out in the market. The problem with Simon was that he only discussed things that were on his agenda at the time. There was very little small talk. You could not ask him on a Monday about the weekend – he would look blank and change the subject."

"We are coming to the end, you will be pleased to know," said Randall before asking the key question: "Did he ever give you a package of papers for safekeeping?"

"No," said Svetlana. "He asked me to send a large envelope of papers by courier to his lawyer in Cornwall. I have no idea what was in the envelope. I subsequently met this lawyer because she handled the purchase of the first apartment, and she seemed like a switched-on sort of lady. She was certainly wasted in provincial Penzance. Simon did not want his name mentioned. He was very firm about that fact, and I never discussed our relationship with Susan Robson."

After Svetlana left, Randall and Wendy Thomas sat for a while discussing and digesting the new information.

"I never expected this. Svetlana has opened Pandora's Box. We knew nothing about his personal business activities or the money he was making. From what we now know, he could have been involved with any number of people who might have wanted him dead," grumbled Randall.

"This investigation is becoming complicated. We need time to reflect on this new information. It is getting late; let's sleep on it," proposed Wendy. Randall agreed, quickly finished his third cup of coffee, and jumped up to lock his desk drawer.

Just as Wendy got to the door, he called, "One thing I have just realised is that we cannot take Svetlana's story at face value. She may be telling lies. Or Craig could have told her a pack of lies to impress her."

"Possibly. Not sure how we can check. What we do know is she bought an expensive apartment with money she did not earn."

"Good point, Wendy. Okay, see you tomorrow."

It was a warm evening, and Randall walked slowly back to his apartment in Pimlico while thinking about the case. He stopped at an off-licence for a good bottle of Italian wine. He had some beef ravioli in the freezer and tomatoes, lettuce, and cucumbers in the fridge. He planned a quiet evening watching the Champions League game between Arsenal and Real Madrid. Lisa was at her mother's house and would probably phone after she knew the game was over. She respected his passion for football and knew better than to phone in the middle of the game. She was not very interested, but she understood that he still loved to watch the top players. She often wondered whether he regretted not taking the chance to play when he had it. His father told her that they had offers from good clubs, but Richard was not interested. He always maintained that he would not have made the grade, that he would have wasted the most important part of his life. Lisa suspected he was not comfortable in the company of footballers and would have had trouble settling in at a professional club.

CHAPTER 12

As soon as Svetlana got back to her apartment, she called Susan Robson using a pay-as-you-go SIM card. Susan answered quickly and Svetlana said, "Call me back on this new number."

A few seconds later, Susan asked, "How did it go? Did he believe you?"

"It went as planned. He is a decent guy and not pushy at all. He was very surprised to hear that Simon was … moonlighting. Isn't that what you call it? He seemed to find it hard to believe that Simon was rich and successful. When I told him, he used an expression you may understand – something to do with cats and pigeons."

Susan Robson said with a laugh, "He probably said something like, 'That has put the cat among the pigeons.' It is good. It means that the theories they were working on up to now will have to be questioned. That's exactly what we wanted."

"Yes," said Svetlana, "those were his words."

"Did he ask you whether Simon left you any documents?"

"Yes. I said that nothing like that had been left with me, but I told him about the large envelope Andrew asked me to send to you."

"Excellent. I am sure you were more or less his last hope of finding copies of those documents."

"Where do we go from here?" asked Svetlana.

"I think it is time to start ruffling some feathers. Where is your uncle Peter at the moment?"

"He is in Cracow. I spoke to him yesterday. I told him we would need him very soon. He is ready."

"I want him to meet a guy called Hans Weber and put some serious pressure on him. He spends most of his time in Dubai. We need to get him to meet your uncle somewhere less secure. I will send you an e-mail later tonight outlining the plan. We need to make the e-mail cryptic, as if we're referring to an old friend. You will need to interpret what I am saying and give your uncle his instructions."

"Okay, Susan. Understood. Please call me about this time tomorrow for an update."

Later that night, Susan sent an e-mail to Svetlana explaining that Hans Weber was an expert on competition law and had recently retired from a top job in the relevant EU department. She said he should be asked to give a series of lectures on the subject to companies and law schools in Poland. She gave Svetlana the e-mail address. According to her, that was the most professional way to contact him. Susan said the e-mail should mention a substantial fee for his services and that an urgent meeting was needed to finalise a programme that would start in September. Susan then sent an SMS to Svetlana asking her to talk to her uncle and agree on the best way to convince Weber it was a genuine proposal.

* * *

"You see, Irina, I am still needed," said Weber as he looked up from his iPad and smiled at his wife.

"Of course you are, my dear. I need you. My family needs you for some money for a few essentials."

"You mean your sister wants a new $2,000 designer handbag?"

"Of course. But please tell me what made you so happy this morning as to smile at me."

"I got an e-mail inviting me to do a series of lectures in Poland."

"Do you speak Polish?"

"No, but they want them delivered in English. They will arrange interpreters, although most law students speak English well."

"Do you speak English well enough?" Irina asked with a laugh, knowing he spoke it like a native.

"I want to do it, Irina, and I need to meet the organisers very urgently."

"Okay. After a week, you are already bored with Ukraine and my family, so bugger off to Warsaw and enjoy yourself."

"If you don't mind, I will. I like the idea of earning a little more money and giving lectures."

"You go dear. Please don't forget to leave me with some pocket money and a little extra for some basics for my large and very poor family," replied Irina. She bent over, kissed the top of his head, and whispered, "Five should be enough for a few days. That is *thousands* of dollars. It should be enough to help me through the misery of you being away."

Weber grunted. She knew he would gladly give her the money to make her happy. He set about replying to the e-mail. He said that he was in Ukraine and could easily visit Warsaw. He proposed a meeting two days later and waited for confirmation.

Irina, he thought, *is not entirely correct about my feeling towards Ukraine. I have a certain fondness for the place, particularly Dnepropetrovsk.* In fact, he had made many visits to the city since meeting Irina.

Despite it being an ugly, polluted, urban sprawl with large areas of grim-looking concrete blocks dating back to the social housing projects of communist times, he appreciated the spirit of the people who endured the cold winters and inadequate housing. Weber particularly liked the main shopping street, Karl Marx Avenue, where the wealthy could shop for famous and elite brands in designer stores. He had a favourite restaurant there as well, where the service was as good as anything he has experienced in any other city. He liked to walk along the riverbank during spring and summer evenings when hundreds of families did the same. There, they found the space that was missing in their cramped, high-rise apartment. Despite his wealth and privileged life, Weber was not a snob. He derived real pleasure from seeing ordinary families enjoying simple things such as evening strolls.

In truth, he got bored anywhere after a few days. It was not the fault of Ukraine. Retirement was proving tough for him, and the lecture tour promised to be just the distraction he needed.

* * *

The text from Andrew Ball was a surprise to Randall:

> *"Richard, this is Andrew Ball. I am using this Egyptian number. Please call me when you have a moment. I have some information you may find interesting.'*

Randall called straight away using his office landline. He introduced himself and then asked in a pleasant voice, "How are you? How is Cairo?"

"I am fine, thanks. Cairo is warm, polluted, congested, and challenging … as usual."

"Have you sorted out the problem for NESC?"

"Nearly. In process. But the issues are quite complicated. Most of the problems I would call a legacy of Simon Craig."

"Interesting. Tell me more," prompted Randall.

"He had a business partner here, an Egyptian guy called Ahmed. They were very close friends and drinking partners. Ahmed says they were like brothers. I have befriended him, and we have been out together on some pretty heavy drinking sessions. Ahmed drinks whisky like it is going out of fashion, and then he becomes maudlin and affectionate. He tells me I am his new brother, sent to replace Craig. When he is drunk, he clings to me, hugs me frequently, and won't let me go home. Anyway, you get the picture."

"Yes, I can imagine the scene late at night when all you crave is sleep and all he wants is company."

"You've got it. But there are some interesting parts to Ahmed's confessions. The first is that Craig controlled the sale of NESC products in Egypt through an exclusive agent. The agency company was owned by Craig and Ahmed. NESC paid between 3 per cent and 5 per cent commission to this company. Craig drew up the agency contract and signed it on behalf of NESC. He had the delegated authority from the board to appoint agents and negotiate terms. Last year, according to Ahmed, they received around $200,000 in commissions for doing virtually nothing. Ahmed simply visits the five or six main distributors in Egypt once per quarter and offers NESC products at very competitive prices. The contracts of sale are between NESC and the distributors, so the agent takes no credit risk. It's easy money."

"Do you think Craig had similar arrangements in other countries?" asked Randall, remembering Svetlana's revelations about Craig and his wealth. He did not want Ball to know he had another source of information, so he asked the question openly.

"Yes. Ahmed told me that Craig was doing the same thing in many countries, and he also held shares in distributors in some markets. He sold to them on very favourable terms and took a share of the profit. In one or two small markets, he made the companies he partly owned the exclusive distributor for NESC."

"But surely NESC must check these things. They must know if an employee owns shares in a company that they sell to. Also, they must monitor market prices and know whether the salespeople are doing a good job," said Randall, sensing he already knew the answer.

"Craig was the most senior salesperson in the company. His boss, Redder, was a figurehead and boardroom strategist. Craig was trusted, and his results were good. He was smart because, according to Ahmed, his shares were all held in offshore trusts. Even if NESC had bothered to look, they would not have found his name on the share register of any of his customers. But there is another point I want to discuss with you, and it may be more relevant to your investigation."

"What you have told me already is very useful background and shows Craig to be much more clever and devious than I had ever imagined. He probably had a considerable amount of money scattered round the world that we cannot see and is not part of his estate. It also means he probably made enemies along the way. Please tell me about the second point."

"According to Ahmed, Craig was very disillusioned with his job in NESC and wanted to get out and concentrate on real estate speculation. Apparently, he already had some successes and made big money. He thought that was his future, and he told Ahmed he planned to devote himself full time. Ahmed said he pleaded with Craig to stay in NESC because the agency was his only source of income. He feared that, without Craig to provide cover and handle the internal politics of NESC, the scam would be exposed very quickly by Craig's successor. Ahmed said there were other people in the network set up by Craig who wanted him to stay in his job. They were also making a good living, courtesy of Craig. The interesting thing is that Ahmed thinks that Craig did not care what happened after he left NESC. He told Ahmed he would strike a deal such that they would never investigate his past and certainly not try to punish him."

"Okay for him, but that would have left his network very vulnerable. Sounds like they had passed their sell-by date, but Craig didn't care," interrupted Randall.

"Yes, he told them to work something out with his successor or move on to pastures new. This seems to be typical of Craig. For example, he told Ahmed that he would ensure his own family had more than enough money, but he would not live with them or spend much time in France. He said he loved his children, but he didn't want to be around during their teenage years."

"Incredible. And everybody thought he was a decent family man," said Randall.

"I suspect Craig only thought in terms of giving them enough money and a good home. Material, not emotional support," replied Ball.

"Yes, I read somewhere that people who live complex lives are usually very good at compartmentalising things and people. From what I can gather, he had a family compartment, a mistress compartment, a professional compartment, and a private money-making compartment."

Ball laughed and stated, "In an earlier life, which I will tell you about one day over dinner in London, some of us were actually trained to think like that, to run parallel lives that never converged. But I don't think Craig was trained; he was just born that way."

"I look forward to that dinner. Did Ahmed say or hint at anything else?"

"Yes, Craig told Ahmed that he was sick to death with Europe. He said he would only do business in the Middle East and Far East in the future. He talked to Ahmed about the hypocrisy of the EU. Apparently, the steel producers have something they call *the club*. It seems Craig had been attending their meetings for many years, representing NESC. Ahmed does not know a great deal more, but he understood it to be a price-fixing ring. He said that Craig was going to use his knowledge of the club to bargain with NESC to get a decent pay-off."

"It all fits," said Randall. "But why bother with blackmail? He seemed to have made himself very wealthy. He wanted a new career in real estate speculation. Why not just quit? I don't get it."

"Yes, I struggled with that until I spoke to an accountant friend. In a way, the answer comes back to the subject of compartments. He wanted to spend money on this house in France to improve things for his 'compartment' family. He wanted to be generous to his wife. One can guess that the pay-off would have been sufficient to enable him to do those things. It would have appeared as normal, taxable income. An official payment to a UK or French bank account. However, without that pay-off, he would have had to channel funds into the EU from his offshore accounts. He could not risk that. You probably know how much money he had in Europe at the time of his death. I imagine it was not much, and all of it was traceable to his salary, right? All of it had been declared for tax purposes, right?"

"That is correct, Andrew. So everything earned in the EU could stay in the EU without raising any eyebrows. Anything coming from outside stood the risk of a tax investigation, a future NESC investigation, or a money laundering investigation."

"That seems to be his motive for demanding a totally transparent financial settlement from NESC," summarised Ball.

"Let's go back to the cartel. In your opinion, Andrew, do you think it exists?"

"Yes. If you remember our lunch, I said Craig was going to meetings on behalf of NESC, but no records were kept. That would be consistent with him attending illegal meetings."

"Yes, I remember. It seems to me that we are fast reaching the point where the next step is to let the competition authorities investigate this cartel. Unfortunately, we cannot give them any hard evidence to work with. It appears that anything Craig may have intended as evidence has been destroyed in a mysterious fire in his solicitor's office in Penzance. As far as a murder investigation goes, this one is dead in the water."

"Richard, you mentioned a fire. When did it happen?"

"A few days before Craig's death. Everything that Craig had sent his solicitor was destroyed. We assume that was the evidence we needed, and that it was what Craig had collected for his blackmail attempt."

"So Craig starts his negotiation with NESC. He tells them he has collected sufficient evidence over the years to show he was attending illegal meetings on behalf of the company and that the documents prove the seriousness and scope of the price-fixing. The NESC negotiators try to call his bluff about the evidence, and he tells them it is with his solicitor and will be released to the authorities unless they meet his demands. He probably set a deadline."

"That seems to be it in a nutshell, Andrew."

"It means that someone in NESC ordered the destruction of those papers. We can assume they handled the negotiations on their own. Perhaps they tipped-off the other steel companies. They probably said they were having problems with Craig but could deal with him. Maybe one of the other companies decided on more drastic action in case the documents were not destroyed or Craig had other copies. Another point to remember is that many other people would have been involved in the same meetings as Craig. If any of them were developing a conscience, becoming disillusioned with their employers, or getting greedy, they were a risk. Now those people will think twice before trying to blackmail or report their own companies. So Craig's death serves as an example to the others of what might happen. A deterrent as well as a solution."

Ball seemed to be hitting his stride, and Randall did not interrupt as he listened to the man develop the theory that seemed to fit the facts: "I am no expert, but I suspect those documents would have limited value unless Craig was around to testify or substantiate them with a formal statement. Alive, he would have been a credible witness, but without him, the other members of the club would deny the meetings and say the documents were false. Something like that, anyway."

"Yes, Andrew, it all sounds plausible. But we don't know for sure, unfortunately. Still, your theories make sense. I had not considered the deterrent angle before, but of course you are right. Maybe *that* was the main reason for killing him. Eliminate one blackmailer and frighten anyone with similar intentions." It frustrated Randall that they knew so much but their information was of little use, and he said as much to Ball.

"The information you have given me completes a picture that has been emerging from other enquiries. It's all hearsay, and we certainly do not have the necessary evidence to bring any kind of charges. Please keep your ear to the ground and text me again if anything new comes up. As soon as you are in London, dinner is on me. I am very intrigued to know more about your parallel lives."

Randall ended the conversation and sat for a while thinking about his next move. It would probably be another discussion with his boss. He felt out of his depth with the increasing complexity of Craig's business dealings and saw little chance of bringing police charges against anyone. He believed he had reached a dead end through no fault of his own. Of course, he did not want his colleagues to think he was flogging a dead horse. Because it was his first case as a chief inspector and head of the department, Randall was pretty sure Sawyer would expect him to make the judgement himself without waiting for instructions. A senior officer should know when to move on and close a file. Overall, he felt he had done a good job, so he decided to summarise his progress for Sawyer and make a firm recommendation to drop the case.

* * *

Hans Weber flew from Dnepropetrovsk to the main international airport in the capital, Kiev, on a domestic service, and then he connected with a Warsaw flight that landed early in the evening. They promised to meet him in arrivals, so he was pleased to see a board with his name on it held by a uniformed person who was looking anxiously at every arriving passenger. Weber walked over and introduced himself with a handshake. The driver seemed relieved to have found his man and took Weber's case immediately as he smiled warmly.

"Welcome, Mr Weber, we are most honoured to have you visit us. I understand this is not your first time in Poland. Do you know Warsaw well?"

"Yes, I have visited the city many times, and I admire it very much. I have good memories of my trips here."

"Yes, we are very proud of it and its history. I will drive you to your hotel. It is about thirty minutes from here if the traffic is not too heavy. We have booked you a nice room in the Sheraton."

"Thank you. I like the Sheraton. I always stay there. I really appreciate you meeting me. Am I to see Mr Bisek tonight?" asked Weber, anxious to learn more about the assignment.

"Yes, he wants to start planning things immediately. I will phone him when you are checked in, and he will meet you one hour later in the lobby. You will have time to unpack and take a shower if you desire. Is that acceptable, Mr Weber?"

"Yes, excellent. I will make myself comfortable, and then I am very much looking forward to meeting him."

"Good. He will take you to a very fine restaurant in the old town. There, you will meet some of his colleagues. It should be a very nice and interesting evening."

"I appreciate people giving up their time, and I am sure we will have a pleasant evening," said Weber with genuine enthusiasm. He liked Warsaw and had been there many times when Poland was negotiating to join the EU. He had many fond memories of evenings spent with generous and hospitable people. He also had memories of expensive but beautiful ladies that seemed to turn up just as he was thinking of bed – usually when he was having a nightcap with colleagues in the hotel bar. He had no doubt that the Polish negotiating team told the girls when and where to be, and he figured they believed a happy team would make a more generous deal. And that's what was destined to happen – with or without the girls. Poland as an early escapee of communism was a big prize, and the will of the politicians prevailed without any tough negotiations.

His spacious suite was on the third floor with a sitting area and separate bedroom. The bathroom was large and offered the option of a tub or shower. He unpacked quickly, carefully hanging his spare trousers and shirts in the wardrobe. He took a shower and afterwards felt refreshed, relaxed and optimistic about the evening ahead.

Exactly an hour after being dropped off at the hotel, the receptionist phoned him to say Mr Bisek had arrived and was waiting in the lobby. Weber grabbed his mobile, which had been charging, locked his passport and credit cards in the room safe, and headed for the lifts. Weber's first reaction to the man waiting for him with an outstretched hand and warm smile was unease. He introduced himself as Jan Bisek. There were two causes for Weber's concern. The first was the fact that the warm smile did not reach the man's stone hard eyes, and the second was that he looked like an archetypal gangster. He was strongly built and wore an expensive-looking, well-cut, black suit. He did not wear a tie, and his white shirt was open at the collar. Weber guessed he was in his late thirties. His dark hair was shaved very short, and his podgy face was clean-shaven. A small, flat nose and thin, pale lips gave him a mean look that Weber instinctively disliked. He decided to brush aside his misgivings on the basis that most of his dealings in life had been with bureaucrats and politicians; he had no idea what an academic from a Polish university law department should look like.

"May I call you Hans? After all, I know we will become friends."

"Of course, Jan. Thank you for arranging everything so efficiently and thoughtfully."

"It is a great honour for you visit us, and so quickly after we contacted you." Bisek spoke slowly in a deep, heavily accented voice, but his English was good enough. He hesitated as he chose his words, indicating to Weber that he just needed more practice at conversation.

"We are going to my favourite restaurant in the Old Town. They will look after us well. I often go there with friends and family, and I have asked them to do their very best for our honoured guest. You will meet my colleagues who are waiting. I believe they are already drinking some beer. Do you like wine, Hans? If so, the restaurant has an excellent cellar that we will visit. We can select something special."

"Yes, wine is my preference after one glass of beer. You are most kind to take this trouble, and I am sure we will have a great evening," said Weber, starting to relax.

"It is not just kindness, Hans. I have checked you out, and I know you were an important member of the negotiating team that helped Poland join the EU. We are forever grateful to people like you that made the transformation of Poland a reality. It is gratitude, not kindness."

Weber felt a tinge of guilt because he had not played a leading role in the negotiations; rather, he had spent much of his time enjoying the local hospitality. But it was true, he had been involved, and his name was on record as one of the Europeans who enabled Poland to make a relatively trouble-free entry into the promised land.

They arrived at the restaurant and were met by three other men. As predicted, they were halfway through their beers and sitting at a window table for six.

"Is someone missing?" asked Weber.

"Yes, Peter will join us after the main course, in about an hour. He is delayed at work and asked us to carry on and order."

"Is Peter also a colleague at the university?" asked Weber. He immediately sensed that he had asked a dumb question. There was some suppressed sniggering from the three beer drinkers that made him feel uneasy again. Jan gave them a dirty look and stated, "Peter is financing this lecture tour and is being very generous. He accepted the budget we proposed, without questioning some of the little luxuries we included to make your life comfortable while you are here."

"I look forward to meeting him," Weber said, and he noticed amusement in the eyes of the other three, which indicated that he was missing something.

A selection of typical polish dishes were delivered to the table at regular intervals, including some things Weber recognised from previous visits.

"This is grilled oscypek?" he asked.

Bisek nodded and asked, "You like it?"

"Yes, it is wonderful. If I remember, the cheese is smoked. It goes so well with this grilled apple and cranberry sauce."

"That is correct. The cheese is made from sheep's milk from the Tatra mountain region of Poland. You should also try the bigos, which is a meat stew. The chef here makes the best I have ever tasted. It is served with mashed potatoes. Leave some room for Sernik, though, because Polish cheesecake is very filling."

Weber nodded and sipped the wine they had selected. They had chosen a robust, Spanish wine that they hoped would pair well with heavy, traditional food.

Gradually, the tense atmosphere of the early evening eased, and a relaxed conversation developed among all five people sitting at the table. Just as coffee was being served, the mysterious Peter arrived. He did not apologise even though he was more than three hours late. Weber guessed Peter was the only sober person at the table, and when he ordered tomato juice, he wondered whether it had been wise to drink so much before meeting the man who held the purse strings for his lecture tour.

CHAPTER 13

Irina often told herself that she was a bitch, but a clever one. She thought the way she had won over Weber was masterful. To get the maximum possible reward and enjoy the process before hooking him was satisfying. She did like him, though, and she could almost tolerate his sexual demands without feeling revulsion. He was an old-fashioned, conventional man who treated her with respect and generosity. At times, the banter could get out of control, and occasionally, after too many drinks, he would insult her and her family. He loved to tell her that she came from a family of losers in a country of losers. It was partly true, but it was not something she needed to hear from him. However, he was always respectful in public and treated her like a lady.

She was financially secure as a result of his generosity and could afford to dump him anytime and survive without needing a job. Her moral compass was a little wayward, but it was good enough to guide her to reward his kindness with warm companionship and occasional sex. She did admit to friends that she had become lazy – a maid did all the cleaning and ironing. She rarely cooked, and when she did, she made only traditional Ukrainian dishes. If they dined at home, he prepared the meals, served her, and loaded the dishwasher afterwards. She rarely spent any of her own money. The monthly allowance he gave her for personal shopping was deposited promptly into one of her many bank accounts. If she needed something, she took him to the shop, selected what she wanted, put it by the till, and walked away (leaving him to pay, of course). She often wondered whether she could cope when he became old and needed more care. She doubted she would stick around for that, but judging by his general health, she hoped he would stay active for at least ten years more.

Irina came from a typically poor Ukrainian family. Her family had lived hand to mouth since the collapse of the Soviet economic system. The last one hundred years had been tough on Ukraine. Both her grandmothers were alive and talked about the misery of Nazi occupation. They still spat if they heard a German voice in the street.

She remembered how Ukraine had first tried to go it alone as a sovereign state. She recalled the chaos and shortages. The country had struggled ever since, despite a few years of progress before the world financial crisis. She did not think highly of the economy, which had stumbled from disaster to disaster and needed continuous support from International Monetary Fund loans. Consequently, she kept little money in Ukraine.

Like many of her friends, she understood virtually nothing about the political system that seemed no more stable than the economy. She had not believed in the Orange Revolution when it was happening, and as she expected, it proved to be a false dawn that was quickly followed by more chaos.

Her father was a product of the Soviet system; he had trained in the army as an engineer. He enjoyed the golden years of the Soviet Union, when its sportsmen were dominating the Olympic Games and its military capability instilled fear throughout the world. He thought of those years as a time when people believed their system had a winning formula and that the decadent West was rotting and dying. Irina supported his views and tried to persuade Weber that most of what had been achieved in Dnepropetrovsk was during communist times. He was reluctant to admit she was right, but he could see that many of the universities, apartment blocks, and roads were built then. Now they were being allowed to decay under a twisted form of capitalism.

Irina's father was a thoughtful man, but he didn't speak English. One evening, over dinner and using Irina as an interpreter, he explained to Weber that teachers, police officers, factory workers, and others were proud people in Soviet times. Conformity was rewarded with a living wage, a heated home, good education for children, summer camps, and sports facilities. Irina emphasised his point by saying that, in the present day, only a few of her friends were lucky enough to get paid, and even they spent their time trying to milk the system.

When she reflected on her situation, she had to admit that Weber had saved her from becoming another loser. In short, she was lucky he walked into the bookshop in Kiev.

The one bad period during her time with Weber was when her friend, Anna, visited them in Dubai. Weber was generous to Anna, and she got, courtesy of him, a two-week, all-inclusive holiday that included some clothes, a pedicure, and a manicure. On the last night, Anna and Irina sat up drinking long after Weber went to bed. Anna goaded Irina into opening the safe and checking how much money he kept in it. There was $30,000 in large notes. When Irina tried to shut the door of the safe, Anna held it open with her left hand and grabbed the pile of money. Holding it above her head, she pushed past Irina like a crazed demon, rushed to her room, and locked the door. Irina did nothing because she did not want to wake Hans or betray her friend whom she assumed was just being a drunken fool. She decided to wait and plead with Anna in the morning.

During the night, Anna disappeared with the money. Irina was horrified. She felt she had betrayed her husband's trust. She could have phoned the police and had Anna stopped and searched at the airport. She decided against that course of action, though, and instead rushed to her bank in Dubai Marina Mall as soon as it opened. By the time Weber came back from golf that morning, $10,000 was back in the safe. She had ordered the balance to be ready for her at the bank later in the day.

That evening, he had taken her for a meal at their favourite restaurant in Dubai Mall. He had been in such a good mood that he agreed to stand with her before dinner for two performances of the famous choreographed fountain. She loved the fountain and the music even though it only lasted a few minutes. Weber was not such a big fan and thought it childish of her to want to stand with the crowds in the heat and watch something so predictable. But that evening, he had smiled and pretended to enjoy watching the water, sound, and light show. Most of all, she remembered the dinner conversation vividly.

"Irina, I know what happened last night. I planned to change some dollars today, but I found an empty safe. Later during the day, I checked and saw $10,000. And later, I saw $30,000. Of course, I expected to see Anna at breakfast. I expected her to thank us and say her goodbyes. But she had disappeared, I assumed she ran off with my money."

"I am so sorry, Hans. I am so ashamed of myself for opening the safe and allowing it to happen. And I am so ashamed of my friend. You were so kind to her, and she betrayed us both."

"Irina, you put things right the only way you could. I have always loved you, and now I love you even more. I will give you back the money as a present, but I never want to see Anna again. Unfortunately, she is a certain type of female – an opportunist with no morals. She is the worst kind of whore ... one who would steal from her client's wallet while walking out the door."

Irina cried over the main course with relief and gratitude. It had been her most stressful day since meeting her husband.

* * *

Randall's meeting with his boss held some surprises and disappointments. He updated the case briefing note he used before with a summary of the interviews conducted since their last meeting. At the end of his report, he drew some conclusions that he hoped Sawyer would accept. He then made a final recommendation that the investigation be closed.

"Firstly, I agree with your conclusions regarding the Craig case. I also support your recommendation that we stop spending time on the investigation. We are never going to prosecute anybody because we have no hard evidence. We know a lot about many things, but not enough to present to the Crime Prosecution Service. We are not going to catch the killers, and we are not going to identify the conspirators unless someone confesses. The list of possible conspirators is longer now we have information from the Polish lady and Andrew Ball about Craig's secret business activities."

"Yes, sir, that seems to be the situation. We have two versions of almost the same story. He was a private entrepreneur doing a job for NESC that enabled him to line his own pocket."

"Okay, let's agree on finishing the investigation right now. Your interviews and discussions with people like Ball, Ms Craig, the solicitor, and the lady from Poland have been conducted well. You know how to ask open questions and win their respect. In this particular investigation, there was no reason to get tough with anybody ... except, perhaps, the NESC people. You were dealing with well-educated, successful, professional people throughout this case, and you were at ease because they are your sort of people. Your next case will take you out of your middle-class comfort zone, and I will be interested to see how you cope. We will discuss that case in a minute."

"I understand your comments, sir, but I did experience the rough and tough of city policing on my way to this job."

"I know that, Richard. Don't be defensive. I want to help you because I believe in you and want to see you climb to the top of the heap."

"Thank you, sir. Do we need to discuss the Craig case anymore?"

"Yes, I have not finished giving you my advice. You see, Richard, there is one thing about ending the investigation that really worries me, and it is something you should have in the back of your mind every time you stop working on an unsolved case in the future. Your decision is right, and I support it. I would order it closed even if you hadn't made that recommendation."

"Your point is that someone else may solve it and call me an idiot?" suggested Randall, feeling uncomfortable with the direction of the discussion.

"More or less. The most dangerous *someone else* is the press. Imagine a scandal breaks concerning price-fixing and they connect the involvement and subsequent death of Simon Craig to the scandal. Immediately, our journalist friends will want to know about the police investigation and which idiotic police officer missed the clues and dropped the case. If it turns political and embarrasses a government minister or two, scapegoats will be found, careers will be damaged. It's probably a small risk, and we have to back our judgement, but it's still a possibility. All I am saying to you as an older, wiser man, is that you should always think about this angle when throwing in the towel."

"Point taken. I must confess, sir, I had not given it a moment's thought. Your kind advice will stay with me for the rest of my career."

"Good. One more thing: I have talked to my boss, and he has talked to his boss. We want your help in giving someone a good, old-fashioned warning of a clip round the ear."

"Whose ear will we be clipping?"

"The chairman of NESC. He is a good, reasonable guy with a long and respectable career behind him. Honours and awards are in the offing. He will expect something meaningful like a knighthood or peerage. You will meet him with two very senior civil servants. The three of you will see him alone. We are pretty sure he does not know what has been going on behind his back."

"What is my role in this?" asked Randall.

"You will present the findings of your investigation, including your theories about why Craig was murdered. You will not mention Craig's extracurricular activities in Egypt or anywhere else; rather, you'll stick to the story that it was all about price-fixing and *the club*. The civil servants will do the rest. We want the chairman to know what his people have been up to, that we believe a consequence of their activities was the death of Craig. We will give him the chance to put his house in order. Someone from the Home Office will contact you when the meeting is fixed."

"Intriguing. I will wait for their call. You mentioned a new case?"

Randall listened with growing interest to Sawyers description of the new investigation he was required to lead. He was to take over a murder enquiry from the city police force in Lisbon, Portugal. A British man had been kidnapped while on holiday, held for three weeks, and then murdered without the criminals ever contacting anyone to demand a ransom. The assumption in Portugal was that he had been kidnapped to stop him from doing something or getting somewhere. They had handed the case to the British believing the reasons for the kidnapping would be found in the United Kingdom.

Randall returned to his room feeling a little down about the conversation concerning Craig, but he was excited by the prospect of starting a new investigation. From a personal satisfaction point of view, he would have liked to have gone further with the Craig investigation, to have finished the story even if no prosecutions could be made. But he knew that, as a professional, it was right to stop and focus on something else. Sawyer's observations about him operating in his comfort zone had also hit home and left Randall feeling that he still had a lot to prove. And top off the flurry of emotions, he was feeling down because Lisa was due to fly to Washington the next day.

The previous Saturday, he and Lisa visited his parents. As expected, they were delighted by the news of their engagement, but they were disappointed that the wedding would be delayed for more than a year. Despite them saying all the right things to Lisa, he could tell by his parents' tone that they did not approve of her trip to Washington. His father understood Randall's weakness very well and knew how easily he could become depressed. He doubted Lisa had witnessed his black moods, and he hoped she never would, but he was sure her absence would be much harder for his son than for her.

Randall sat in his office reflecting on the visit and his situation; fearing the next twelve months. He then took out his notebook and scribbled a few lines to prevent the negative thoughts from overtaking him:

Our lives changed forever:
Kind fate bringing us together.
Mutual respect and sharing,
Much support and caring.
Achieving things with pride,
Not drifting with the tide.
Parting full of sorrow,
Worry for tomorrow.

He knew the poetry wasn't very good, but that was not the point – when he finished, he felt more positive. He decided to read the poem to Lisa over dinner that night and hope for the best.

* * *

Ricardo Denso had tracked down Andrew Ball without the help of Barker. It was simple. It took one phone call to the NESC sales office in London during which he pretended to be a customer and close friend. Via that call, he established that Ball used to work there. Denso just asked to speak to him, and he let the helpful receptionist do the rest.

"Andrew Ball is no longer based here. He is now working as a consultant on a special project concerning one of our subsidiaries in Cairo."

"Do you know when he will be back from Cairo?" Denso asked, "I really would like to catch-up with him soon."

"Not for a few weeks, I believe. I can give you his office number in Cairo," she offered, and he gladly accepted the digits.

To Denso, the conclusion was obvious: Ball had worked for Craig, and he was a close enough friend that he wanted to visit Craig's family in France. If he was a close friend and colleague, he would probably know too much for comfort because Craig would have confided in him. Denso's caution bordered on paranoia, but he didn't want to leave anything to chance. Regardless, he was bored, and a trip to Cairo would give him something to do. Thus, his next challenge was to devise a cover story. He needed to meet Ball and build his trust, and he could try some well-chosen trick questions on him. He doubted Ball was very bright; after all, he had been a salesman throughout his career. Furthermore, his brain was probably addled by alcohol as a consequence of entertaining clients for forty years.

He arrived in Cairo International Airport on a direct flight from Zurich. The airport was chaotic – the much-needed third terminal was still under construction, and the other two were unable to cope with the volume. He spent nearly an hour in an immigration queue before reaching the crowded arrivals hall where he began his search for a taxi. But chaos was what he expected, especially on the roads. The fifteen-kilometre drive from the airport to the centre of the city took more than an hour. Drivers were changing lanes illogically and honking their horns rather than making progress. *Typical Egypt,* he thought, *chaotic, hot, dusty, and run-down. Not like my beloved Zurich.* (Although he did sometimes complain to friends that Zurich was too much at the other extreme: unnaturally organised and polished.) He needed the trip to Cairo to remind himself what untidiness looked like, to appreciate order and cleanliness.

He checked into the Cairo Marriot in the Zamalek district, close to the city centre. He decided to spend a week on his mission. He needed time to win over Ball and get him talking. Also, he wanted to enjoy himself – the outdoor swimming pool, good food, and a casino were all he needed to entertain himself.

By the time he reached his room, he was starting to relax. He threw down his briefcase on the bed and waited for his luggage to be delivered. The view over the Nile from his balcony was impressive, but the heat and the noise of the city did not make it a good place to sit. He shut the sliding doors and poured himself a beer from the minibar. He decided a good dinner and an early night would set him up nicely for his first meeting with Ball. He had phoned Ball from

Zurich and arranged a breakfast meeting for the following day. The pretext was that Swiss Metals had a special project for him and would pay well for his consultancy services. Ball sounded enthusiastic and agreed to meet Denso in the lobby of the Marriot at 8:00 a.m. It seemed to Denso that Ball liked consultancy work and the thought of earning extra money.

The next day, the lobby was busy with check outs, but there was only one man who fit the description of a semi-retired Englishman. Denso approached him with an outstretched hand and a broad smile.

"You are Andrew Ball, I think. I am Ricardo Denso."

"Yes, I am. And I am pleased to meet you, Ricardo."

Ball was wearing an open-necked, blue shirt, dark grey trousers, and black shoes. He had not bothered to wear a suit because he did not consider the meeting an interview, more a sharing of ideas and exploration of possibilities. Anyway, he did not want to look too keen because he doubted he would be interested in working with Denso. Denso's first thought about him was that he looked like an ex-military man. His assured manner, his good posture, and his choice of clothing were all good hints.

After introductions, they were taken to a table in the dining room. It was a buffet breakfast, and the food was arranged on several islands. Ball chose only from the fruit island and sat down quickly with a plate of melon, pineapple, and apple slices. Denso had to wait for the chef to prepare an omelette filled with peppers, onion, and tomato.

"I assumed an Englishman would have sausages, egg, and bacon," joked Denso.

"Not this one, Ricardo. Ten years ago, I would have, but now I try and eat healthy food during the day and then have what I like for dinner."

"Sounds sensible. You look slim and fit. Perhaps I should try your approach. Do you like working in Cairo?"

"Not really. It is an interesting place to do business and I've learnt a lot, but I am here at the wrong time of year to enjoy it. It is too hot for golf or sightseeing. Give me Europe in summer anytime."

"Well that brings me to the purpose of our meeting. Let me explain the background." Denso had finished his small omelette in a couple of bites, and saw little point in more small talk. He started with an explanation of his role: "I am head of security, and I report to the chief executive officer of Swiss Metals. He is a no-nonsense guy, and he asked me to look at the senior sales people in the company and advise him whether I thought they were honest and loyal."

"That is a tough assignment – honesty cannot be measured easily. Sometimes it is very difficult to know whether the salespeople are getting you a good deal or favouring customers. Loyalty is also difficult to check, and disloyalty can come in many forms," commented Ball.

"Exactly the problem. I have twenty guys working for me, and their main occupation is watching purchasing people and salespeople – the two areas where big money can be made from bribes and kickbacks. By *kickbacks,* I mean giving selected customers a low price in return for money. My people monitor mobile phones, e-mails, and behaviour."

"What do you mean by *monitoring behaviour?*"

"We know how much people earn and their family situation. For example, if a purchasing guy with a modest income and a wife at home looking after the children buys an expensive car, we will look more closely. Through our networks, we can find out whether the person borrowed the money, paid cash, or saved up for it. My people also hang around bars that our staff use and listen to conversations. It is amazing what people say to and about their friends after a few drinks. Naturally, we have a few spies in the critical departments as well who feed us information about their colleagues."

Ball was surprised and interested that so many resources were put into detecting such things. NESC also had a large security department under the infamous Ronald Barker, but he doubted they were so committed. He asked Denso, "Does NESC have more or less the same thing, Ricardo?"

"Yes. Like us, they have a front office security department with people you would see and know. Behind the scenes, there is another layer of security based in a secret location. You would never meet those people unless by accident, and you would not know their job. Usually they're ex-policemen or ex-intelligence officers."

"Amazing. I would never have expected the problem to be so large."

"This is the irony of our work. It is not a big problem because we stop it from getting out of control. I think you English might say we *nip it in the bud.* What we know from studying corruption in Eastern Europe and Africa is that it is like a disease, and if it's not dealt with early, it spreads and becomes an epidemic."

"I understand. So where might I fit in?" asked Ball.

"My boss thinks we are missing the big fish. They are the clever and sophisticated guys who create a network and use their business school know-how to build their own enterprises within our company."

"Do you have any examples?"

"Only suspicions, Andrew, and an understanding of how it could be done. We think some of our senior salesmen have appointed agents and distributors on the basis that they will be allowed to take a cut from commissions or profits. It is difficult to prove because they channel the money into offshore vehicles and do not repatriate it through their own bank accounts. They reinvest through nominees or their offshore companies."

Ball was not sure where the conversation was going, but he had an instinctive dislike of Denso. His training in the intelligence services prepared him for such situations – situations in which giving information could yield more from the other side, but giving too much, too quickly could reduce your value in the equation. He thought long and hard, and then he said, "I came across something like you are describing here in Cairo. Very sophisticated. I soon discovered the same thing was going on in other countries. I assumed NESC was losing several millions to middlemen created or supported by a senior salesman. Yes, in our case, the man became a big and wealthy fish using his job with NESC to build a vast business empire."

"Then my boss is probably correct," said Denso. And when Ball didn't add more, he asked, "How did you discover what was happening?"

"I came here to sort out a problem of slow-moving stock and falling sales. The closer I looked at things, the more concerned I became. I was suspicious of the way the office was being run and the nature of the customer relationships. It is always interesting to look at who is not being sold to and ask why. The answer may be that they are not prepared to share their profits or provide kickbacks. Therefore, I made friends in Cairo connected with the steel industry, and I drank and ate with them. Basically, I kept my ear to the ground and pieced together what was going on." Ball's explanation was not the whole truth, and it made him seem smarter than he was. Most of what he had discovered came from Ahmed rather than from clever research. In reality, the business fell apart because of Craig's death and the vacuum that left. There was no one to operate the systems and networks he established. He did not want to introduce the subject of Craig, though. He suspected Denso would, in his own time.

"Andrew, the work you have done here in Cairo is what we think we need to do. We should have an experienced person like you looking at what our salespeople are doing. We need someone to talk privately to those who know and understand the business in each market where we sell our steel. It is like intelligence gathering, and it would mean a lot of travel and time. If you are interested, I will talk to my boss later today. I hope you are, because we would work well together. If he agrees, I will put together a proposal for you to consider, and perhaps we can meet for dinner tomorrow evening."

"Sure. I will be your host. We will eat on one of the very good floating restaurants not far from here. Local people eat quite late, so the best atmosphere is after nine o'clock."

"Okay, where shall we meet?" asked an eager Denso.

"The restaurant is called Le Pacha 1901. It's the large floating palace that you can see from this hotel. It is brightly lit at night. Anyway, I will meet you in the lobby at nine o'clock. We can walk from here."

They parted in the hotel entrance with Denso adding a friendly pat on the back to his firm handshake. Ball smiled to himself. *Just like the old days, except I am the source this time,* he mused. *They want something from me, but not consultancy work.*

CHAPTER 14

Weber noticed that no one spoke after Peter arrived, and there was a long period of silence before Weber decided he should offer his thanks: "We have had a most excellent dinner, and the arrangements for my arrival were very kind and efficient. I thank everybody for their part in making me so welcome."

Peter looked at him long and hard. He was wearing an immaculate, dark grey suit with a white shirt and pale blue tie. His hair was shaved close to his scalp. He was average height and slightly overweight. His large chest and broad shoulders reminded Weber of a nightclub bouncer he upset in Dusseldorf once. "I am pleased you are pleased," he grunted sarcastically. "Unfortunately, Mr Weber, there are some people who are not pleased with you, and they have asked me to meet you and explain what makes them unhappy. However, I have given you the benefit of the doubt and treated you with respect and generosity – that is because I know your type, Mr Weber, and negotiation is second nature. You will avoid confrontation at all cost; you are a diplomat by character, and compromise is your watchword."

Weber's mind was fuddled by the wine and tired from the journey. It was almost his bedtime, and he felt groggy, but he managed to say, "So the welcome and kindness was a ruse and I am here under false pretences?"

"Yes, you are. We will talk again in the morning. We will go for a long walk together in Kampinos Forest. It is a wonderful place to walk and think and talk. We will discuss the details among dunes and marshlands. The weather forecast is good, and I will bring a picnic. Do not panic, though, because there is a solution. However, should you panic and want to rush to the airport, we have accessed your hotel safe and removed your passport and credit cards. Should that make you panic enough to go to the police, you would be wasting your time because they are my friends and ex-colleagues. They will occupy your time taking statements and seeming concerned, but they will not help you recover your possessions. And should you rush to the your consulate looking for help, you will deny yourself the opportunity to know what we know about your past criminal behaviour and risk becoming the culprit in a fascinating story of corruption in the EU that is about to be published in an American newspaper."

Weber felt frightened and confused. They put him in a taxi and sent him back to the Sheraton. During the journey, the message started sinking in. His stomach tightened at the prospect of the walk in the forest. He stopped in the hotel bar for a large Cognac before heading for his room. The barman's attempts at friendly conversation were rebutted, and Weber found a seat that was far from the bar. He dreaded going back to his room and finding confirmation that the men with whom he spoke were as good as their word. Sure enough, the safe was empty.

In the meantime, Peter phoned Svetlana to confirm that contact had been made, and she said, "What is he like, Uncle Peter?"

"A fairly typical, long-serving government official. Well-educated, well-mannered, and sophisticated. The other guys said he was a good conversationalist when relaxed." He laughed.

"Will he cooperate?"

"For sure. When I spell out the options tomorrow, he will seek to please."

"Good luck. And thanks."

Svetlana smiled to herself. Things were going to plan. Revenge for the misery of Craig's death was part of her motivation, but she genuinely thought that they were right to expose the businessmen who believed they were above the law. If her uncle had to use intimidation, it was a necessary evil. She looked around the apartment and the personal good fortune it represented. She felt a pang of guilt because Craig had been a great friend and lover, and she missed him badly. But her material reward was impressive, and she was proud to own two valuable properties in London.

She poured herself a drink and decided to phone Susan Robson. She could tell immediately that Susan was on edge and keen to get something off her chest.

"I was talking to an old colleague in London. He took over from me on the competition law consultancy work. He is very busy, but you know, Susan, the reasons companies want advice has nothing to do with wanting to comply with the law. They just want to know enough to avoid being caught."

"You mean they intend to carry on as before, but they want to know the risks?"

"And how not to leave evidence. When I was involved, some companies organised shredding parties to destroy old documents that could be used as evidence. The authorities have the right to raid offices without warning. These raids are popularly known as *dawn raids,* but they usually take place during normal office hours."

"How do they know where to raid?" asked Svetlana as she visualised senior managers standing over shredding machines, not daring to hand the task to assistants.

"If they have a suspicion that an illegal meeting has taken place, they look for confirmation by raiding companies they think were at the meeting. If they find diaries or travel documents of a senior executive linking the date and place, they're golden! If they are lucky, they'll find meeting notes or an internal briefing document describing the meeting."

"So part of your old job was telling them not to leave incriminating stuff lying around."

"I never looked at it like that when I was doing it, but yes. Some companies called back retired employees and trained them in the investigation techniques of the competition authorities. I am ashamed to say that I helped them simulate raids. Any employee we discovered with documents I thought might be incriminating was disciplined."

"Did people hide documents as some kind of insurance policy against getting fired? I would have," said Svetlana, only half-joking.

"Yes, I'm pretty sure they did. What makes me particularly bitter is that many companies appointed compliance officers on my advice. All they seemed to do was send out personal warnings and threats about the consequences of getting caught. It was done to cover their boss's arses when, all along, the bosses wanted the collusion to continue. It seemed that free competition was too expensive for them."

"You take it too much to heart, Susan. You were just doing your job."

"I think that is what certain gentlemen pleaded at their trials in Nuremberg," she said with a laugh.

"By the way, Susan, I almost forgot: Uncle Peter and Hans Weber have met, and Peter is certain he will cooperate."

"Good. Then we can wreak havoc on some egos and careers."

* * *

Denso was in a light-hearted mood at dinner in the Le Pacha 1901. He seemed to enjoy the atmosphere, the food, the belly dancing, and the traditional music. He said nothing significant until the main course had been cleared away and they had finished the first bottle of wine. Ball had ordered a decent bottle of Beaujolais, and that provided the cue for Denso: "That is a very nice wine, Andrew. Do you normally drink French wines?"

"No. Often, but not normally. In restaurants, I usually drink South American wines because they can be very good and a better value. I saw this particular Beaujolais on the list, though, and knew it would be excellent. I decided to spoil us with something a little special."

"Do you like France?"

"Very much. I was there a few weeks ago visiting friends on the way here."

"You drove here?!" exclaimed Denso.

A warning bell sounded in Ball's ear. It was not a loud one, but it was strong enough to cause him to think about why Denso had made that assumption. Few people would drive from London to Cairo on a business trip. Ball had said nothing about travel during their first meeting nor used his BMW since arriving in Cairo. He was using a NESC car registered in Egypt because he feared his BMW would get damaged in the chaos of the city. There was nothing to suggest he had not flown to France, met the family, and then flown on to Cairo. That would be the normal thing to do. Denso did not seem aware of his mistake, and he was actually delighted with Ball for confirming his trip to France without too much prompting. It seemed Ball was not trying to hide anything, but Denso needed to ask a few more questions to be sure.

"Yes, I drove. I had plenty of time, and I wanted to enjoy myself. I love rural France. Of course, I also saw quite a bit of your country before catching the ferry in Naples, which was also very interesting."

"Do your friends live in Paris?"

"No, a long way south."

Still not hiding anything, thought Denso, and he sipped the last of the wine in his glass before changing the subject: "The guy you told me about yesterday, the guy who was building his own business out of his NESC responsibilities – was it Simon Craig?"

Again, Ball was hearing warning noises. Denso's subconscious seemed to have associated the friends in France with Craig. Ball picked up the wine list to give himself time to think before replying. He pretended to read it. He thought, *there are two possibilities: Denso knows I went to see the Craig family or he is guessing.* Ball decided to let the conversation develop, but not before calling the waiter and ordering another bottle of wine.

"Yes. In fact, it was his widow and children I went to see in France."

"You must have known Craig very well."

"Craig was not the sort of man you got to know well, but he was a good boss."

"But well enough to make a big diversion on your journey here."

He knows where the family lives, Ball thought. He wondered whether Denso would be so transparent in his own language. If he was thinking in Italian and translating at the same time, he might be giving himself away accidentally. The other possibility was that he trusted Ball and wanted to confide in him to bring him closer as a potential employee. For a reason not yet clear to Ball, he rejected the last possibility.

"I was not able to go to the funeral. I wanted to pay my respects to the widow and check how she was coping. I had met her a few times, and it seemed the right thing to do. Craig had few close friends in NESC, and the people who went to his funeral were figureheads doing it out of duty."

"NESC did not ask you to visit the family? Maybe check a few things?"

"No. What do you mean by *check a few things*?"

"Well no one knows why he was killed. Perhaps Mrs Craig had been contacted or found out something to explain his death."

"NESC did not know I was visiting her."

"Why does she think he was killed, Andrew?"

"Despite all the speculation going on in her head, she has no idea."

"Do you think she is telling the truth? Perhaps Craig told her more than she is letting on," prompted Denso. He leaned forward in his chair and looked Ball straight in the eye.

"I doubt it. She seems genuinely confused," replied Ball, holding eye contact.

"Did NESC give her good support?"

"Financially, yes. What upset her was that some of the people sent to help her seemed more interested in what she knew about some documents. They even asked the eldest girl if she knew her father's secret hiding places."

"Did they find anything?"

"She said they did not. She thought they were half-hearted attempts, though. They told her they were looking for important company papers, and she gave them permission to search anywhere. She told me they were not thorough. It upset here at the time, but she had plenty of other things on her mind. Afterwards, after they had gone, it really hit home: she started to have nightmares about her husband's secret papers and what might be in them. She did a very thorough search herself. She said it became an obsession to find something or find nothing. She spent three days looking, though, and found nothing."

"I guess NESC were not really expecting to find anything," said Denso thoughtfully. "I guess they were checking rather than searching. And checking on her and how much she knew."

"Perhaps. It is a very strange story that we may never get to the bottom of."

"My boss asked me to check out the Craig murder in case any of our people were at risk. You know, from some kind of anti-steel terror campaign," Denso lied.

"What did you conclude?"

"That it was a one-off," replied Denso with the confidence of a man who knew for certain.

Ball said goodbye to Denso at that point, declining the latter's offer to join him in his hotel casino. As they parted outside the restaurant, Denso handed Ball an envelope containing a draft consultancy contract. He did not bother opening it that evening because he had no intention of working with Denso. The dinner conversation had given him food for thought, though. He needed to phone a contact in Paris, but when he checked his watch, he decided it was too late.

* * *

Uncle Peter was waiting in the lobby at nine o'clock in the morning when a sour-faced Weber descended in the lift. Peter spoke first, oozing goodwill: "Good morning, Hans. I am pleased you decided to join me this morning. I have a very special picnic in the car, and I am sure we will enjoy ourselves and come to a mutually satisfactory arrangement. And the weather forecast is good."

"I am not sure I will enjoy myself, but I am prepared to listen and understand what you want from me." Weber was regretting the cognac. When paired with the worry of the picnic in the forest, the drink had kept him awake all night.

"I think you will come to understand, Hans, that we mean you no harm. We simply want to work with you on a project that is very important to our sponsors."

"Sponsors? Who are your sponsors?"

"I can't tell you that, but I can tell you they are two very determined ladies who want justice and retribution. I warn you that they are dangerously committed to their cause. They are intelligent and know a lot about you and your activities over the last few years. Now let's stop this discussion until we are walking in the beautiful forest."

Weber was nervous as the car pulled away from the hotel. It headed northwest towards the Kampinos Forest. The forest was part of a national park. The park had a special significance for the people of Warsaw because it contained mass graves for those secretly killed there during the Nazi occupation of Poland. Weber did not want to end up in a single or mass grave, and he wondered what was expected of him. He also wondered how much he would suffer if he refused. He could think of nothing in his past that justified his present situation and the threat he felt hanging over him. And then he remembered Craig and felt his blood pressure starting to rise.

They left the car in a parking area close to the forest entrance. Peter gave the driver instructions to set up the picnic in an hour at a specified location in the trees. Normally, Weber would have enjoyed such an outing, but on this occasion fear ruled out any pleasure.

Peter started the conversation with a statement about the rules they would follow: "First, you will listen and not try to contradict or deny what I accuse you of. We know much more than you think we know. Protesting your innocence will not work with me."

Over the next fifteen minutes, Peter horrified Weber with a very accurate and complete list of his wrongdoings during his career in the Competition Inspectorate. Weber had to admit that the research was sound and filled with details he thought he had hidden. Weber did not interrupt, and at the end of the monologue, he heard the punchline: "Hans, we know a lot about you and what you are. In exchange for our silence, we need your help. It will not be challenging for you, and I think you will soon appreciate how reasonable we are prepared to be given your criminal behaviour, disloyalty to your employers, and disloyalty to the people of the EU in general."

"What do you want from me?" grunted Weber.

"Three things. First, we want three hundred thousand euros to cover the expenses our ladies are incurring. You can afford this easily. We know your assets and bank balances."

Again Weber grunted, and then he asked for the second and third demands.

"Second, we want the names of five people from different industries who you think would be prepared to cooperate with us to expose their own secret clubs and cartel operations. Third, we want you to approach these five people and tell them to help us or become victims themselves. Tell them great purges will follow the publicity and embarrassment our ladies plan to deliver to the unsuspecting masses. Politicians and senior bureaucrats will be looking for scapegoats, and the courts will be full of those they hold responsible. Anyone who helps end this nonsense will be identified by us and labelled a hero. We promise to portray you as a good guy, Hans."

"Am I to understand you plan to take this evidence to the competition authorities?"

"Certainly not. They would organise a cover-up of something so embarrassing to them."

"I agree. You should stay well away from them. If I do not cooperate, I will be exposed as an organiser and supporter of these cartels, I'll be considered a corrupt official who took money to protect companies from investigation."

"Exactly," agreed Peter.

"If I do cooperate, I will still end up being investigated, but I will have already confessed and helped expose the problem. There's not a big difference; both lead to humiliation and ridicule."

"True. But if you help us, you will be a seen as a man who saw the light after retiring. We will say you came to us full of remorse and confessions. We will arrange for you to give some television interviews. As the heat dies down, you should be able to negotiate a deal for yourself, either immunity or something to let you avoid being charged with anything serious. If you do not help us, the press will chase you and portray you as scum because we will say you were a leading figure. Which you were. Then you will be arrested. You will be photographed getting in and out of police cars with a blanket over your head. You will probably be the top scapegoat. They will freeze your assets and put you in prison for a few years. The press will also chase Irina and pressure her to give them the inside story on her husband. You will be able to read about your sex life in prison and see pictures of Irina pouting at the cameras." As Peter calmly explained the options, Weber was trying to see a way out but struggling.

"Put like that, I do not have many choices. Of course, I could confess now and be in a better position for immunity."

"You could, but their internal investigation will take much longer than we need to get our story to the public. We will do it with or without your cooperation. We will lean on people ourselves if you do not help, and then we'll exaggerate your role. We will make you the central figure. If they promise you immunity before the story breaks, they will have to break their promise; otherwise, it will look like the old boy's network conducting a cover-up."

They walked without talking for a while, which gave Weber the chance to think before he asked, "How good is the evidence you already have?"

"Very good. It was written by a man now dead, and there are plenty of supporting documents to substantiate his claims. But we want to update the story and show it is still going on, that people alive today are involved. These are people that can be identified, investigated, and punished. It will be more newsworthy."

"I guess the dead man is Simon Craig?"

"Yes," confirmed Peter.

"Few people were more involved than him. If he provided the information, then it is good. Which industries other than steel are you interested in?"

"Cement, paper, pharmaceuticals, footwear, mobile phones, and anything else you recommend. You know where the strongest cartels operate." Peter offered Weber the chance to use his inside knowledge. It seemed from his comment about Craig that Weber recognised the strength of their position. And his last question suggested he was on board, ready to cooperate.

They walked slowly through the forest and arrived at a picnic area where the driver had laid one of the tables with white linen, cutlery, and champagne glasses. No one else was around, and all they could hear were the sounds of the forest. And then the silence was disturbed by a loud pop indicating the removal of the champagne cork. Nervous, Weber jumped at the sound before realising it was not a gunshot. The driver poured like a well-trained waiter, and Weber felt himself relaxing. He did not want to spend the rest of the afternoon in a bad mood. Despite the unpleasantness of the situation, he liked Peter and wanted to enjoy his company over lunch. He had already decided that, because he could not beat them, he may as well join them. Thus, there was no point in sulking.

* * *

The meeting took place in a conference room in the Goring Hotel in Belgravia. Randall did not know why they could not use an office, but he guessed neutral territory was more suitable for an off-the-record conversation. Anyway, it was a short walk for him, and the overstated Englishness of the place was quite amusing. There were four of them in a room big enough for ten people. There was a strong smell of wood polish and leather that Randall found suffocating. Stuart Baxter started the meeting with introductions while opening a window. It seemed he also wanted to change the air, and a cool breeze quickly removed the staleness from the room.

"You know who I am, Stan, and you know Peter Cook, my colleague from the Home Office. Let me introduce Chief Inspector Randall from the Metropolitan Police, based in Scotland Yard. Let me add that this is a private, off-the-record discussion."

"Good morning, everybody," replied the chairman nervously. Rarely was he called Stan, except by his wife and friends. *Stanley* was more appropriate in such a situation – even *Mr Jones* would suitable – but he suspected Baxter was sending him a message … something about ego and status. He knew Baxter from meetings he had attended at the Department of Trade and Industry. He was a top guy, very sharp and in control. He continued, trying to sound relaxed, "I am curious why such senior civil servants and a police officer want to meet me privately. What have I done?"

An unsmiling Baxter moved directly to the matter at hand: "Chief Inspector Randall will give you a summary of his investigation of the Craig murder. We believe we fully understand the motive. It is very relevant to you as chairman of NESC. You may question him at the end, but please do not interrupt his report."

Over the next thirty minutes, Randall ran through the main points of his investigation and the conclusion that Craig had tried to blackmail his employers. He explained the fire and said that he firmly believed that event had been organised by NESC. He finished by stating that, though they had no evidence, they suspected that either NESC had arranged the killing or the chairman's colleagues had tipped-off other companies in the cartel. He speculated that, most likely, another company had not trusted a negotiated solution and wanted to eliminate the risk and issue a warning to others. Stan, the chairman, sat listening. Periodically, he shook his head in apparent disbelief.

When Randall finished, Peter Cook spoke for the first time, "An excellent and balanced summary of the case, Mr Randall. You will understand, Stan, why we brought this to your attention. The lesson for everybody is that once people cross the line into lawlessness, they become vulnerable to more lawlessness. There is no justification for thinking sophisticated white-collar crimes are different from common crimes, and it seems – as with the murder, as with the fire – that they can easily morph."

"Yes, I do. I am horrified; I am disgusted at the behaviour of my own people and with myself for employing and trusting such people."

Stuart Baxter nodded as if understanding and sympathising. He then spoke in an unemotional, monotone voice usually associated with television caricatures of civil servants.

"Our fear, Stan, is that, one day, the press will get a sniff of this story. Too many people know part of the story, and a good journalist could research or guess the rest. We need hard evidence to bring a prosecution about, but newspapers can destroy reputations with just rumour. You have a good reputation, and I am sure it will soon be rewarded with high honours—"

"Unless this story breaks first," Jones interrupted, finishing the sentence for him.

"Yes. The question is, what can you do now to help protect the reputation of your company, yourself, and the businessmen of this country?"

"I am not sure what I can do, but any advice would be welcome. And rest assured, I will do whatever you advise me to do. If you think I should resign earlier than planned, I will resign."

"No. To resign a few months earlier than planned will draw attention at the wrong time. Your replacement cannot start earlier than January. You need to clear out a few senior people so that, if the story breaks, at least they won't be your employees – you will not have to defend them. We think Barker, Redder, and Jackson knew exactly what was going on and handled the negotiation with Craig. We think one of them orchestrated the fire at the solicitor's office and tipped-off the other companies regarding the negotiation with Craig. It does not matter which one of them it was, if you flush out all three."

"I understand. But sacking three board members will also lead to speculation and draw attention to the company," argued Jones.

"Yes, but it is the lesser of evils we are trying to deal with," answered Cook. "The company results are not good, and you can say you discussed it with the new chairman and agreed with him that action was needed immediately. We will brief him, and he will support your story."

"Are you going to tell him everything you have told me today?"

"No, it will be an abridged version. He is a good friend of this government, and I am sure he will help us through these difficulties, especially if we make it look like he is already getting involved in NESC matters and preparing the ground for his arrival. He will get credit for being proactive."

The meeting broke up with a humbled chairman agreeing to follow their advice. Randall had mixed feelings. He admired the way the matter was being handled, but he regretted the fact that he had not completed the investigation to the point that prosecutions were possible.

CHAPTER 15

Ball arrived in London a day later. Before leaving Cairo, he told Denso he did not want to commit his time to more consultancy work. He said that he had been called back to London and left Denso scratching his head in his hotel with a few more days of his business trip to kill.

Apparently, Denso had won nearly a thousand dollars in the casino and thought he was on a run of good luck. As far as Ball could make out, he was sleeping during the day and playing roulette by night.

Ball arranged to meet Randall in a pub in Belgravia at eight o'clock. They planned to have a beer before heading for an Indian restaurant Ball liked in Knightsbridge. Randall explained on the telephone that the investigation was on hold, but he said that he would be delighted to have the long-promised conversation on parallel living and catch-up on events in Cairo. With Lisa being away and no football on television, he was grateful for the company of a man he had grown to like and respect.

They both arrived at the pub at the same time by separate taxis and shook hands on the pavement before entering the dark interior of The White Horse. Randall ordered their drinks, and they found a corner table. Ball set the agenda for the evening: "I have a few things to tell you about the Craig case that we can do here over this pint. And then I propose we head for the restaurant and discuss parallel lives, football, and cricket."

"Okay. I cannot switch off from Craig even though, officially, the investigation is finished. My boss thinks it may come back to haunt us, perhaps through a newspaper story. By the way, I get the impression he knows you from somewhere. Whenever you came up in conversation during my progress reports, he reacted as if you were an acquaintance whose opinion he respected."

"What's his name?"

"Fred Sawyer. He is a chief superintendent."

"Yes, I know him. Not well. Anyway, we will discuss this when we cover parallel lives," said Ball with a smile.

"Update me on Cairo and Craig."

"The thing you will be most interested in is that Rachel Craig's phones were being tapped. I have an old colleague in Paris who arranged for the landline and her mobile phone to be checked."

"You are very resourceful! What made you have them checked?"

"The head of security of Swiss Metals visited me in Cairo with a story about wanting to hire me. His name is Ricardo Denso. Instinctively, I did not like or trust him. During a dinner conversation, it became obvious he knew I had visited her. It puzzled me at first, but not for long. I had called her to ask permission to visit the house. Of course, I had to introduce myself."

"Seems your instincts were right. They probably made you aware of his mistakes."

"Yes. I think he was not as cautious using English as he would have been in his native tongue. Another thing about Denso was that he seemed too interested in whether Rachel Craig had found out anything new. The questions were reasonable, but the intensity on his face and in his eyes suggested it was more than a passing interest. If I am not mistaken, this guy is paranoid about something."

"So you think his main reasons for seeing you in Cairo were to find out what you knew as a colleague of Craig, to figure out why you visited the family in France, and to discover what she may have told you?"

"Yes. He asked me if NESC sent me to see Rachel, to check a few things out. Those were his precise words."

"It seems as if this Denso does not feel comfortable, as if he fears something will crawl out of the woodwork," suggested Randall.

"That, I think, is the cause of his insecurity. He is looking for an early sign of trouble so he can prepare and act accordingly. He told me he comes from a humble background, so he is very proud to have made serious money and to live well in Zurich. But his biggest fear is losing everything and ending up back where he started … or worse."

Randall sat thinking for a minute, staring down at the nearly finished beer in his glass. He then said, "It does not make sense. If Denso organised the killing of Craig, he would have done it skilfully, with plenty of anonymous cut-outs between him and the assassins. So what does he fear?"

"I guess his biggest fear is that it was all for nothing – a waste of time, money, and someone's life. Suppose the story Craig wanted to tell breaks anyway and his employers are under investigation, then he failed to protect his boss and his company. And all the time, at the back of his mind, will be the worry that his perfect crime was not quite perfect. With all the publicity and the connection with Craig's death, he will assume someone somewhere is going to expose his involvement. It will haunt him even if the probability is virtually zero. Presumably, his boss gave the order to deal with Craig. Perhaps he will make a deathbed confession and name Denso. Who knows? I am just speculating. But Denso will always have this worry."

"Interesting," said Randall. "We get a lot of training in interrogation techniques and the mind-set of criminals during questioning. I remember a psychologist telling us that the suspect across the table is probably not worrying about what you are asking, they're worrying about what you are *not* asking. In other words, they know the full extent of their guilt, and they are wondering if you do. They wonder where the next question will lead."

Ball laughed. "I have never been very fond of shrinks. Give me an example."

"Let's say we arrest a guy for stealing a car. And let's say, the week before, he mugged an old lady who was seriously injured. He answers questions about the car but he keeps wondering if we can connect him to the mugging. As the interview goes on, you sense he is relieved to be talking about stealing the car. He starts to relax. That is the signal to dig deeper and start applying pressure. Normally, we start mentioning serious crimes he may or may not have committed with the implication that we have evidence to connect him. And then you watch for signs of anxiety."

Ball interrupted, "I guess what you are saying is that, even when Denso has dinner with me, he is thinking I could know more than I am admitting. Any minute, I might mention something to worry him and feed his paranoia."

"Yes. I presume his earlier career was either in the police or an intelligence organisation so suspicion is second nature. Let's head for the restaurant."

They left the pub and strolled through Belgravia to Sloane Street. It was a warm, humid evening. Neither had an umbrella or raincoat, but there seemed little prospect of rain. By English standards, it was turning out to be an unusually dry summer. Ball spoke almost wistfully of the pleasures of being in England when the weather was good: "At the risk of sounding sentimental, there are few better places to be in summer."

"You got homesick in Cairo?"

"Yes. Usually my business trips were a few days or a week at most. I was too long away this time, and Egypt is not my idea of fun."

Eventually, they arrived at the restaurant called Haandi. It was half past nine o'clock, and the place was almost full. Ball was relieved to see that a table for two in the window had a reserved sign. He was pleased he had taken the precaution of booking and requesting a good table. During the meal, Ball told Randall about his intelligence work and how he got into it. He was a little more open with Randall than he had been with Rachel Craig because he knew that Randall would better understand the kind of work he had done and the risks involved. They cracked their way through a plate of poppadum before the first course arrived. Randall let him complete his story before raising his glass of Tiger beer in salute. He stated, "Congratulations on a long and successful parallel career. It can't have been easy living a double life for so long, but you seem to have managed it well. I am proud to say that I sensed you had some special qualities and inner strength when we first met."

"Thank you. It is very kind of you to say that. These days, they use me as a wise man and invite me to the odd strategy meeting or policy discussion. Otherwise, I am retired. But I'm still in reserve. If some undercover work fits my profile, they'll call me. I hope that never happens."

"What you have told me is an interesting example of history repeating itself."

"In what way?" asked Ball

"I have just finished a very good book on spying in the run-up to the First World War. It seems many British travelling businessmen were part-time spies for the different and competing intelligence agencies. As they travelled around, they gathered information on rebel groups or the military activities of foreign powers. They sought to identify threats to the Empire."

"Sounds like a good read. Thankfully, the thing that has changed is that the agencies usually work together now. But even in my early days, it was a problem. Opportunities were lost due to the fact that we did not share information."

"Why were people so protective of a given domain?"

"Mainly because too much information was leaking, and no one knew who the moles were. So there was a deep distrust within and among agencies."

Changing the subject, Randall asked, "How do you know Sawyer?"

"Our paths crossed several times at intelligence briefings. He seems like a good, thoughtful guy. I think you are lucky to have him as your boss. His type and your type have to be the future of policing; otherwise, the distance between the general public and you guys will just become greater and greater. Even now, there are too many wooden tops in senior positions. When they give press conferences and speak in public, they sound like robots. If the public gets angry about a serious crime, people want to see and hear anger from the police."

"Yes, I like working for him. As far as press conferences go, the problem is that we have to be so careful what we say in public. We always have to consider how the media will interpret the information."

"I know, but there must be a better way of handling public relations," concluded Ball.

They had both ordered dhansak as a main course accompanied by pilau rice and another Tiger beer. Randall could feel himself reaching his limit of beer consumption. *Wine next,* he thought, *or water.* He was missing Lisa and did not want to trigger a black mood by drinking too much. There was not much chance with Ball as company, but later, at home, if she had not e-mailed, there was a risk. He checked his watch and calculated that it was only the middle of the afternoon in Washington. Two days without communication from her was agitating him, but he hoped she would send a message that evening, after she got home from work.

He could always SMS or telephone her, but he was reluctant to seem too possessive. He had shown her his poem before she left. She liked the message and did not care whether or not it was good poetry.

In fact, she asked for more. *Tonight,* he thought, *I will send my latest scribbling whether or not I hear from her.* He quickly ran through it in his head while Ball was in the restroom:

Dinner time:
This, the saddest time;
Now, when I sit and dine.

This, the frightening hour
With thoughts turning sour.

This, the saddest time;
The only voice, mine.

This, the frightening hour,
Only hope having power.

Why must it be like this?
Because it is you I miss.

He knew it was sentimental, but he hoped, like last time, she would appreciate the message.

"Cheer up, Richard. You look glum," Ball said upon his return to the table. "You remember you mentioned Craig's solicitor in Penzance? The one who had a fire? It was not difficult to find a report of the fire and identify the solicitor. I am going to meet Susan Robson tomorrow."

"Why? Are you doing some private investigating?"

"Sort of. I have an appointment with her in the afternoon. Ostensibly, I want her to draft my will. I told her my old boss had recommended her months ago and I wanted to get the job done. When I told her my boss was Craig, she hesitated but agreed."

"To refuse would have been strange, but what do you want to learn from her?"

"It is a matter of instinct again. I know Craig had a mistress called Susan. It was last year at some point, and the relationship didn't last very long. This Susan was also a lawyer who practised in London. That is all I know, but it is a coincidence worth checking."

"Certainly," said Randall, "Susan Robson moved from London to Penzance a few months ago. You may be on to something. Do you have a theory about her?"

"If she is a former mistress of Simon Craig and was dumped by him, there will be some bitterness. Therefore, I doubt she did not read the documents. It is human nature to be inquisitive, particularly about former lovers, and this would override any ethical considerations. Perhaps she even kept the papers and has plans for them."

Ball's logic impressed Randall, and he added, "I probably should not tell you this, Andrew – it is supposed to be a secret – but we met with Stanley Jones and explained what we knew and suspected. We told him to put his house in order. My boss called it an 'old-fashioned clip round the ear.' He is going to fire a few people."

They finished their coffees and asked the waiter to order two taxis. As they left, they agreed to meet at the same time and place the following week. They had forgotten to discuss football and cricket, but a real bond was developing. It offered Randall a rare chance at fostering a friendship ... one he thought would last and never become too onerous.

* * *

Rachel Craig's life had developed into a state of practical, if not emotional, equilibrium. Working in the garden was a form of therapy that helped her put things in perspective. Recently, she had become angry with Simon's memory for bringing so much misery into their home. She could no longer feel the sorrow of those first few weeks. She was convinced he had brought the trouble on himself and resented him for it. Occasionally, she remembered the happy times, the early love affair, the birth of Amy, the creation of the home in France, some good holidays, and other special moments. But most of all, she remembered her jealousy. It was an emotion that had eaten away at her for years. Long before he died, the jealousy overshadowed any remaining feelings of love; it pervaded her every thought. She was jealous of his success, of him controlling the money, of his good looks (which improved with maturity), and of his freedom to travel. She was jealous that he could come and go as he pleased. His self-confidence irritated her. His special and gentle relationship with their children confused her: he switched roles in front of her eyes from loving father to indifferent husband. It was as if he did not recognise that the children were the product of her womb, of her constant attention, of her total commitment to their well-being. But no warmth was shown, no gratitude expressed, and no emotional support given. She was jealous of the other women she imagined he loved or used. She remembered the phone calls from different cities. The background noise overheard when he was at bars and restaurants and airports. She would listen for a female giggle or a voice beckoning him back to bed, anything that would confirm her fears and feed the green-eyed monster.

She rested against the spade and checked the time. She had another hour to work in the garden before the children would return. It was too hot for digging, but she needed to keep active and achieve something. It was one of her bad, introspective days when she examined herself and reached too many negative conclusions. She imagined the years after the children left home, when the great motivator called parental responsibility no longer pushed her forward. *Take each day as it comes,* she thought. That was the usual advice, but living like that was not in her nature. For years, she had been planting seeds and nurturing them to become something beautiful or edible. That was her nature: plan and act for the future. Her latest gardening book had gone to the publishers, and she did not wish to write another. She had considered going back to England, but the idea did not appeal. Anyway, the children needed to finish their education in France.

She desired wise and mature advice, not the babble of friends, family, and psychologists. She wanted the advice from someone who had no emotional involvement or doubtful training. She stared at the ground she had just dug up and realised what she had to do. She grabbed her mobile phone. She knew it was impulsive and rather selfish to impose her problems on him, but nevertheless, she sent a text to Andrew Ball: "I need some advice, please. May I call you? When?"

He replied immediately: "I will call your landline around eight o'clock your time, okay?"

She confirmed and felt strangely excited. She respected him and what he had achieved in life. She had enjoyed his visit and the fascinating story he told about his double life. She was sure he would provide wise counsel – certainly better than her neurotic mother, her apathetic father, and patronising psychologists.

* * *

Ball picked up a copy of *Financial Times* from WH Smith on Paddington Station and the book Randall had mentioned over dinner. It was his reading material for the journey. He was looking forward to the trip and to a visit to the local Tate Gallery. He had booked a hotel room in St Ives, which meant he would have to leave the train one stop before Penzance, at St Erth, and change for the local service to the seaside town. He would then check in at his hotel, have lunch, and take a taxi to his afternoon appointment with Susan Robson.

Settling in his seat, the front page of the famous, pink newspaper carried one article that immediately caught his attention. It was about three resignations from the board of NESC. Inside, there were more details and pictures of Barker, Redder, and Jackson. The report said that the present and prospective chairmen agreed to the changes given the poor performance of the company. Ball was amused. It seemed that Randall's 'clip round the ear' had taken effect. Barker had been there forever and was due to retire along with the chairman. Barker was an expensive buffoon, but he was not directly involved with company results. His job was to smoodge with investors and manage the press office and security departments. Ball could see no reason to humiliate him at this late stage of his career. Unless, of course, the chairman was forced to do it after the police spoke to him. Ball muttered to himself, "All this upset at a time when Old Stan was anticipating a life peerage at best and a knighthood at worst. Poor man!"

He fell asleep with a smile on his face and woke up as the train stopped in Exeter St Davids. He still had three hours to go. He found the lunch menu and looked around for someone who could take his order. Seconds later, a smiling lady with a strong East London accent asked him what he wanted. She reminded him that there would be no more than trolley service after Plymouth. He ordered a sandwich and coffee. He was enjoying himself, feeling relaxed and alert after his sleep. The best countryside and sea views were yet to come, so he decided not to start his book until the evening.

Unlike London, the sky was dark and the air was damp when he left the local train. A mist hung over Carbis Bay, making the coastline invisible. His taxi driver to the hotel assured him it would clear by the middle of the afternoon. The following morning, he planned to visit the St Ives Tate Gallery before heading back to London. The weather was not particularly relevant to him, but he hoped for a dry stroll before dinner and a quiet pint before finding a licensed fish and chip restaurant in the harbour. To a man used to being on his own, the prospect of a sitting with a glass of wine, a book, and a meal didn't concern him. Depression was not something he suffered from, even though he still missed his dead wife and daughter. Missing them was something he came to terms with many years before. Pain still struck him when memories were triggered, but not in a way that undermined his natural optimism.

The text from Rachel Craig arrived just as he reached the front door of the solicitor's office. He paused in the doorway to send a prompt reply. He rightly guessed that she would be anxiously waiting for his answer and fearing he would not want to get involved in her problems. He sighed, imagining the difficulties she was facing. He hoped he could help. He then put the phone back in his jacket pocket and climbed the stairs to Susan Robson's office. There was no receptionist on duty, and the door to a large, well-furnished office stood open. Susan Robson was sitting at her desk and rose quickly to greet him with a disarming smile. The taxi driver had been right about the weather, and the view from her office window showed a sunlit harbour and glistening seascape beyond.

"Nice office, Mrs Robson, and a great view," he said after introducing himself.

"Thank you. The weather was grim this morning, but it has turned nice now. I am flattered you came all the way from London to consult me. Are you taking a break for a few days as well?"

"Just one night in St Ives, but I love train journeys through western England, so it is a pleasure to make the trip here."

"So you want me to draft your will?"

"Not really. We could have done that by e-mail. Anyway, I already have one."

She looked anxious as if feeling vulnerable in the office on her own. She looked out towards the reception area. "My assistant will be back in a few minutes. Please tell me why you have travelled from London to see me if it is not about a will."

"I think you have played the innocent for too long and used your professional status and feminine charm to deceive a few people. It will not work with me."

"What do you mean, Mr Ball? You are talking in riddles."

"You were Simon Craig's mistress for a short time, and you also became his solicitor. Despite the fact he moved on emotionally, you remained his solicitor. You received some documents from him, read them, and knew their significance. You did nothing before he died, and you have been hoodwinking since he died. I think you still have the papers and intend to use them."

"Complete rubbish, Mr Ball, but what is the point you are trying to make by telling me this untrue story?" She had become red in the face with either anger or embarrassment. It did not deter Ball.

"I am here to advise you and warn you. If you send the documents to the relevant authorities, they will cover-up the whole story. There will be no investigation. Too many reputations are at stake; too many European companies are at risk of huge damages claims. There might be blacklisting in America. Furthermore, if you go to a newspaper, you will need at least one person alive and kicking to substantiate the evidence – preferably two or three credible witnesses to what Craig's documents allege went on. Do you agree?"

"I am listening, Mr Ball, just listening."

"Well as you know, there are unexpected consequences of Craig's attempt to blackmail NESC: a chain of events involving arson and murder. Craig's opportunism has caused things to reach a level of full-blown criminality that he never could have imagined. If he had, he would still be alive."

"Is there more, Mr Ball?" she asked when he hesitated.

"I am pretty sure I know who orchestrated Craig's murder. The guy has a connection to organised crime and thinks like a gangster."

"Is there a punchline, Mr Ball?"

Her arrogance was getting on his nerves, but he sensed she was listening. He also sensed that, under the tough facade, there was a nervous woman.

"If I am right in everything I have said, if you go in search of witnesses, word will spread. Unless you have an established chain of command with information cut-outs between you and those representing you, it will only be a matter of time before you are identified."

"Are you talking about cells like they created in the French Resistance? Even under torture, people cannot expose the whole chain, right?"

"Yes, but it is very difficult to organise. People still need to be properly informed in both directions along the chain."

"You have experience?"

"Purely theoretical knowledge from my days in the army."

"I appreciate you coming to see me, Mr Ball. The message is loud and clear. Hypothetically speaking, assuming you wanted justice and retribution, assuming you held these businessmen who thought they were above the law in complete and utter contempt, and assuming you wanted a few EU officials locked up for taking bribes, what would you do?"

"Hypothetically speaking, of course, exactly what you are doing. But I would be taking extreme care and expecting trouble at every turn. I would need a strong and experienced team to help me because success would require working very quickly to get the story to the public. Only then will you be safe."

She smiled for the first time since she greeted him. "Nice to meet you, Mr Ball. And thanks. I have a good team, and I agree with your point about speed."

"One last thing: three directors of NESC resigned or were fired yesterday. It is in today's *Financial Times*. I have it here; I will leave it with you. The one that is really interesting is Ronald Barker – I have put a ring around his photograph. Your team may want to have a closer look at him. I suspect all three were involved in the negotiations with Simon Craig. Perhaps Barker's role went further than that. After all, he was in charge of their security department and may have issued instructions that led to the fire here. Perhaps he also tipped-off other members of the club and indirectly instigated Craig's murder. I can assure you, there is a direct connection between those guys quitting yesterday and the recent shelving of the Craig investigation."

"You seem to be a very well-informed and well-intentioned man, Mr Ball. I will take everything you say seriously and discuss your advice with my team."

After leaving her office, Ball headed down Market Jew Street looking for a taxi. He carried his jacket over his shoulder and walked slowly, relishing the smell of the sea and enjoying the quaintness of the town. He was walking eastward and shops and offices provided shade from the afternoon sun. He thought about his brief conversation with Susan Robson. There was little doubt about what she was trying to achieve, and he hoped she had taken his advice seriously. There was no more he could do. He found a taxi at the railway station standing in a queue of more than ten. On the way to the hotel, the driver explained that it was a slack time of day because no London trains were due for over an hour. As Ball sat nodding off in the overly warm taxi, he realised there was something he could organise to help watch her and her associates' backs. He smiled to himself, and a few moments later, he fell asleep.

CHAPTER 16

Ricardo Denso was irritated. He was bored with Cairo and had lost his thousand dollars and another two thousand trying to get it back. He could afford it, but he was annoyed with his stupidity. He had also failed with Ball, and his boss was not pleased with him. Denso was not sure how much value Ball could bring, but he wanted him alongside to help watch his back and to try to find out whether Ball knew more than he was letting on. He knew he was worrying too much, but it was in his nature. Anyway, he liked Ball and needed a friend. He would have taken Ball to dinner in Zurich and invited him to his house. Ball would have been a calming influence, he guessed. Plus, his presence would allow him to avoid eating in restaurants alone. He would have had a British friend, and they could have spoken English, which would improve his fluency. There were many positives that would stem from having Ball as a colleague and friend. Since his wife had left him for a rich Frenchman, he had been pretty lonely. She was living in a mansion in Zug, just thirty minutes from Zurich by train, but she may as well have been on another planet.

Suddenly, his mobile rang. It was a UK number. He picked it up and heard the following: "Andrew Ball here. Ricardo, good evening."

"Good evening, Andrew. I was just thinking about you."

"Positive thoughts, I hope, because two days in England have convinced me I will quickly get bored with retirement."

"You will work for Swiss Metals?"

"Yes, if you still want me."

"Fantastic news! The boss will be pleased, and I am delighted. We will make a great team. Let's meet in Zurich on Monday. I will introduce you to the boss, and you can both sign the contract there and then."

"I will be there. Looking forward to it. Sorry to muck you about, Ricardo – put it down to old age. Goodbye."

Denso was very happy and decided that, after dinner, he would have one more try in the casino before finding himself a woman for the night.

* * *

Rachel Craig served an early dinner. Afterwards, Sophie settled at the table to complete her homework. Sophie was very self-disciplined; she usually started work as soon as she got home from school and finished after dinner, before heading for the television for some well-earned relaxation. The burden of homework was far greater than Rachel remembered from her schooldays, and she hoped Sophie would not rebel against it before reaching university. The school environment suited Sophie, and Rachel prayed she would get through her teenage years as a sensible and committed pupil. Amy was in her first year of junior school. They were both truly bilingual. Amy, the youngest, had been in France all her life and did not have a hint of an English accent when she spoke French. Sophie was not so lucky with the accent, but she was equally fluent.

At eight o'clock, the phone rang. She felt a tingle of excitement. It was unfair to expect him to have a solution, but she hoped for a little guidance. "Andrew, thanks for calling. I hope this call will not cost too much," she began.

"Don't worry. I have three hundred minutes of free international calls under my contract, and I have not used any of them this month because I was in Cairo."

"Look, I am sorry to trouble you with this, but I was wondering if you have any advice. I am living day-to-day, and it is no good for me. I need a plan, something to motivate me. I need something to give me ambition and long-term objectives."

"I understand. You feel you are drifting through life, and you worry about what purpose you will have after the children are fully committed to school and then university. Am I right?"

"Exactly right. I have taken advice from numerous people, including psychologists, and they all think it a question of time. It's almost as if fate will decide everything for me."

"I suspect that is complete rubbish. I believe we must drive ourselves forward by identifying something that excites us and brings us fulfilment."

"Okay. Do you think there's a process I should follow to find that *something* you talk about?"

"I'm no expert, but let's try and see where we get to in this discussion. Tell me, Rachel, what you are good at. Don't be modest; think back over the years. Bringing up the children does not count; writing doesn't count. Look at other aspects of your life. Remember what success felt like and the glow it gave you."

"First, I love experimenting with food. Second, I like gardening and have developed a nice and varied garden here. Third, I trained as an accountant and like managing people. It has been years since I have done it, but I think I was a good manager when I worked for NESC. Finally, I like solving problems and removing barriers, like when we first moved here and I had to deal with all the bureaucratic hurdles – things like living permission, health care, schooling for the children, permission to improve the house. Simon was away most of the time, and I was proud to sort it all out."

"Good Rachel. Got it! Open a restaurant and never look back. Think about it: it fits with all your strengths. It is a long-term project, you have the cooking skills, and you will enjoy the creativity of developing different menus. There will be tremendous bureaucracy to deal with, but you will sort it out. You will have a few staff to train and manage, and you'll have to keep the books. You can even supply your own vegetables or herbs or table flowers or something from your garden. I really believe this idea would work for you."

"It is and interesting and exciting idea Andrew. It ticks all the boxes. Thank you."

"Give it some thought. Hope I have helped, Rachel. Goodnight. Dream about a name for your restaurant."

He hung up without another word, but his enthusiasm was catching. Rachel Craig knew he was right and went to find the children and hug them. They were surprised, and Sophie quickly squirmed out of the hug to concentrate on the television. Amy smiled at her obvious happiness. She was ready to try, and she was sure the children would support and encourage her. She started to think of names, and she spent the whole night awake, planning her next steps. *Motivation at last,* she thought.

* * *

Hans Weber was anxious to get his passport and credit cards back and return to Ukraine. After the picnic, they went to Weber's hotel and used the Wi-Fi connection to make a funds transfer from one of his Swiss bank accounts. The transfer was made to a company account in Ras al-Khaimah. Weber was given an invoice for a boat he had not bought. Peter was all smiles and slapped Weber on the back as he hurried to a taxi and asked for the airport.

Relieved to get away with his passport and credit cards, Weber made it to the airport just in time to buy a ticket and catch a Ukrainian International evening flight to Kiev. He decided to stay in Kiev and travel to Dnepropetrovsk in the morning. He was looking forward to seeing Irina, but not to explaining that he had to make a number of trips to Europe. He wondered how much he should tell her. *On the one hand,* he contemplated, *if she knew the full story, she might give me some useful advice and support. On the other hand, she might see me as a loser heading for deep trouble. If the latter turns out to be true, Irina will be gone. But better sooner than later.* He imagined her friends and family laughing at his demise and saying they always thought he was arrogant and too good to be true. He imagined her checking her reserve funds when the Weber cash machine broke down. He knew he was being cynical, but the last few days had shattered his confidence in everybody, including himself.

On the flight from Kiev the next morning, he made up his mind to tell her everything. As a product of the former Soviet Union, she would understand opportunism. She would see his behaviour as normal – making extra money a privilege of being successful. To her, the only sin would be getting caught.

She was waiting at the airport, looking beautiful in a blue summer dress. It nearly broke his heart just to look at her standing there and smiling. Her fair hair was blowing across her face, and hid her shining eyes momentarily. The sight of Irina and her enthusiastic greeting confirmed to him that trust was the best option.

"Smile, Hans, or I will think you don't love me and have found a better woman in Warsaw." She grabbed his hand and looked him in the eye. He forced a smile and said, "I am glad to see you, Irina, and there is no better woman anywhere."

"Okay, I believe you. Put your bags in the car, and we will drive to the riverbank and have lunch there. You can tell me what's wrong. I know you, Hans, and I know when you need cheering up."

The restaurant she chose was on the right bank of the River Dnepr and the English translation of its name was *The Coast*. It was newly opened and had a terrace overlooking the water. Despite its depth and width, the river normally froze during the winter. In summer, it was a slow-moving, smelly waterway that carried industrial waste south to the Black Sea. The terrace was a popular meeting point for local gangsters, but she didn't see any bodyguards hanging around black Range Rovers and guessed they were doing whatever gangsters normally did when they were not meeting, eating, and scheming.

They both ordered grilled salmon and potato puree, and Irina chose a Chablis Grand cru to loosen his tongue and ease his nerves. Over lunch, he told her the whole story, omitting the detail of the funds transfer. Such wasted money would make her angry. She listened carefully, occasionally shaking her head and looking at him with sympathy. When he finished, she asked for his hand and held it firmly for a few moments before offering her opinion: "You poor thing. You must have been so stressed when they took you to the forest. You did right to tell me – never doubt that. Now we need to find a solution."

"I wish I could think of one, Irina."

"The first thing that comes to mind is the fact that Craig was an Englishman. He collected this so-called evidence before he died. So let us assume it is still somewhere in England. You said two ladies are seeking justice or revenge or something, and you said that the plan is to publish a story that is so damning and so complete that the authorities will have no choice but to investigate and prosecute."

"That's a good analysis," sighed Weber, "but not a solution."

"Be patient, Hans. There is some logic to check before we rush to a solution. Who will be most harmed by the disclosure of this sorry tale?" Irina asked.

"The companies involved, the individuals taking part in the meetings, and EU officials (past and present)."

"Only the companies have the resources to protect themselves, and presumably that is why Craig was murdered: a company or several companies protecting themselves."

"Agreed," said Weber, "I think you are saying we need to warn some of the target companies they intend to name and shame in the article."

"Yes. We need to move very quickly. You will have to do what this Peter told you to do. Your hands will be tied working for him. I will go to work on the real agenda of finding these ladies and dealing with them and their evidence. That means that, if I fail, you will still have the deal Peter offered to you and the hope of being seen as a reformed person, even a hero!"

"Irina, you said you will go to work on the real agenda. I can't ask you to do that."

"No matter what you ask, I will do my best to stop these ladies. No more discussion on that point. I cannot do this on my own, and we don't have much time, so I have to find some shortcuts and some help."

"Perhaps Irina, but you must be careful," Weber said. He was unhappy, but he saw her point. She was deep in thought, not listening to him. And then she looked up with a smile of satisfaction and said, "Ukrainian companies have big security departments. They are paranoid and listen to phone conversations, read e-mails, and spy on employees. Do European companies have something similar?"

"Yes, but probably on a much smaller scale."

"I want to find a head of a security department that takes my story so seriously he is anxious enough to agree to meet me. That way, we may be able to find some of those shortcuts to the ladies."

"What is your story?"

"Close to the truth. My husband was a senior official in the Competition Inspectorate and has been tipped-off that an article is about to be published linking the Craig murder to one particular company in the steel club. I'll say that the intention of the article is to expose the cartel, connect it with the murder, and name the company responsible for having him killed." She looked around the restaurant to check whether anybody had tuned in to the conversation. It was unlikely because they were speaking English, but it still seemed like a good precaution. "This will be a game of bluff, and I am gambling that the only people capable of hiring assassins would be security people. If I am wrong, then I will be wasting my time,"

"It is worth the gamble. You are guessing all but one of the guys you talk to will not be interested? The cartel part of the story is not of interest to them, even if they understand the significance. But if one of them has blood on his hands, he would be stupid to ignore you."

"That's the way I see it, and we just have to hope it works. If he agrees to see me, I will fly to wherever he works and explain the true story about the two ladies, Peter, and what you have been forced to do."

"It will be a race between you and me, which I hope you win," said Weber, feeling both anxious about her involvement and proud of her loyalty and commitment.

CHAPTER 17

Simon Craig had not died a contented man; his ambition was far greater than his achievements. He was leading a complicated life and starting to feel the stress of spreading his time and loyalties too widely. He was making money and keeping a few people happy in the process, but he felt no great attachment to anything or anybody. The children were special to him, but as they grew older, he knew the joy they brought would turn to sorrow as their teenage frustration and detachment grew stronger. He remembered his own childhood and just how quickly he had grown to resent his parents and their stifling affection. He loathed it when they fussed over his school reports, observed his every move, dictated what he wore, and challenged his teenage opinions on music, books, and relationships. He wondered how his son had coped and what sort of rapport he had with Cindy. He hoped Cindy's optimism and enthusiasm had rubbed off on Colin. He regretted that they had not met him, and he was surprised and disappointed that Colin had never tried to contact him. Craig hoped Colin was waiting for the moment when his instincts led him to contact his father. He doubted that a child could have any kind of bond with a father he had not met, but he supposed it depended upon the story his mother told and the way she portrayed him.

He had not been back to Australia since escaping Cindy more than twenty years before. He had read about her success as a photographer and even seen some of her pictures in a magazine. It had surprised him greatly that the vivacious and spontaneous person he had known had turned into a highly respected photographer with all the focus and dedication that implied. With his usual conceit, he liked to think it was a positive outcome of their relationship. He mused that, without his emotional cruelty to her, she would not have been inspired.

After returning from Australia, he had set about finding a job in England. He was undecided on a career, so earning money was the priority. His father nagged him to be sensible and join a bank or insurance company, but the more he nagged, the less Craig listened. His first job was a hotel receptionist in a four-star hotel in the King's Cross area of London. The place was seedy and in need of renovation, and most guests were dissatisfied from the moment they arrived. The tasks were not challenging, but many of the clients were. He learned to tame his tongue and deal with complaints, tantrums, and rudeness with admirable self-control. He found a house share advertised in an evening newspaper, was interviewed, and joined a bunch of ex-students just starting jobs in London.

One of the more serious and ambitious members of the household suggested he join him on the NESC graduate training programme. Craig took some persuading, but he signed up when he discovered the money was twice what he was earning as a hotel receptionist and the work was likely to be less demanding. His father was contemptuous, saying there was no future in British manufacturing – least of all in industries such as steel. Craig carried on regardless and found the programme to be like an extension of university with a large group of like-minded, young people with whom he connected.

He met Rachel when she was a trainee accountant in NESC. He was a newly promoted sales manager. In retrospect, he doubted he ever really loved her, but somehow, they fell into a comfortable relationship. Marriage was the outcome. He admired how she coped with her job and raised Sophie. Craig liked Sophie with her non-stop chatter and positive outlook on life. They got on well, and he felt like he had acquired an instant family. He looked forward to their weekends as a threesome as much as they did. They took Sophie to museums, the seaside, and on the London Eye; they attended picnics and children's parties.

His career was progressing slowly, so planning the marriage ceremony and buying a house added some purpose to his life. By then, Sophie was five years old. She enjoyed the preparation for the ceremony and the event itself. In contrast, his parents did not; in fact, they were reluctant to grace the occasion with their presence. They finally agreed to attend, but only the church service. Evidently, they did not want to be part of the reception and meet Rachel's family. To them, she was the irresponsible mother of an illegitimate child, and she was far too wayward for their wonderful son.

Initially, they would not accept her as part of their family and refused visits if she was around. Craig was infuriated with them and vowed to get his revenge by denying them access to any future children. Their attitude changed when Amy was born, and they tried to ingratiate themselves so they could play grandparents, but he blocked them out and refused to speak to them. Rachel maintained a polite relationship and even visited them with the new-born baby. This annoyed Craig – he could not understand why she was so forgiving when it was her they had insulted most.

After she qualified as an accountant, Rachel's career moved forward quickly. She was soon managing a team of trainees and growing in status and confidence. The birth of Amy put a stop to her progress, though, and she quit NESC rather than taking maternity leave. With Amy and Sophie to bring up and Craig beginning to earn good money, they decided she should take a break and concentrate on the children and her writing hobby.

In the meantime, Craig was tasting success and a number of promotions got him as close to the top as he wanted. He was able to travel and create the network of small businesses that eventually gave him the money to live well.

By then, Rachel was in her thirties and settled with the children in France. She was becoming increasingly jealous and suspicious of him. Ultimately, he decided to exploit his freedom and prove her suspicions valid.

The affair with Susan Robson started well but ended quickly when he met and successfully pursued Svetlana. He felt a bit sorry for Susan because she was desperate for a partner after splitting up with her husband. For a time, she probably thought he was the answer. She may have thought she could win him away from his wife and children. Svetlana ended those fantasies.

The last great act of his career was trying to blackmail NESC. But whether through arrogance, stupidity, or naivety, Craig never fully considered the risks.

* * *

Ricardo Denso sighed and pushed back his chair. He liked his top-floor office with his view over Lake Zurich. The sun was shining, and he had been feeling pleased with himself. Ball was due to arrive soon, and the $3,350 worth of casino winnings were sitting in his safe at home. To come away a winner gave him great satisfaction even though it had taken him hours to accumulate the winnings with the usual ups and downs of roulette. He accepted the fact that there was no skill involved, but that did not matter to him. He had to keep proving to himself he was one of life's winners. It was not important money for him, but it would be appreciated by his parents. He would wire it to them when he had a moment.

But all that optimism had vanished with the last call to his landline. He banged the table and spoke out loud, knowing no one could hear him outside his sound-insulated, bug-free room.

"Who is this crazy woman? What does she know? Is it a bluff?"

He sat thinking, and then he checked airline schedules on the Internet and dialled the number she had given him.

"I will see you. Come to Zurich. You say you are coming from Vienna, so catch the Austrian Airlines flight arriving here at 10:10 a.m. I will meet you at the airport. I will carry a board with the name *Irina* on it. Look for me in the arrivals area."

He hung up as soon as she said *okay,* and he banged the table again, muttering, "Now I am a bloody driver with a name board. Irina, your story better be good."

Her English was excellent, but her accent suggested she came from east of the Danube. *Perhaps Russia,* he thought. *I don't want to get involved with Russians – dangerous people.* A horrible thought then crossed his mind. He did not know the nationality of the Craig assassins because everything had been arranged through third parties, but there was a high probability they were from Central Europe or Eastern Europe. His paranoia was working overtime, and a pain started to throb above his right eye just as his assistant announced the arrival of Andrew Ball.

* * *

The previous afternoon, Ball had phoned his old boss in MI6. They had arranged to meet for a pint in the Dickens Inn in St Katherine's dock. It was another dry evening, and they sat outside. Ball had worked for Daniel Davis for many years. As a reservist, Ball was on call for him. During the phone conversation, Ball had recommended that Davis call Fred Sawyer and ask for a copy of the Craig file. Sawyer knew Davis, and as expected, he was keen to cooperate. Sawyer sent it to Davis by dispatch rider, and he read it in the back of his official car on the way to the pub.

"Update me, Andrew. Tell me why you are so concerned and what you plan to do."

He told her about his meeting with Susan Robson, his suspicions about Ricardo Denso, and how he planned to work for Denso to keep an eye on him and determine whether he was a threat to Robson or any of the people with whom she was working.

"Andrew, you are concerned this situation will get out of control and that this Robson woman is playing with fire and needs her back watched. You are going to be working undercover in Denso's organisation to monitor his next move. All the while, he will be watching you because he believes you know more than you are letting on."

"Yes. I know it all sounds a bit surreal. Another point is, I do not see any good will come from publishing the article she proposes."

"I agree. If they plan to expose a broad range of industries and companies, then the fallout will be too damaging. The Americans will have a field day, bang damages claims on every company identified, and blacklist a few for good measure. They will ridicule the EU, which they enjoy doing at the best of times. What's more, the Chinese will see it as an excuse to do what they like, and our Russian friends – who are getting stronger by the day – will mock the self-righteous attitude we direct at their corrupt institutions."

"A potential mess. The problem is that Robson is evangelical about her cause and obsessed with the idea of justice and revenge. If we tried to warn her off or frighten her, it would make her more zealous. And those doing the frightening and warning could get egg on their faces later if the story gets out," Ball said with a sigh.

"Yes. It's definitely a matter for us, not the police. We must avoid any more deaths, and at the same time, stop this story from being published. For good measure, we will also try to nail Denso. Probably, nailing Denso and protecting Robson and her people will go hand in hand, but stopping the article is more difficult. Perhaps that is one for the politicians when we have a complete picture to give to them.

If she plans to publish in a foreign newspaper, it will be more difficult to stop."

"I think we have about a week before Robson has enough evidence and witnesses to satisfy a newspaper editor."

"You said you are going to Zurich in the morning. I agree with the approach you are taking. What resources do you need?" asked Davis.

"I want two experienced field operators. Old-school people who know my tradecraft and don't look like intelligence officers or bodyguards. People who can tail and not be seen without needing lapel microphones. I also want an MI6 contact in our consulate who will do what I ask for a few days."

"No problem. To blend into the background in a place like Zurich and to work with your old-fashioned methods, you need people around your age. If you have any retired colleagues you would like to work with, I can probably get them on a plane tomorrow – assuming they are not out of the country."

"Jim Cunningham and Dave Smith would be my choice. Then Peter Dixon if one of them is not available."

"Right. All three are on call, so I have their numbers on my laptop in the car. I will phone them tonight and let you know. I will send my car for you in the morning to take you to the airport. I will leave an envelope with the driver that contains the contact details of our people in Zurich."

When he got home, Ball received a cryptic text: "The first two okay. On the way tomorrow. No 3 on call in the UK. The names and contact details of two friends in the organisation you mentioned in the pub are with my driver. They will give you all the help they can. The car will pick you up at 6:00 a.m. Have a safe trip."

Ball was relieved. He had the support and resources he had hoped for. He just prayed he was right about Denso being the key man to watch.

* * *

Irina got to Vienna at exactly 4:35 p.m. She booked the flight as soon as Denso confirmed the meeting. She had taken the daily flight from Dnepropetrovsk, and the journey took less than two hours. She booked the NH Hotel at Vienna Airport to catch the early flight to

Zurich the next day. The hotel was opposite the arrivals area and the most convenient airport hotel she had ever encountered: it was less than five minutes' walk from the terminal building. She was proud of herself for taking action to protect her husband and pleased she arranged the meeting with Denso so easily. *My bluff seems to be working, at least on Denso,* she thought. She was surprised at her feelings of affection towards her husband. She wanted to win the battle; her fondness for him had surfaced the moment he looked horribly vulnerable and helpless.

Not wanting to sit in the hotel all evening, she took the city express to the centre and joined the tourists packing into St Stephen's Square. As had been the case for many years, part of the cathedral was under renovation and shrouded in printed cloth that showed an image of the hidden part of the building.

She had been to Vienna many times and knew an authentic, family-run, Chinese restaurant not far from the square. She ordered a set menu for one person and a glass of red wine. Her arrival had attracted a few stares and nudges from a group of four middle-aged males. She ignored them, opened her iPad, and propped it up with her plate. She had downloaded an e-book for the journey and was very content to eat, read, and block out the noise around her.

* * *

Denso took Ball to meet his boss, Maurizio Moretti. He seemed friendly and enthusiastic about Ball working for Swiss Metals. They both signed the consultancy contract, which included payment for accommodations and expenses. It was ridiculously generous, and Moretti made it even more so by giving Ball five thousand euros as an advance payment against future expenses.

"Ricardo has booked you a good room at the Dolder Walhaus hotel, close to where he lives," said Moretti. "I phoned the manager this morning and insisted that you get the best room with the best view."

"That is very thoughtful of you, Maurizio," replied Ball, genuinely surprised that such a powerful man would take the trouble.

Ricardo was beaming from ear to ear as if introducing his star pupil to the headmaster. "Tonight, Andrew, we eat together. I will choose the wine. We will celebrate. In the meantime, let's go back to my office and work out a plan for the next few weeks."

At the end of the afternoon, Denso drove Ball to his hotel. The exterior of the hotel was ugly. It was a mid-century, concrete construction looking down and across Lake Zurich. The lobby was plain and functional. *Typically Swiss,* thought Ball. But his room on the fourth floor was large and impressive. It had two balconies, one facing east and one south. He liked it very much, and the corporate discount given to Swiss Metals made the room rate very reasonable.

Denso had insisted on seeing the room and ensuring its suitability. He seemed satisfied. "Unpack, take a shower, and relax. When you are ready, walk to my house so I can show you my home. It is only a five minutes' stroll from here. Turn left out of the hotel, go past the big wheel standing outside the Dolderbahn station, and look for my house. It is the white house with the red-tiled roof straight ahead of you on Kurhausstrasse," instructed Denso.

"Thanks, Ricardo. I will be there in about an hour."

Ball was quite tired after late nights with Randall and Davis, and he was already bored with Denso's company. Nevertheless, time was running out, and he had to stick to Denso like a limpet. His plan for the evening was to get Denso as close to drunk as he could while staying sober himself (yet appearing full of alcohol-induced bonhomie). It was not easy, but Denso seemed ready to cooperate judging by the greeting Ball received upon arriving at the house. Denso welcomed Ball at his open front door with two glasses of recently poured champagne. Judging by the still rapidly rising bubbles and slight froth, Denso had been watching for his arrival from a window and poured the drinks as soon as Ball approached the house. A cloud went across Ball's mind as he suddenly recalled an evening when his wife had greeted him in such a manner on their first day in their new home. He clenched his fist to retain self-control in the way he had taught himself after the tragedy. The cloud passed, and he smiled warmly at Denso.

The house and furniture were impressive. It was really a small mansion and offered wonderful views of the lake from the upstairs windows. The enclosed garden at the back was nicely planted, and there was a small terrace with just enough space for a barbecue, a table, and some chairs.

"I am sandwiched between two roads, so there is not much room for a garden," explained Denso. "But I think the house compensates."

"It is a wonderful home. The furniture looks to be nineteenth-century Italian, and it seems to be of the highest quality."

"Thank you, Andrew. It is. Mostly craftsmen from Milan, but some of the more exotic pieces originally came from workshops in Florence."

"You live alone?"

"Yes. My wife ran off with a rich Frenchman a little while back, and lives in Zug."

"I am sorry, Ricardo. That's tough. Is not Zug famous for its billionaires?"

"Yes. And he was one of them, the bastard."

They both laughed and finished the bottle of champagne. Denso phoned for a taxi, and they headed for the old town and a restaurant Denso had talked up in the office.

The conversation in the restaurant was polite but facile, and Ball was struggling to stay awake. He found Denso's life history mildly interesting, but thirty minutes sentimentally describing his wonderful parents left Ball with glazed eyes and an overpowering desire to yawn. Still, Ball estimated that Denso was consuming wine at about twice his rate and showing no signs of slowing down.

"Tomorrow, you will be on your own for most of the day. Please read through the personnel files of the top fifty managers, and then wander around to meet people. Maurizio sent an e-mail informing people you have joined my department as a consultant and that they must cooperate with you in any way you ask. I will be back in the office around four o'clock, and we will swap notes and discuss your first impressions." His speech was slightly slurred, and Ball could tell he was finding it more and more difficult to assemble the right words in English. He decided it was safe to press Denso a little on his plans: "No problem. Are you out of the city tomorrow?"

"No, I'm meeting an old girlfriend at the airport and taking her to lunch." He was lying, but his smirk added credibility to his story.

"Good luck. Nice lady?"

"Oh yes, very beautiful. She is Austrian." He was making it up as he went along, but he was still smirking as if he were talking about a real woman.

"Let me try and guess her name," joked Ball, "I know a few Austrian girl's names."

"You will never guess, but try."

"Hannah, Sophia, Katharina, Isabella, Julia, Maria," Ball stated.

"No, she is called Irina. You would never have got it."

They finished their wine and coffee and headed into the night air. Denso wanted to walk a little before finding a taxi.

"Have you an early start, or will you be able to begin the day gently?" asked Ball, knowing Denso would wake up with a dull head and a raging thirst.

"She arrives at ten o'clock from Vienna. So not too early, thank God."

As soon as Ball got back to his hotel, he put a new SIM in his phone and called one of the contact names Davis sent with his driver. He dared not do it from his room because he had no doubt it was bugged. Instead, he sat in the dark, empty bar area.

"Sorry to wake you, Sam, but this is Andrew Ball. I need some urgent help."

"I was expecting a call. What can I do for you?"

"How good are your relationships with the border police at Zurich Airport?"

"Excellent. We have cooperated on a number of money laundering projects."

"Good. Tomorrow, a lady named Irina is arriving from Vienna at ten o'clock in the morning. Second name not known. I am not sure which airline, but the timing should solve that problem. She is travelling alone. I need a copy of her passport page, plus any of her visas. Ask them to detain her for as long as it takes, but be very apologetic. Try not to make her too suspicious."

"No problem. Do you want me at the airport?"

"Not to meet her, but yes. I'll need you there to get the copies. Please phone me on this number when you have them."

His next call was to Jim Cunningham. They had already made contact to confirm each other's arrival and whereabouts, so no pleasantries were required. He explained what he wanted Jim and Dave Smith to do the following day. Finally, he went to bed very tired but pleased with himself. He hoped Denso would forget some of the details he had given Ball and wake up with a fuzzy memory.

* * *

Irina arrived on schedule and queued in the *other passports* line. She was expecting a speedy entry.

"Good morning, Madam," muttered the immigration officer after taking a long, hard look at her name and then consulting a piece of paper.

"You are Ukrainian, but your visa is issued by the Polish authorities. And yet you have no stamp of entry into Poland. Why is that?"

"My first trip to the Schengen Area was supposed to be Warsaw, but I had to cancel it at the last minute," she lied.

"Please wait on that seat over there, and I will be back in a few moments when I have checked with my boss."

Five minutes later, he returned full of smiles and said, "I am very sorry. My mistake, I thought your first point of entry had to be in the issuing country, but apparently your type of visa does not require that. Once again, sorry for delaying you. Welcome to Switzerland."

Denso was getting anxious by the time she finally appeared. He had been holding the name board and hoping not to meet anyone he knew. His hangover was starting to fade with the help of some caffeine and sugar. He had arrived early and drunk two large, strong, sweet coffees before taking up a position alongside uniformed drivers with name boards. His first impression of Irina was that she was stunningly beautiful; his second impression was that she was not Austrian; and his third impression was that she was wealthy. Her Gucci handbag and shoes, her designer dress, and her expensive luggage spoke loudly. *She will fit in well in a place like Zurich,* thought Denso, wondering where her home was and fearing it might be Russia. She approached him with a heart-melting smile and apologised for being late.

"They don't seem to like Ukrainians," she complained as she looked him straight in the eye.

"Obviously, they have no taste," he said instinctively while weighing up the new piece of information. He decided it was bad news.

"We need to talk privately, Mr Denso, and we need to be honest with each other. Otherwise, we will both regret the consequences."

Denso was not sure whether the statement was meant as a statement of fact or a threat. *Probably both,* he thought. "I propose we find an outside terrace where we can sit by the lake and have coffee and talk. I will take you to lunch, show you the old town, and drop you back at the airport in time for your return flight."

"All right, but the last part of your plan will depend upon our conversation. We will see."

* * *

By the time Denso and Irina exited the airport, Ball was listening to a description of Irina's passport: "Ukrainian lady. Irina Shevchenko is her name. She is an astounding looker and not short of money judging by her appearance. I watched through the two-way mirror, and she seemed very relaxed, not fazed by the delay. She has a resident's visa for the United Arab Emirates, and the others are visitor visas for the United Kingdom, the United States, and Schengen Area," Sam told Ball.

"The UAE visa is interesting. Who is the sponsor?"

"It just says spouse. No name."

"Okay, please call our people in Dubai and get them to contact the immigration department to confirm whether the husband's name is the same as hers. She may or may not have changed her name when she married, so we should not assume they match. I remember someone telling me that it is a bureaucratic nightmare in Ukraine, so some people don't bother. I hope they do not match because her second name is very common in Ukraine and Russia, and we will be looking for a needle in a haystack. Then check him out as best you can."

"I will Andrew. It may take an hour or two."

"Fine. And thanks for the good work at the airport."

Ball was beginning to think he might be barking up the wrong tree, however. He failed to see how a Ukrainian lady could be involved. *Perhaps she really is Denso's ex-girlfriend,* he thought. *But Denso said she was Austrian, and there was no reason for him to lie. Jim Cunningham and Dave Smith are watching them, but it will be difficult to learn much from a distance. My only hope is that Denso changes his plans or does something unexpected as a result of the meeting. Perhaps he'll even tell me what this is about.*

* * *

Denso and Irina sat by the lake with Cunningham observing from another table. He would sit there for twenty minutes, and then Dave Smith would take over by ordering a coffee at a free table. There was really nothing to see except an animated conversation. Denso was doing a lot of head shaking, but she seemed relaxed and faintly amused by his reactions.

"Look, Irina, I agreed to see you because it is my job to gather information and weigh up threats to my company."

"You agreed to see me because I mentioned Craig."

"It does not matter what you think. There is no evidence to link me to the Craig murder because I was not involved, so let's stop bullshitting."

"But what about everything else I have told you this last hour? What about my husband and the ladies looking to publish a story. Does that worry you?"

"Yes. It will do too much damage to many people and many companies, including mine. I also doubt they will be able to protect your husband the way they told him they would. He was a senior official and had responsibility for enforcing the law; instead, he took bribes and joined the game of subterfuge. He will be hung, drawn, and quartered in public."

"I agree. So you want to protect your company, and I want to protect my husband against the same threat. We must work together."

"Maybe. The first question I have is simple: who are these ladies who think they are in such a strong position? We need to flush this Peter out and find out how he is connected to the ladies. Maybe he will lead us to them."

"Hans told me he has been instructed to meet with a guy called Barker, an Englishman. Apparently, this man has been sacked and may be persuaded to tell his side of the story. One of the ladies was tipped-off that he is the person who knows most about what happened. This Peter is going with Hans to the meeting with Barker to apply some pressure. The meeting is tomorrow."

"Now that is interesting, Irina. Barker knows more than most, and it is his stupidity and incompetence that has left the door open for these ladies to annoy us. Barker believed he had destroyed all the evidence Craig was going to use. What none of us knew was whether there were more copies. Barker assured us there were not, that he had searched and was certain. As time passed, people thought he was right. I never assumed anything and kept my eye on the situation and a few people. One of the ladies in question could be Rachel Craig, another could be an unknown mistress, and another could be his solicitor. We need to know. Let's have some more coffee and take a walk. I will take you to a very fine restaurant for lunch. It is in the hills above the lake. You will like the views and the food. After that, we will finalise our plans and swing into action tomorrow. I will fly to England tonight."

"I will come with you," said Irina in a voice so firm that Denso didn't even consider arguing with her.

* * *

While they were at lunch, Ball got the information he needed. Irina Shevchenko's husband was Hans Weber, a one-time senior official in the Competition Inspectorate in Brussels. They lived in Dubai, but according to immigration records, they were both abroad having flown out of Dubai International Airport one week before. Their destination had been Ukraine via Vienna on Emirates. They had travelled business class. Some of it was superfluous information, but it gave him an idea of how well the authorities in the UAE monitored the comings and goings of their residents. He knew from past experience that Dubai was a very secure place with a strong, uniformed police force and many secret servicemen who ensured it stayed safe.

After receiving the information, he felt sure he was on the right track. But understanding the connection between Shevchenko and Denso and anticipating their next move was a problem he couldn't crack. Dave Smith had reported that they were at lunch and seemed to be getting on well.

An hour later, a call from Cunningham gave him the information he needed: "Denso went back to his house while Shevchenko waited in the taxi. He came out after ten minutes with an overnight bag. Perhaps they are headed for a romantic night in a hotel somewhere."

"I somehow doubt it. Let's assume they are heading for the airport. Jim, you stay with them and send Dave ahead to the airport. If you lose them for any reason, he should be able to spot them arriving at the taxi drop-off. She is due to leave for Austria this evening, so I'm assuming they will not split until they reach the departures area. The interesting thing is where Denso is heading – see which airline check-in he uses. Anyway, I will get Sam to request the passenger lists through official channels, but it is possible he will buy the ticket at the airport, which will negate advanced warning."

"Thank God for the war on terror; otherwise, this information would not be available to foreign intelligence agencies."

"True. I remember the days when it was virtually impossible to get passenger lists from airlines. Good luck and keep in touch."

Ball waited. His Swiss Metals Blackberry was on the desk, and his private Samsung was in the breast pocket of his business-like white shirt. Via a pre-arranged timetable, Ball and his two fieldsmen changed prepaid SIM cards every two hours at ten minutes past the hour. Ball felt relaxed and in control. The company dress code did not require ties, except when meeting customers, so his collar was open. The files Denso gave him were on the desk in front of him. It had taken him barely two hours to scan them. He had an exceptional memory for the written word, and he was prepared to answer any questions Denso might throw at him about their employees. He had also walked through the offices and introduced himself with friendly smiles and warm handshakes. A question here and a question there brought cheerful responses, and he sensed no animosity or reluctance to talk. He had not visited the procurement or sales departments because he wanted to establish a benchmark of the employees' general attitude towards him. He would then measure that against the mood in the critical areas of the company where Moretti believed his problems to be. If he encountered resentment and evasiveness, he would start digging – that is, if he still needed a cover story to continue watching Denso. If not, he would quit. His guess was that he only needed a few more days before matters would be resolved one way or another.

* * *

Denso and Irina Shevchenko headed straight for the British Airways ticket desk. They were hurrying and seemed agitated. Cunningham looked at the departures board and saw a BA London flight scheduled for 4:32 and a Glasgow flight at 4:56. He looked at his watch and recognised that boarding had already started for the London flight. He guessed they wanted one of those spots, which explained their agitation. He knew the girl who served them issued their boarding passes because they came away from her desk carrying the printed sheets and big smiles. Denso was leading the way, and he pointed at the sign for the departure gates.

Cunningham walked slowly back to the exit and then returned through the doors marked *entrance,* almost running to the ticket desk. He tried to play it off like a harassed traveller. Thankfully, the girl was not serving another passenger and looked up with a smile.

"I was told to meet Mr Denso by this desk. He was supposed to give me his car keys. It needs urgent repairs; I will be shot if I miss him."

"I am sorry, sir, but they have already gone through. They had to hurry to catch their flight."

"Oh my God. He didn't leave the keys with you?"

"No, sir, but he will be back later in the week. Surely it can wait until then."

"Why did he have to go to Glasgow today of all days. I will be shot. This is my second mistake with Mr Denso's car; I will meet him here when he comes back to apologise."

"Your decision. If it helps you, he will be back from London, not Glasgow, on our 9:20 p.m. arrival on Friday."

"Thank you, thank you!" Cunningham exclaimed. And he meant it.

* * *

Ball listened to Cunningham's report with admiration. It was no less than he had expected from a good man he had successfully worked with many times. He debated in his mind whether Cunningham and Davis should go back to England or stay in Zurich to await Denso's return. He decided to delay the decision. He was tempted to fly to London himself, but he feared a wild goose chase. He needed a clue as to where they might be going ... and for what purpose. He needed to understand why Shevchenko had changed her plans and was travelling to London with Denso.

It was six o'clock in the evening, and the offices were empty. Ball went back to his hotel, changed, and headed for the bar. He studied the framed menu displayed in the lift and decided to eat in. The bar was empty, and no barman was there to serve him. He waited five minutes, and then he went to the lobby.

"Is the bar open?" he asked the girl at the hotel reception desk.

"Yes, sir. It opens at five o'clock," replied a girl with a bad complexion and scruffy hair. She looked about fifteen and spoke in a patronising tone.

"But I have been there, and there is no one serving."

"Yes, sir. The barman serves at the tables during busy times."

"I am going to eat in the restaurant, but first I would like a drink in the bar."

"Have you booked a table, sir? We are very busy."

Ball was starting to get frustrated and could not be sure which of them was being more pedantic. He wanted a drink in the bar, and she was not prepared to lift a finger to get someone to serve him. She must have sensed an impending confrontation, though, because she quickly proposed a compromise: "Look, sir, if you go to the restaurant, book a table, and explain what you want, I am sure they will do everything to help you."

He decided to beat a retreat and give her the benefit of the doubt on the grounds that she was young and probably resented having to work rather than be out with her friends. "Thank you," said Ball, and he smiled sweetly at the obnoxious girl.

The restaurant manager was helpful and promised Ball a table as soon as he was ready. He also relieved the barman of his waiting duties and sent him to the bar. Almost as soon as Ball had settled with a whisky and ice, his mobile rang.

It was Sam, and he stated, "Weber has booked a flight to London from Düsseldorf. He arrives around nine o'clock in the morning at Gatwick Airport. Presumably, he is going to meet up with his amazing wife."

"Thanks, Sam. It looks like everybody is converging on London. I need to work out why, but I doubt it is for romantic reasons."

CHAPTER 18

Weber regretted booking such an early flight as soon as he found out Peter could not make it to London before lunchtime. What was worse, Peter was flying to Heathrow Airport and expected to be met. Weber tried to change his flight, but the BA customer service call centre apologetically explained that the two Heathrow flights that morning were fully booked. He tried Lufthansa and got the same response. He resigned himself to a taxi ride around the M25 from Gatwick in the south to Heathrow in the west. He would be in no hurry, which was just as well given the road works and congestion on the notorious motorway.

He was surprised at the willingness of Peter to fly to London. He had no idea where they were going except that they would visit a man called Barker. It seemed out of character for Peter to be so openly involved, but he guessed the ladies had given him instructions.

As required by Peter, Weber had met with some people he hoped to persuade to support the newspaper story, but no one was interested. The general attitude was that they would take their chances rather than betray friends. They had all stated doubts that any promises of protecting their interests would amount to much with journalists. As one contact put it, "If the story breaks, it will be dog eat dog, and every newspaper will want to name and shame. There will be no heroes and no innocents."

Weber tended to agree, and he was starting to think he should have walked away in Warsaw. But he had more to lose than most: he still accepted Peter's argument that he would be the number one scapegoat once the world knew how many properties and how much money he had accumulated as a result of not investigating what he was paid to investigate. He was sure he would be one of the first to be thrown to the wolves as politicians washed their hands of any blame. In one recent nightmare, he heard an imaginary speech delivered in the European Parliament: "We had a rotten apple in the Competition

Inspectorate's barrel. Many companies are also at fault, and they are being investigated. But a top official was corrupt, and an evil environment was created by him. It became an environment where the rule of law was disregarded with the apparent blessing of the man paid to uphold it. He made money by not doing his job; he will go to prison, and his assets will be seized. Rest assured, members of this Parliament, Hans Weber will be punished severely. He will die a disgraced man."

Peter had a point: as an accuser and a reformed man willing to confess to the world, his chances would be slightly better – particularly if the world believed it was a widespread problem. It would be difficult to find the original bad apple if whole barrel was rotten.

The one good thing to come out of the debacle was Irina's attitude. He had spoken to her on the phone after she got to London with Denso. She was positive and said everything would be sorted out very quickly. She was also affectionate and said she looked forward to meeting him in London. He was close to tears by the time they hung up. It seemed that adversity had brought them closer together. Weber liked expressing himself in something approximating poetry, and over dinner, he scribbled some lines on the back of the menu. He e-mailed the following words to Irina as soon he got back to his room:

Good memories of being together,
Of things that seemed would be forever,
Of sitting at a table with food and wine,
Of talks free of trouble in happier times.

Good memories of going to many places,
Of planes and trains and foreign faces,
Of cities, beaches, shows, and walking,
Of being together and forever talking.

Good memories of strolling by the bay,
Of cooling breezes blowing heat away,
Of the moon rising as if a ghost,
Of hearing what each wanted most.

Good memories of trust and sharing,
Of fondness and mutual caring,
Of wanting to talk and be great friends,
Of dreaming a future that never ends.

Her e-mail reply was instant: "Thank you. It is wonderful. I love you, too. Goodnight. By the way, I call your friend *Polish Peter* because we still don't know his second name."

* * *

Ricardo and Irina arrived at Barker's house by taxi at the agreed time. Denso had phoned the evening before, and at first, Barker had refused to meet them. After Denso explained the purpose of the meeting and the threat they all faced, though, Barker agreed reluctantly.

The house was a mock-Tudor mansion with a long, gravel drive that swept from gates to the left of the house to the front door before forming an arc that passed the double garage and ended to the right of the house, at another set of gates. The front garden was planted with flowering shrubs around a well-kept lawn. There were plenty of signs of prosperity, including the location of the house, the dark blue Bentley parked on the drive, and the two gardeners working away. The scene suggested money was not in short supply.

Ronald Barker answered the door. He was immaculately dressed in grey flannels and a blue blazer, and he only lacked a tennis racquet to complete the impression of a PG Wodehouse buffoon. His face was drawn, and his eyes looked tired and rheumy. *It's from a combination of too much alcohol, too much stress, and too little sleep,* thought Denso.

"I was supposed to play golf this morning. Pity to waste a lovely day sitting inside. Anyway, come in. I will not say you are welcome, Mr Denso, but this lovely lady with you may make me change my mind."

Irina was smiling, clearly enchanted by him. Denso guessed the man looked how she imagined the archetypal Englishmen to look.

"Thank you. This is Irina, the wife of a German gentleman called Hans Weber."

"I will call you Irina rather than Mrs Weber. *Weber* is such an ugly name for such a beautiful lady," said Barker, turning on his old-school charm. "Where are you from, Irina? Certainly not Germany. Now let me guess, somewhere famous for beautiful ladies – Ukraine, perhaps, or Belarus?"

"You are very kind, Mr Barker. I am from Ukraine."

"I know the name *Weber* from somewhere. I think I met a Hans Weber once at a conference in London."

"Possibly," said Denso, wanting to keep control of the conversation. "Irina's husband worked for many years for the Competition Inspectorate in Brussels."

"Oh yes, that's the guy. Seemed a decent sort, very knowledgeable, good speaker. But Irina, he is much older than you, so I will add *very lucky* to my description of him. I hope he is rich and treats you well."

Denso groaned at the crassness of the man's flattery, and then he changed the subject by summarising the problem of the sponsoring ladies, Polish Peter, and the task Weber was being forced to do. At the end, Barker nodded as if he already knew part of the story.

"I had a call this morning from a lady who said she was a researcher for a business magazine. She asked me to meet one of their journalists this afternoon. They want to interview me about changing attitudes in regards to international business, my reflections on the last forty years. She said he would be accompanied by a photographer."

"Did you agree to do the interview?" asked Denso.

"Yes, I was flattered. I am also very bored with retirement, and a good article may get me some consultancy work."

"But surely you think it is too much of a coincidence, right?"

"It does seem to be. The lady had a foreign accent; perhaps Polish. The story you have just told me and a request to meet a journalist—"

"I agree," interrupted Irina, and then she continued, "My husband is on his way to London today and will meet with Polish Peter at Heathrow soon." She hesitated and then explained for the benefit of Denso, who looked shocked and annoyed. "He called me this morning from Düsseldorf Airport."

"You should have bloody told me!" snapped Denso, banging his fist on the arm of the chair.

"There was no point. He has no idea where he is going or why he is here. But I think we can now guess from what Mr Barker has told us."

"Now, now, Mr Denso, no swearing and no Italian temper tantrums in my house. That chair was expensive," said Barker in a gentle tone, hoping to wind-up Denso even more. The look of hatred on Denso's face changed the mood in the room. He was showing a side of his character that Irina had not seen before. She suspected his temper could be dangerous, and based upon the reaction she had witnessed, it could be triggered quite easily.

"Let's move on," said Irina, trying to restore the calm. "It seems you have two choices, Mr Barker. The first is to do nothing and await events, and the second is to meet with Polish Peter and my husband to see what deal they have to offer. After that, you can help us kill this story before it surfaces."

"I was never involved in the sort of thing Craig was doing. He represented NESC at all the club meetings, and that had nothing to do with me."

Denso joined the conversation after calming down. "The sensational part of the exposé will be the connection with Craig's murder. Without it, the story will be weak and uninteresting to most people. I do not think they will directly accuse you, but I am sure they will lead the readers to the conclusion that you were responsible for causing his death."

"But why lay the blame at my door?" pleaded Barker.

"Because, somehow, they know. My chief told me that you tipped him off about your problems with Craig. Presumably, you spoke to other bosses and they told colleagues. Before long, it is common knowledge," replied Denso. He wanted Barker to think he was under pressure. He doubted Polish Peter and Weber knew as much as he claimed. He assumed their visit would amount to grasping at straws; they needed plausible witnesses, and there did not appear to be many willing candidates. After all, Irina told him that Weber was failing in his mission to find people prepared to cooperate.

"I did not want or expect anybody else to get involved. I said we were dealing with him by negotiation and some local actions. I just wanted our friends to know we had a problem, but that the situation was under control."

"Unexpected consequences," said Denso wryly, "and pretty sensational ones at that."

"So what will your husband and his friend want this afternoon, Irina?"

"They will offer you a deal if you help them substantiate their evidence and accusations. They will give you the opportunity to tell your side of the story and limit the damage," Irina replied before Denso could jump in with his version. He was not quiet for long, however, and he spoke to Barker in a friendlier tone: "You should meet them and find out what they know and assess how vulnerable you actually are. Try and find out who is sponsoring them – the names or some hints about the identities of the ladies. We will meet you this evening and decide what can be done to eliminate these threats once and for all. I will not sleep until I know that all of Craig's documents are destroyed."

"I agree. My wife will be here this evening, so I think we should meet somewhere else. One look at you, Mr Denso, and she will think I have befriended the Mafia."

Denso snorted in anger, and his face turned dark again. He was about to speak when Irina sent him a calming signal with her right hand. Barker continued, pleased with himself for getting under Denso's skin: "There is pub by the river called The Old Crown. It has a large garden and the seats are spaced far from one each other. Let's meet there at 7:30 p.m. And Mr Denso, I guess it was you that arranged Craig's murder. Why else would you be here and so concerned? Please don't reply, I don't need to know."

Denso stomped out of the room and headed for the front door without bothering to shake Barker's hand. Irina delayed the farewell to confirm the meeting at The Old Crown.

Barker watched them walk down the drive to the waiting car. He sat down abruptly in the first chair he could reach, put his head in his hands, and sobbed. He felt as if the whole world had suddenly decided to punish him. He was normally strict with himself about drinking before noon, but he poured a brandy and drunk it quickly as the clock chimed to indicate it was eleven o'clock.

He had not felt good for some weeks, and the final diagnosis had confirmed his worst fears. His adventures in Thailand had resulted in AIDS. It had been a bad two weeks: he had lost his job in a humiliating way only months before he was going to have retired with dignity; his illness had been confirmed; and now he faced exposure as some kind of conspirator to murder. The sound of ridicule from his wife, former colleagues, and the golf club members would be deafening. He remembered lying by the pool in Thailand and his premonition of a humiliating end to his life. He had drunk brandy then and cheered himself up, but this time he was using it as an anaesthetic.

He was proud of the way he had maintained a stiff upper lip with Denso and Irina, but beneath the self-confident facade was a man in deep distress who thought himself beyond redemption. He thought of his life and tried to remember when he had last been relaxed and happy. *Not for a long time,* he concluded silently, *and I'm sure it won't be possible in the future.* For the last few years, he had gone to work knowing he was not respected and considered a relic of a bygone era. His responsibilities had diminished and he no longer got a buzz from being one of the top men in a big and important company. In private, his wife treated him with contempt and showed her resentment by avoiding his company and promptly leaving any room he entered. He poured himself another brandy and steeled himself for the task ahead.

* * *

Weber and Peter took a taxi from London's Heathrow Airport to Weybridge. The distance to Barker's house was only about twelve miles by road, but the journey took forty-five minutes due to road works and traffic jams. Weber did not like the outer parts of London. To him, it was a scruffy and congested urban extension of a great city, a characterless approach-zone that gave a disappointing first impression to visitors. From any of the main airports, the views were similar. He discussed it with Peter in the taxi, and the latter replied drily, "I recommend that friends making their first visit to London close their eyes when they get off the plane and open them when they arrive in central London." It was advice Weber thought both humorous and wise.

He met Peter at the airport without delay or difficulty and got the impression that Peter was genuinely pleased to see him. He reflected on his first impression in the taxi and wondered why Peter was not criticising him for his lack of progress. He speculated that, perhaps, Peter was not as committed to the cause as Weber had first thought back in Warsaw. He chanced a question: "Are your sponsors disappointed by my lack of progress?"

"Yes, but I warned them that it would not be easy. They have now switched their attention to this Barker fellow. Someone suggested he is a key figure. Again, I think they are being optimistic. In my opinion, your input will be enough."

"Unless I change my mind and refuse. I could do that if they have nobody else on their side."

"You could, but then you would have broken your word to me. We had an agreement, and I let you leave Poland in good health with your passport and credit cards. You will stay in England with me until the article is published. It will be published with your full cooperation."

"I guess that, behind that statement, is a threat. And if I run away?"

"You are forcing me to spell it out when I don't want to. I like you, Hans, and I enjoy your company. I want you to work it out for yourself so I don't have to make threats. Let me just say that my influence has a long reach, and any services I require can be bought easily."

"Okay, I get the message."

"I hope so because I hear your wife is very attractive and has a big family in Ukraine." The thinly disguised threat sent a shudder through Weber's body.

* * *

Denso was keen to get back to London. He urgently needed privacy and a reliable Wi-Fi signal. Without warning, he said, "Irina, we will go back to the hotel. I need to write some e-mails and keep in touch with things in Zurich. We will return here by taxi this evening."

Back at the hotel, he worked quickly. He had about three hours to get a team organised. He called a Reading-based security firm he had used before and arranged an urgent bank transfer of $20,000 from an unnamed account in Liechtenstein as a prepayment. Once the money was received, he called back with Barker's address. Their task was to tail the two men who would be visiting Barker that afternoon. The chief of the security firm said his name was Steve, but based on his accent, Denso thought it was more likely to be Ivan or Vladimir or something else Russian. Anyway, Steve confirmed he had enough resources available to do a professional five-men-on-two tail. He said that, by the evening, his men would be watching their hotel and mingling in the dining room and bar. He promised to follow them if they left. Denso was satisfied. *If they got separated,* he thought, *there will be enough followers to handle both targets.*

Denso congratulated Steve on his proposal and then raised a question: "If I asked you to subcontract a more challenging task, would you be able to help?"

"Call me back on another number. I will text you the number," replied Steve.

When they reconnected, Steve answered Denso's earlier question: "Possibly. Anything can be arranged if the risk and reward are balanced sufficiently in favour of those taking the risks."

"I need them to deal with a difficult client. Your people will soon know the client; they will see him at the house today. The final task of dealing with this client should take place in the next twenty-four hours. Your subcontractor can choose when, how, and where."

"That is a tough assignment. It leaves little time for preparation. These guys usually like to do a survey and plan the project properly."

"I understand. Can it be done?"

"Of course. The advantage we have is that my men will already be in touch with the client. Of course, they will disappear at the critical moment. Which of the two clients we are meeting today is the difficult one? We need his first name."

"Hans. The older man. He's a grey-haired, tanned, and fit-looking man. He's well dressed."

"For a project of this size, we will need a prepayment of another $100,000 and a completion payment of $400,000. The bank details will be different from the one you just sent the money to."

Expensive, thought Denso, but he agreed anyway. He hoped his boss would think it worthwhile, but he could not wait for his permission. He phoned his bank and warned them that he would be making a large transfer. (Without the call, he would have been limited to $100,000 per day.)

The one thing that made him nervous was that he had no idea what Peter looked like. Irina had shown him a recent picture of Weber, though, and the description he had given Steve was accurate. He just hoped Polish Peter did not look too similar.

* * *

As they approached Weybridge, the surroundings improved and tree-lined, suburban streets gave the impression of wealth and well-being. Weber and Peter reached Barker's house, knocked on the impressive front door, and waited. The Bentley was still parked on the drive. One of the gardeners came over to them after a few minutes, seemingly anxious to gossip.

"He's at home. He never walks anywhere other than between tee and green. Perhaps he's asleep. No golf today because he had visitors this morning. He will not be happy at missing his daily four-ball."

"We have an appointment with him in twenty minutes. We're a little early. Is there somewhere we can wait?" asked Weber.

"Our Mr Barker does not get many visitors, but one of them this morning was a well-dressed lady who should be a model. Or perhaps she is – talk about eye candy. John, over there, couldn't work for an hour while thinking about her. He said he had fallen in love. Anyway, there's a bench under that willow tree by the pond. You should be comfortable there for a while. It is clean and dry."

"Thank you, thank you very much," Peter said, patting the gardener gently on the shoulder. He smiled warmly, but he wanted to end the mind-numbing chat as fast as possible.

Weber had listened to the gardener with increasing trepidation in case Peter realised that the lady in question was Irina, but he did not seem suspicious. He walked over to the bench, made sure it was clean, and sat down.

They stayed there for twenty minutes, and then they tried knocking again. Peter put his ear to the door, but the only sound was a chiming clock confirming that, according to the household's time, they were punctual to the minute. They went back to the bench.

"I am going to have a look around. You stay here. I am sure there is an outside toilet these guys use. I will ask." Peter walked off in search of a gardener. Weber sat depressed. The conversation in the taxi was confirmation that there was no easy way out for him.

Peter asked the gardener for directions, and he pointed to the garage. Sure enough, set in the side of the garage, there was a small toilet and washbasin. Without using it (and out of sight of the two workers), Peter slipped around the back of the garage and tried a rear access door. The door opened. He hoped there would be another unlocked door leading into the house. But he needed to go no further. There was enough light from a barred window set high on the left-hand wall for him to see a body hanging from a cross beam. He shut the door and hurried over, making a mental note of the scene. There was an older man, a thick rope, a good noose, a pair of stepladders kicked away, and a nearly finished bottle of brandy on the floor close to where the ladders must have been placed. It was a world Peter knew and understood. He checked the man's clothes for signs of a struggle and tried not to step in the puddle of urine directly under the feet of the body. The smell of the last bodily functions running their course was disgusting, but Peter was unperturbed. He felt the skin temperature and concluded that the man had not been dead for more than an hour or two. He then turned back to the rear of the garage and walked into the sunlight. In his professional opinion, it was suicide. He returned to the bench and whispered in Weber's ear, "Barker is dead. Hung himself in the garage. We need to get away from here. We must not get involved with the police. Act normally; knock on the door again and wait a minute or two as if you expect an answer. I will stay here looking bored. Then we will leave."

Weber tried to remain composed as he banged firmly on the door. He waited and shook his head in the direction of Peter after a minute had passed.

Peter walked over to the gardener and said, "We can't wait any longer. We have to go to the airport."

"Going anywhere interesting?" asked the gardener innocently.

"Yes, Canada. Do you know where we can get a taxi?"

"It's a ten-minute walk to the railway station. There will be plenty there. Turn right out of the gates and right again at the junction of this road and River Lane. That will take you to the high street and station."

"Thanks," said Peter. He turned and strolled casually towards Weber, who was heading for the gate with a worried look on his face."

"They will be able to describe us to the police," complained Weber.

"So what? We have done nothing wrong. And when they conclude it was suicide, no one will be interested in his visitors. Remember one thing: police like suicides and hate murders. Murders are time-consuming and expensive affairs; suicides are not. By tomorrow, it will be another statistic, a grieving or not grieving widow, and work for the undertakers. Life moves on, and those that are privileged but still choose to end it early are seen as pariahs. Think of the film and rock stars who opt out – there is little sympathy because they have what others dream of."

Weber nodded, seemed to remember something, and said, "When you came back to the bench, you smelt foul. It was like you had rolled in dog shit. I hope the gardeners didn't notice."

"Stop worrying, Hans. Please stop fussing; everything will be fine."

They walked in silence to the railway station. The properties they passed became less and less desirable as they neared the town centre. Detached homes like Barker's became terraced houses with no front gardens and only the street for parking. Weber commented, "This is the problem with England: too many contrasts; too much good and too much bad."

"You are spoilt, Hans, by Germany and Dubai. I like England and the mix of people. It is very international and very tolerant. Many Poles live here and do very well for themselves."

They could have grabbed a taxi at the station, but Peter decided it would be quicker to take the train. They bought tickets and climbed the steps of the bridge that crossed the tracks to the London-bound platform. The electronic board indicated they had only five minutes to wait.

"Waterloo is suitable? You know the place?" asked Peter.

"Yes, it is on the south bank of the Thames. We can take a taxi from there to our hotel."

As they were talking, two of Steve's men joined them on the platform, one of them talking on his mobile, the other reading a timetable notice board.

CHAPTER 19

Denso and Irina found a table in The Old Crown at exactly 7:30 p.m., and Denso ordered drinks. The bar had a low ceiling with solid beams just above their heads. According to the notice on the front door, it had been an inn for more than three hundred years. They took their drinks outside to the riverside gardens and found a picnic table with benches.

"I think we should eat here as well, but after we finish with Barker, The menu looks good by English standards," said Denso

"Yes, I like it here by the river. I had heard about English pubs, but I'd never visited one. It is a very nice tradition to have a meeting place for conversation and relaxation. To me, the English are very mysterious people, and I like sitting here and observing them."

"Mysterious, maybe, but also aggressive, conservative, and irritatingly self-confident."

"You say *aggressive,* but compared to Russians, they are not."

"Probably true, but don't ever think you understand the English because they don't understand themselves. They appear to have liberal attitudes on immigration, sexuality, and just about any modern trend, but in their hearts, they are reactionaries waiting to justify a return to traditional values. Listen to their politicians. They live in the present and excite each other by calling up the past. They still talk about the glory of two world wars and their defunct empire."

"I will form my own opinion, Ricardo, but compared to Germans, they are open-minded, exciting, and progressive people. I admired them from a distance as a child in the Soviet Union. I admired them for their music and films and traditions. Now I want to admire them close at hand; I want to sit in this pub garden by the River Thames and let the atmosphere sink in."

By eight o'clock, Denso was getting restless. He did not think Barker was the kind of guy to be late for an appointment without phoning. Thirty minutes later, he had had enough and tried Barker's mobile again. It was still switched off.

"You stay here, Irina, in case he turns up, but I am going to his house. It is no more than a ten-minute walk, and I want to know what his game is. I don't care if his wife's at home."

Irina was relieved to see him go. His constant fidgeting and inability to enjoy the moment was getting on her nerves. She wanted to sit, admire the surroundings, and observe people. After all, there was nothing in Dubai nor Ukraine with such character, history, and atmosphere.

Denso walked through the quiet, tree-lined streets. It was still light but becoming cooler as sunset approached. He was fuming at Barker for keeping them waiting. Eventually, they'd have to get back to central London, and they'd need to eat first. *Perhaps we should have eaten at the pub earlier,* Denso thought, but he did not expect to spend the whole evening waiting. English pub food was not usually to his taste, but he had to admit that the menu at The Old Crown looked modern and international, not limited to shepherd's pie and bangers and mash.

On the way, he smiled to himself as he remembered a short holiday he took in London with his brother. They were both students with little money. They found a cheap hostel in Fulham and worked their way through the full repertoire of English-style food in the local pubs. They eschewed anything that tried to imitate Italian dishes.

As he approached Barker's house, he noticed a small group of people standing on the street, beyond the closed gates. A police officer stood inside the gates and chatted with them. There were a few long-lens cameras on display and a crew from the local radio station was sitting in a van on the opposite side of the road. The van was decorated to promote their morning chat show – it depicted a smiling lady.

Denso joined the group by the gate and listened. He turned to a friendly looking, middle-aged man carrying a dog-eared notebook. He looked like he had eaten too much pub food and downed too many pints of beer. He turned his podgy face towards Denso, smiled, and mumbled, "Don't recognise you. Are you from one of the nationals?"

"No, an Italian business magazine," lied Denso, guessing that *national* was the man's term for a daily newspaper.

"You got here quickly."

Denso laughed and said, "No, I was here already. I was waiting for him in the local pub to do a short interview on his career. He has just retired."

"Yes, he was a well-known figure around here and quite a big fish at the golf club. Unfortunately, he topped himself this afternoon."

Denso noticed the use of the past tense and assumed the use of the expression *topped himself* meant Barker was dead. Still, he queried, "Topped himself?"

"Sorry, a bit colloquial. It seems he hung himself in the garage. His wife found him when she came home and opened the doors to put her car away. It must have been a horrible sight, him hanging there, twisted face, tongue hanging out."

"Terrible. Why would a successful man with this wonderful house do that? It seems he had everything."

"An age-old question, but there is not much doubt it was suicide. The police are treating it that way. You can tell: their actions are low-key, there's no murder scene, and there's no door-to-door questioning. They did do a routine interview with the gardeners because they were here all day. I spoke to one of them. They heard and saw nothing except some unknown visitors to the house this morning and two more this afternoon. He did not answer the door to the second lot … for obvious reasons. Apparently, Barker's wife was out all day, so she knew nothing."

"Sad. I always wonder what can drive a person to this. Anyway, I must get back to the pub. I left my wife drinking wine, and I don't want to have to carry her back to London." Denso then shook the man's hand and walked back the way he came.

"Shit. Another door closes on finding out who Weber is working for. But then again, there's one less witness to cause trouble in the future," he muttered to himself as he walked back to the pub. He was hungry, and his mind turned to the menu at restaurant.

* * *

Susan Robson called Svetlana as soon as she saw the report of Barker's death in *The Telegraph* the next morning. She had woken early to see the boys off on a school trip to Arundel Castle and some nearby Roman remains. They would be away until the weekend.

Svetlana spoke first: "I was going to call you as soon as I was sure you would be awake. I got a text from Peter late last night saying Barker killed himself. There was no meeting."

"His death is reported in my paper. Not much information – some glowing tributes from the chairman of NESC and a few other ex-colleagues. That's why I phoned. Where do you think that leaves us?"

"It's good news for us. Perhaps it's not good for his widow, but it helps us. We have another victim to help sensationalise our story. We can accuse Barker of everything and anything, and he will not be able to defend himself. Nobody else will stick up for him because they will not want to be tainted by association."

"Svetlana! You are thinking like a mafia boss!" exclaimed Susan with a laugh. "Shall we tell Peter and Weber to stop what they are doing and concentrate on Weber's confession? A living Weber and a dead Barker should be enough. He has to say that this was a widespread problem involving many industries and companies. I do not want this to be a steel industry story. I want to illustrate that the whole system is a mess."

"I agree. I will tell Peter to take Weber to a nice hotel by the seaside and get him writing. I will go there and tape an interview with him."

"Good idea. Use two sound recorders and a camcorder. Run them simultaneously. I don't want him denying the authenticity of the tapes later."

"Now who's thinking like a gangster?" joked Svetlana, and they said their goodbyes.

* * *

Davis called as Ball was selecting fruit from the breakfast buffet in his hotel in Zurich. "Barker killed himself yesterday afternoon. It is in the newspapers."

"Without doubt suicide?"

"Yes. I contacted the local police, and I have their report in front of me. Apparently, he left a short note of apology to his wife."

"Interesting timing," observed Ball. "I would like to know if he had visitors yesterday – and if so, their descriptions. Perhaps Barker's house is where our friends were heading."

"I have the incident report in front of me. Two gardeners were working when Barker's wife came home and opened the garage doors. They were asked to give statements and mentioned two people in the morning and two in the afternoon. They commented that it was unusual for him to have visitors. The door was not answered to the afternoon callers, and they left after waiting a while in the garden. No other details or descriptions."

"Thanks. Perhaps the morning visitors tipped him over the edge. Or maybe the prospect of the afternoon meeting was too much. Maybe he had already decided when he got up in the morning that it was to be his final day. We will never know. It would be useful, though, to get descriptions of the visitors and a transcript of the conversation the visitors had with the gardeners."

"Agreed, Andrew. I will get the local police to go back and interview them properly. What are you going to do?"

"Denso e-mailed me last night saying he is in London and will not be back before the weekend. He says there are problems in their sales office that need investigating. I will come back to London today with Dave and Jim and work out what to do. It looks like the United Kingdom is the place to be for the next few days."

"Yes, Andrew. Unfortunately, we have another body connected with Craig, even if Barker's death is self-inflicted."

"What worries me – and you can call it a ridiculous superstition – is that these things tend happen in threes."

"I hope you are wrong. See you in London."

* * *

Denso thought highly of Irina. He found her quick wits and determination admirable. He enjoyed being with her and being seen in her company. In fact, he thought it was better than wearing the most expensive watch money could buy. It boosted his ego to see men staring at her in admiration and then glancing at her partner. He knew they would assume he was rich, famous, or both. He knew no ordinary, middle-aged man would be with such a lady unless it was his daughter. And she did not look like his daughter. She had Slavic features and a slim figure, and he had Latin colouring and a dumpy, overweight body. No, he was sure they presumed her to be his wife or mistress. He felt good about the situation, to say the least.

To Denso, one of her disappointing characteristics was her naivety. Another was her apparent devotion to her husband. And he knew that, whatever happened, he could not risk Weber helping the ladies with their story. Even if he and Irina could get to the evidence and destroy it, Weber would still be around, would still be a risk. If he was ever investigated and decided to cooperate with the authorities, he could cause a lot of trouble. Denso did not want to be haunted by Weber's knowledge for the next ten or twenty years. He blamed himself for not being aware of him and his deep involvement in the dark side of business. *The man would never have reached retirement,* thought Denso. *And I think I made my situation worse by agreeing to meet Irina. She assumed I arranged Craig's death. Soon, she will be accusing me of something worse.*

It was a new day, and he was sitting in the lobby of their London hotel. By the time they got back from Weybridge the previous night, it was late. After the mild shock of visiting Barker's house and hearing of his death, he recovered and enjoyed grilled salmon with mustard dressing, mashed potatoes, and broccoli that he washed down with a good Rioja.

Irina was subdued and drank little. She said that, in her culture, suicide brought shame on the friends and family of the victim. Denso tried to change her maudlin attitude by saying, "You hardly knew him, Irina. Yes, he was charming to you, but it was an act. He must have already made up his mind. The British call it keeping a stiff upper lip."

"Think what mental torture he must have suffered while he sat there talking to us. Perhaps our visit tipped him over the edge?"

"No, Irina. I read that most people contemplate suicide at some time in their life, but they do so as a reaction to things that happen to them. Those who actually go through with it are reacting against a worsening situation. I don't know, it may be bullshit, but I think a tough character like Barker would need to face something worse than a little public disgrace."

He failed to change her mood. She left most of her food on her plate. It was the first time he had seen her dejected. The barman called them a taxi after that, and she fell asleep as soon as they got in.

* * *

"How are you this morning, Irina?" he asked as she joined him in one of the armchairs near the concierge's desk.

"Fine. Much better. I think I was tired last night. I slept well, and upon reflection, I agree with what you said about Barker. I am sure his reasons were more private than we know. Enough of him, though – what are our plans for today?"

"We can relax and do some sightseeing. I put some people to work to find where your husband and this Polish Peter are staying, and then we will have a nice chat with them. We'll see if we can strike a deal."

"Sounds good. I won't ask how you are going to find them or what the deal is."

"No, don't. It is not your problem, but I am sure you will be pleased to see your husband again. Then you can both go home."

"You sound very confident, Ricardo. I suppose with Barker out of the picture, you can be."

"It helps. But we still have to rescue your husband before he confesses, and we are running out of time."

"I need to get some cash; I can't let you pay for every taxi and every meal, Ricardo."

"I don't mind. It is on expenses, but there is an ATM across the road if you insist. But let's do the normal sightseeing."

"Okay. I will need to do some shopping for presents, so can we sightsee this morning, have lunch, and then go to Oxford Street?"

Denso groaned inwardly at the thought of shopping, but he agreed anyway. He needed to stay with her all day and watch the events unfold. He had no idea how quickly it would happen or how soon she would be informed, but he knew he had to be around when she learned the truth.

CHAPTER 20

Weber and Peter boarded a train at Victoria station after buying tickets to Brighton, on the south coast.

"Why Brighton?" asked Weber.

"Nice change of air, comfortable five-star hotel, and not far from London. I like the place. It's bright and colourful. In places, it is a bit run down, but it has charm. Plus, the sea air will invigorate us. As soon as we arrive, we will go for a walk on the peer. We will walk around the fascinating shops in The Lanes. Perhaps you will find a present for your wife," stated Peter cheerfully.

"Sounds good. And then what will we do?"

"You will write you memoires and talk to some tape machines. I will relax."

"I thought you might say that."

"Cheer up. Did you see the reports in the papers about Barker? I told you no one would doubt suicide. The note he left for his wife confirmed it."

"Yes. Poor sod. Must have been very depressed, lonely, and desperate to do that."

"You are not feeling the same, are you, Hans?"

"Not yet. Who knows how I will feel in a few days' time."

"You have a lovely wife, properties, and plenty of money. I am sure you will be able to keep all that and stay out of prison if you are sensible and continue to cooperate with us. You will meet one of the ladies later today. I think you will be impressed."

The journey to Brighton took less than an hour, and Weber enjoyed the views as they crossed the South Downs. The part of the Ukraine that he knew was flat and cultivated; Dubai was either buildings or desert. What he was seeing was more like southern Germany: no mountains, but it was green and pleasant. *An ideal place to play golf,* he thought. It made him feel a little homesick. He was missing Irina as well, and he wished they were travelling together. When they arrived in Brighton, he was in a melancholy mood.

Their first-class compartment was at the rear of train. They had to walk the whole length of the platform to exit, and by the time they reached the concourse, most passengers had gone to the bus or taxi queues. Some were heading downhill in the direction of the sea that was just visible in the distance. Weber noticed it was cooler and the air was fresher than it was in central London. His spirits lifted a little as they strode into bright sunlight.

There were two black Mercedes waiting at the front of the station. The drivers held boards. "Grand Hotel," they declared. Peter could feel a tingle at the back of his neck. *Something is wrong.* His instinct for danger had saved him before, and he tried to pinpoint his concern. *First, I didn't book a car. Second, not two.* But then he became unsure because the receptionist had asked him how and when he was travelling to Brighton. He had said by train, but he could not remember whether he had given her the times. His mind whirled. *We booked two rooms in different names, so two cars might be logical.* He started to relax, and then he saw a man in his peripheral vision approaching fast from the left. As Peter was pushed hard to one side, a voice shouted, "Hans!" Hans looked towards the voice, and its owner stepped forward and put a knife in his chest. Moments later, three men jumped in the Mercedes and drove off quietly. There was no rush; only Peter seemed to have noticed what happened. Other people were beginning to point at Weber on the ground, but things were happening slowly. Peter looked down at Weber, noticed the position of the knife, and knew he had been killed by an expert knifeman. He smiled ruefully and asked an approaching youth to dial 999. A small crowd gathered as they waited for the ambulance. A community police officer arrived on the scene and asked onlookers to keep away from the crime scene. When he heard numerous sirens approaching, he slipped away from the growing crowd of watchers, went back into the station, and caught the first available train to London.

* * *

Ball was sitting in the business lounge at Zurich Airport when Davis phoned him and said, "Andrew, we have a third body.

Unfortunately, your superstition proved right. It is the guy Sam tracked. The husband of Denso's visitor, Hans Weber. He arrived in London from Düsseldorf yesterday morning and died in Brighton about two hours ago. He was professionally stabbed – one wound and dead. The name, passport number, and date of birth all match."

"Not good. Anybody else injured?"

"No. It was a well-organised event that was carried out efficiently."

"How many attackers? How did they behave?"

"The reports from the few witnesses are confusing, as usual. There were three or four men, two black Mercedes, no panic or fast getaway. It was all low-key, casual. People say it seemed to happen in slow motion and that it shocked them."

"So they were professionals. Classic hit. They minimised the impact of the drama: few people noticed, and even fewer saw enough to remember anything of note."

"Yes, that's the picture I am getting."

"Was he alone?"

"Again, there's confusion on the part of the witnesses. We are checking the security cameras at Brighton and Victoria to see whether we can spot him with anybody else."

"Out of interest, how did you get the information so fast? Two hours is quick."

"We feed names into police databases that continuously scan them. If a local force enters a name that matches our name, we get the report. With common names, we have to do some sifting, but *Hans Weber* is rare in this country. Fortunately, Sam entered the name as soon as he knew his wife had linked up with Denso."

"Smart guy. Has someone told his wife?"

"Not yet. We are trying to find her and Denso. We should find them in the next hour or so – assuming they are staying in a London hotel. Then we will send a police officer to inform her in the usual way. No need for us to get involved. They will interview Denso, put him under pressure because he is with the man's wife and staying at the same hotel. They will tell him we believe he had a strong motive for killing her husband."

"He will have a perfect alibi, but it will be good to make him feel uncomfortable for a few hours. I think Weber's widow may be in danger. I will come to your office in about three hours ... I land at

Heathrow in two. Things are getting out of control, and we need to think this through."

* * *

Denso and Irina were shopping in Oxford Street. Denso liked some of the big stores, such as John Lewis and Selfridges, but not the street itself. The crowded pavement meant he was being jostled constantly by people rushing in the opposite direction. He felt vulnerable, insecure, and out of place in a street full of badly dressed and ordinary people. He was beginning to get frustrated with Irina, too, because she seemed content to wander from shop to shop buying presents for her family. He was waiting outside a shoe shop when he received a text from Steve: "Project completed to everyone's satisfaction."

Poor Irina, he thought. He wondered whether she really loved her husband or just enjoyed the lifestyle he provided. Perhaps he had done her a favour; perhaps she would be pleased to escape nursing him through old age. *Hopefully, she will just go back to Ukraine, sort out his affairs, and worry about her future.* Somehow, he doubted that, though. She would immediately assume he had arranged her husband's death, and she was the type to want revenge. With her money and Ukrainian connections, she could pay people to punish him. Plus, he knew he would be an easy target. Therefore he set about deciding what to do about her. He did not think he needed an answer immediately, though. He opted to help her through the next few days and see how she reacted.

Soon thereafter, he received another positive text from Steve: "We are still with the big bloke. He is back in London."

Denso replied, "Stay with him. Critical to keep me informed of his moves."

Time to destroy this phone and SIM card, thought Denso. It was a cheap Nokia he had bought at Heathrow along with a pay-as-you-go English SIM card. He told Irina he was having problems with his mobile, and they stopped at a Vodaphone shop in Oxford Street. He bought another cheap phone and plenty of credit on a SIM card. He texted Steve his new number and received a prompt acknowledgement. Back in the street, he dropped the old SIM into a drain along with the battery. He figured he could ditch the phone later.

They were staying in The Connaught in Mayfair, which was just a short walk from Hyde Park and Grosvenor Square. Denso liked the place. He liked it even more when the manager offered to upgrade him to a suite for a very small amount of money.

They took a taxi from the Tottenham Court Road end of Oxford Street to Carlos Place, carrying Irina's shopping load into the lobby. Denso snapped at the bellboy for not helping them exit the taxi, and the concierge apologised with exaggerated humility.

They decided to go to their rooms, change, relax, and meet at around half past seven in the bar to discuss dinner plans. As soon as Irina closed the door to her room, the hotel phone rang. *Not Denso changing our plans,* she hoped.

"Irina Shevchenko? This is Inspector Williams of the Sussex Police. I would like to come to your room and talk to you privately."

"Okay, I am waiting," said Irina nervously.

She opened the door to a tall, unattractive woman in her thirties with short, cropped, dark hair that was flecked with grey. The look on her face spoke volumes. She handed over Hans's passport and questioned, "Is this your husband?"

"Yes," said Irina in a barely audible whisper. "What has happened?"

"He was killed this afternoon outside Brighton railway station. I am very sorry to be so blunt, but there is no other way."

"How was he killed?" asked Irina as she dropped into one of the two chairs by the dressing table and pointed at the other. "Please. Sit and tell me."

"He was stabbed through the heart. It was a single wound that killed him almost instantly."

Irina held back the tears and stared at the police officer in disbelief. The message slowly sank in. And then she cried out loud, "I should have been with him! I should have protected the silly, old man!" Finally, she began sobbing. A part of her brain remembered his wonderful poem.

The police officer was trained to cope with such situations and provide support when needed, but she was also trained to be firm to keep the grieving person cooperating. There was a procedure to follow, and Irina would have to go through more horrors before being left alone. Williams waited several minutes, and then she stated, "Irina. Here is a glass of water. Please drink it. I need to ask you a few questions, and then we will discuss the next steps."

"Thank you. I understand you need to talk to me."

"What did you do today?"

"Sightseeing, lunch, shopping."

"Were you with Mr Denso all day?"

"You know his name?"

"Yes. Please answer my question."

"Yes. We were like tourists"

"Do you have any receipts that would show where you were at a particular time?"

"Yes. In my handbag. I will get them."

She handed them over, and Williams looked at each one.

"You went to an ATM close to this hotel at 10:06 a.m., and you were busy shopping between two o'clock and five o'clock this afternoon. What about in between?"

"Working backwards, we had lunch at about noon. Denso paid."

"How did he pay? Was it cash or credit card?"

"Credit card. He carries very little cash."

"We went to Westminster Abbey before that. He paid the entrance fee via credit card."

"Thanks, Irina, that's enough questioning for the moment. We are checking with him now; another officer is with him. It is normal and routine to ask these questions to eliminate people from our enquiries. You understand how it looks to us right now, right? You are staying in a hotel with another man and your husband just got killed. You may be lovers, which could be motive enough for one or both of you to conspire to kill him. We will leave it there for the moment, but the suspicions will not go away just because you both have good alibis. Thank God I did not find you in bed together. Now I must ask for your help."

"I have no close relationship with the horrible Mr Denso. It is purely business. I only met him two days ago. I will try to help, but the news is still sinking in. To me, Hans was a good and generous man. He deserved better than to die in the streets of a foreign country with a knife through his heart. Denso is a creep."

"Actually, I believe you about Denso, but others may not. It matters little; it is entirely academic what anyone thinks. What matters is evidence of conspiracy, and that will be difficult to find. Now to next steps: it is procedure for someone to formally identify the body. You are probably the only person in this country who can do it."

"When should I do it?"

"My advice is sooner rather than later. Anticipation is far worse than the reality. I have a car and a driver. We can go to Brighton now, or I will send a car for you tomorrow."

"I want to go now and see him."

"Good. I recommend we book you a hotel for tonight. A driver will bring you back here in the morning."

"I want a good hotel. The best in Brighton. I will be very low, and I don't need a depressing environment. I will pack some things."

"You are a strong lady, Irina. Stay strong for the next few days, and then you can go home and be with your family. That is, unless we find something to connect you with your husband's death."

Denso answered all the constable's questions and provided as much proof as was necessary to show he had been in London all day. He felt quite smug. He wondered how Irina was coping. He wondered whether she was already accusing him in her mind. When the constable got a call from his boss, Denso was able to deduce from the responses of the constable that they were going with Irina to Brighton that evening. He was relieved. *I'll have dinner and get a little drunk,* he thought. *Maybe I'll go to a club and find a whore. I'm sure the concierge knows the clubs with good whores.*

* * *

Ball arrived at Davis's office at the time he had predicted. Davis handed Ball a copy of the notes taken of the interviews with Barker's gardeners. Ball read them quickly.

"Looks like Denso in the morning with Irina Shevchenko. Weber and an unknown friend in the afternoon. This Irina certainly captivated the gardeners. Their description of her is like poetry. And their description of the unpleasant-looking Denso is totally accurate."

"Interesting comment about the smell on the man's clothes."

"Yes. I think our unknown friend discovered the body and got very close to some shit that Barker produced in his dying moments."

"Yes. That's a bit crude for you, Andrew. You are obviously in a bad mood. But I am sure that's what happened. He wanted to check that it was suicide. It would have been obvious that Barker was dead from two yards. There was no need to go closer. It's the sort of thing a police officer would do, not a member of the public. It means he found the body, ensured he was dead, satisfied himself it was suicide, and calmly buggered off without raising the alarm."

"Looks that way. I am in a bad mood because I am angry with myself. I should have been here. We should have tailed Weber as soon as he arrived. We should have tailed Denso, and we should have known about his unknown friend."

"Just a moment, Andrew. Think it through: we could have followed Denso from here to kingdom come, but what would it tell us except that he met with Barker? We could have followed Weber, but we would not have learned much except that he had an appointment with Barker that never happened. I agree we should know who this fourth guy is. One of my people is working on it; she will be here soon. None of the main characters have done anything yet to define the end game, so we will concentrate on predicting it. Then we will act."

Ball nodded his agreement and tried to summarise what they knew: "It seems we have two couples with different agendas following more or less the same path. Irina Shevchenko is a link between the two teams. For some reason, they converged on Barker. I do not think they had the same goals. In fact, they almost certainly had opposing objectives."

"So try and guess the intentions of the two teams. Speculate."

"I think Weber was going to be a star witness for Susan Robson," proposed Ball.

"Why would he agree to that? From what we know, he was very well off."

"Probably threatened physically or threatened with exposure of some involvement in something corrupt in his past. Anyway, it was enough to get him to cooperate."

"So we will call the team with Weber and the unknown soldier; Robson's team."

Suddenly, there was a knock on Davis's door, and a young lady wearing a black trouser suit entered the room. She smiled at Davis and shot a questioning glance towards Ball. She was quite short, and she had long, wavy, golden-brown hair and dark eyes.

Davis stood up, and with an open right hand, he gestured in the direction of Ball, "Susan, please let me introduce you to Andrew Ball. He is one of us."

"Pleased to meet you, Mr Ball. I know who you are. Something of a legend, actually."

Davis laughed. "Why is he a legend?"

"During my training, some of his intelligence material from the Cold War was used to illustrate best practices when interpreting scraps of information. It was fascinating stuff."

"I am flattered," said Ball while standing and shaking her hand.

"What can you tell us, Susan, about the man we have just christened *the unknown soldier*?" asked Davis.

"It was easy to get a name because he stayed in the same hotel as Weber and also booked two rooms at The Grand in Brighton. His name is Edgars Jansons. The passport he showed at the hotel check-in was Latvian. However, despite it being a common Latvian name, no one has entered this country on a Latvian passport under that name for more than a week."

"He obviously travels with another passport, which means he is well equipped, not an amateur."

"Do we know where he is staying tonight?"

"No. We will keep checking the hotels with this name, but he could use another passport."

Davis thanked Susan and watched as she went over to shake Ball's hand again. She maintained long eye contact with Ball and said, "If I put together a small group of friends from the service, would you have dinner with us and talk about your experiences?"

"I would be delighted. Arrange it through Mr Davis." She smiled and left.

"Bright and ambitious girl. Carry on speculating, Andrew. We have Robson's team. What about Denso's team? And why is Weber's wife a member."

"For some reason, Irina Shevchenko wanted to stop her husband from telling his story. I am not sure whether she was trying to help him or destroy him. As we now know, the latter was the result, but his death may not be her fault."

"How did she find Denso? And why?"

"I struggle with the *how*, but *why* is easier. She needed an associate with certain skills, plenty of resources, and something to lose. Denso is obsessed with protecting his boss and the company, and he has the resources and skills."

"It is his job, Andrew. And at the same time, he protects himself, his lucrative position in Swiss Metals, and his lifestyle in Zurich. You told me he comes from a humble background, so he will fight to stay where he is."

"Yes. He is obsessive and paranoid. He also has an inferiority complex. It's a dangerous combination."

Davis smiled at Ball's psychoanalysis and turned his attention to the question of how Irina found Denso. "We will assume for the moment that Irina wanted to help or protect her husband. When her husband told her he was being cornered into making a confession of his sins, she would want to know the whole story before deciding what advice to give or how to help. He would have told her there was strong written evidence that incriminated him and that it was going to be used in a newspaper article. He would have told her about Craig and what happened to him."

"I understand your logic," interrupted Ball. "So she decided to try and get to the evidence before it was published. The problem is, she needed help. It does not answer the question of how she found Denso and got him involved, though."

"No. It is a mystery. And she must have worked fast. I suspect we will get a chance to ask her very soon. Let's agree on next steps, including how we are going to stop this article from being published. I think they will go ahead with the story without witnesses. They will concentrate on the connection between the three dead bodies – that makes the story even stronger. Dead witnesses are sometimes more powerful than living ones when it comes to sensationalising an otherwise dull story; it's an investigative journalist's dream come true."

"Since we have a murder enquiry underway, does that give us grounds to ask for the article to be postponed?"

"It will be one of the arguments. There are others of a political and economic nature. We are trying to find which newspaper has the story. Now we must find this unknown soldier and get Denso to leave the country. I would like our people to hold him at the airport because we can arrange his demise very easily there. Lastly, we need to give Susan Robson and her family some discreet protection. Then we will go for a drink … it is getting late."

CHAPTER 21

Richard Randall was very excited. Lisa was on her way to London after only two weeks away. He had not expected to see her so soon, and he hoped her return would set a precedent for the future. She explained in an e-mail that she convinced her boss to change his mind about her role. After a week at the new job, she realised it would take years to understand the culture, the system, and the politicians of a foreign land. He agreed and asked her to interpret political events in Europe for an American audience. They both felt it was a much better use of her time and ability than being some kind of student of US politics.

Before leaving Washington, she called Randall and insisted on two things: not to meet her at the airport (she would take the Heathrow Express because it was quicker than making the journey by car) and to have dinner together. The Heathrow Express took fifteen minutes and made the journey every twenty minutes. She phoned him from the airport and estimated that they would both arrive in Paddington at about the same time. Randall left the office after the call and picked up a taxi in Victoria Street. He was at the terminus in good time to meet an incoming airport train. As she requested, he booked a table in the restaurant where she had proposed to him. Her actions indicated to him that she was feeling sentimental, and that put him in a good mood as he watched the arriving passengers.

He had phoned ahead and asked that the house champagne be put on ice. It was the perfect temperature when they sat down at their table and took their first sips. They exchanged news, and he started to relax for the first time in two weeks. She was still the Lisa he loved – there was energy in her voice and her usual, exaggerated body language.

"I missed you, Richard. And I missed London. I like Washington as well, but it is important to separate the novelty of being in such an amazing city from the true value of the experience. I wanted to visit you as soon as possible, and I was lucky to get this trip. There is a big story about to break concerning business malpractices in Europe. We have an exclusive, and I thought they would want a more experienced journalist to cover it. But here I am, pleased to be home and having dinner with the man I love. Soon, I will want bed and plenty of affection."

"The affection bit is guaranteed, but how long can you stay?"

"The evidence we need for the story is back in the States, and all I have to do is some background interviews with key people over the next three days. We want to publish on Sunday. After that, I can take a few days of working holiday, which means I am booked to go back in about eight days."

"What is a working holiday?"

"I must do some research and complete and article by Wednesday. I will use my laptop, and it will not make much difference to them whether I am here or there. They are very flexible, and many people work from home when there are no meetings to attend."

"I am due some leave. We could go away to the coast for part of it," said Randall, smiling at the good news.

"Funny you should say that. I am supposed to make my last interview on Friday morning in Penzance. You could meet me there on Saturday. We can visit the Scilly Isles, stay there a few days. What do you think? Do we have a deal, fiancé?"

"It's a deal," Randall said, and he theatrically shook her hand across the table.

"Great. Always wanted to go there. We will travel by boat. When we get home, I will go on the Internet to book a hotel. The affection thing will have to wait a few minutes because I want this little holiday to be special."

"I have waited a fortnight, so another few minutes will be acceptable … as long as you don't decide to read your e-mails as well," noted Randall with a grin.

"By the way, Rich, it is an amazing story we are going to tell on Sunday. It will shock people to know just how devious senior executives and EU officials in Brussels can be. In this story, we have blackmail, corruption, and even murder by hired killers."

Randall's heart began to sink as he thought back to his boss's warning about ending the Craig investigation and the story turning up in a newspaper. One question remained for him: "Who are you interviewing in Penzance?"

"An amazing lady. A solicitor who exposed the scandal after the murder of her client. Apparently, before his death, her client sent her some papers that told part of the disgusting story. She and a Polish friend then filled in the gaps and sold the exclusive to us. According to these ladies, the police investigation into the death of this guy called Craig was called off. They say the investigating officer was a very charming and well-educated guy, but he was completely out of his depth. I will get his name on Friday; you may know him."

* * *

Fred Sawyer liked to get to the office before 8:00 a.m. And he did not normally like an uninvited invasion of his early morning privacy. His preference was a quiet coffee alone with the overnight reports before the routine of attending meetings and briefings kicked in at 9:00 a.m. He was therefore surprised to find Randall waiting in his outer office. He hoped Randall would not make a habit of it, but he guessed by the worried look on the young man's face that there was a genuine problem

"Good morning, sir. I apologise for intruding, but your warning about ending the investigation and then reading about it in a newspaper has very quickly proved very relevant."

"Come in, Richard, and tell me about it," Sawyer said, pointing the way to his office.

After Randall left looking very miserable, he phoned Davis. Davis had the name of the newspaper and the publication day. Davis was relieved because he had several days to marshal the arguments and apply the right pressure in the right places. Davis had proposed they meet for a drink the following Monday when the dust settled. But Sawyer felt sorry for Randall. He had done the right thing, but if his fiancée found out, he doubted she would forgive him. And if her newspaper found out, he doubted the bosses would forgive her.

* * *

The same morning, Ball sent a text to Denso's company mobile: "Give me a ring. Amazing news re Craig."

Ten minutes later, a drowsy Denso called back.

"You sound rough," joked Ball, "Have you been enjoying the London nightlife?"

"Something like that. What's the news?"

"I met with a friend last night whose girlfriend is a journalist," he began. "Apparently, an American newspaper is running a story based on Craig's documents. They have surfaced thanks to his solicitor. They are making a connection between the murder of Craig, the suicide of an old colleague of mine, and yesterday's killing of a retired, top-level EU official. It will be a sensational story."

"You are in London, Andrew?"

"Yes, came back last night to meet these friends for dinner. An annual get-together of old colleagues – pure luck I met this guy." He hoped his lies were convincing.

"Are you sure about this?"

"Yes, the journalist has an appointment with the solicitor tomorrow. She was supposed to interview Barker today, but he's dead."

"Yes, I read about Barker committing suicide. Very sad."

"And what is worse, she was planning on interviewing the EU guy who was murdered yesterday *this morning*."

"Too many coincidences. The fact that she is here on the ground and bodies are appearing around her will make her report all the more sensational," muttered Denso.

"The solicitor is now under armed protection until the story breaks on Sunday."

"When are you going back to Zurich, Andrew?"

"Today. I will be heading for the airport in a few minutes. I will be there by lunchtime." It was his third lie.

"I will be there later than you, but let's meet for a drink tonight. I should feel better by then. We can catch-up on all this news. It sounds like a lot of people are going to have egg on their clothing, including me and my boss."

"I think you mean egg on their *faces*, Ricardo. But I agree. Sunday will be a bad day for many people," Ball said, knowing the article would never get published. He hoped Denso would keep to his word and try to go back to Zurich.

Indeed, the call had the desired effect: Denso checked out of the hotel and headed for the airport. His hangover was immense, but he was starting to the think clearly. It slowly dawned on him that the murder of Weber was a big mistake. It would feed the story, give it legs … and it would run and run. In the hands of the media, it would become an uncontrolled, hysterical monster. Even worse, the political and international dimensions of the murder would put the British police under huge pressure to solve the case. And then there was the Irina factor – whether she would set the wolves on him.

He made it to passport control, Heathrow Terminal 3, before sensing he was being followed. The border control officer looked at the passport for several seconds before nodding to two men who had closed in on Denso from behind. "Come with us, Mr Denso. We would like a chat," they stated gruffly. Two armed soldiers watched from a distance, their guns hanging by the straps on their shoulders, their hands gripping long riot sticks. Denso guessed they were there to step in at the first sign of him making any trouble. The men took him to an office with two-way mirrors looking out over the border control area. There was a uniformed customs officer waiting in the room. Judging by the stars on his shoulder, he was a high ranking officer.

"Mr Denso, my name is Brown. My colleague's name is Smith. Common names, you will realise, and definitely not the ones we were christened with. We work for an intelligence agency and have the authority to detain you for a limited period of time unless we find reason to have you charged with a crime. We have been advised that you are carrying drugs. We will search your bags in a moment, but we must give you the opportunity to cooperate."

"I am not carrying drugs," replied a wary Denso.

"Then please hand me your bags. Place them on the desk, lift the lid, and stand back."

Denso knew the game and realised that Ball's call had been about getting him to the airport. Sure enough, a hand emerged from one of his cases with a large packet of white powder. The customs officer stepped forward and nodded, and then they took his mobile phones, including the Nokia he had intended to throw away.

Denso guessed the situation was not only about charging him with a drugs offence. He suspected they would detain him while they investigated Weber's murder. Denso sat down and resigned himself to a tough few months ... or years. For some reason, he thought about Irina and wondered what she was doing.

* * *

Susan Robson met Svetlana by platform three of Bristol Temple Meads station. They hugged and held each other fondly before turning towards the exit and the main street. Susan had waited more than an hour between her train arriving and Svetlana's pulling into the station. They had agreed to meet in Bristol so that neither of them had an overly long journey. Susan killed the time by drinking a coffee and reading *The Bristol Post* and *Daily Mail*.

"Any updates?" queried Svetlana when she noticed the newspapers placed between the straps of Susan's handbag.

"I got a very early edition of *The Telegraph* at home, and it carried a simple description of the murder and Weber's career. These later editions have much more detail about him and his work. He was quite senior, and he was obviously trusted and respected."

"How wrong they were. If we believe Simon's version, he was at the centre of all that was wrong."

"I think the fact that he was killed confirms Simon's version was true. Weber must have known a lot about many people and many companies across many industries."

"Where are we staying?" asked Svetlana, changing the subject.

"The Thistle. It is in the centre. We are sharing a room. I think we will both feel more secure."

"Yes. Until this is all out in the open, I will not sleep well. When are you seeing the journalist?"

"Eleven o'clock. I am catching the first train, so don't let me drink too much wine."

They walked the rest of the way in silence, Susan remembering her last visit to Bristol many years before. Her father had been studying for a postgraduate degree at the university, and she had travelled from London with her sister to spend the day with him. He was a mature student and quite lonely in his rented room while he worked on his research project. Susan remembered his pleasure at seeing them. He gave them a tour of the university's physics laboratories before showing them the Clifton Suspension Bridge and the Avon Gorge. All the time, he talked about the wonders of a new type of microscope and how it was helping his research. Susan remembered that she and her sister giggled every time he mentioned the new machine. In hindsight, his seriousness and single-mindedness was admirable.

Svetlana interrupted her thoughts by saying, "Peter is hoping to get here by seven o'clock. He is coming by bus from London. He is nervous about using the train because he thinks he was caught on video yesterday travelling with Weber to Brighton and then on his way back to London. The police know he booked two rooms in Brighton, so they will want to interview him and ask why he did not wait by the body after Weber was killed."

"Peter should have waited; he is now a suspect. They will think he was a conspirator who led Weber into a trap. He is now a prime suspect, and they will be monitoring the railway stations and airports."

"He stayed with me last night and is very nervous about us. He is not too worried about being arrested as long as we are safe. He said he would tell the police that he was in shock and ran away. He will argue that, as a foreigner, he did not know the system."

"He will get away with it as long as they have a better line of enquiry. If not, they may prefer to pretend to the public that they have arrested one of the conspirators, if only to show progress. This is a front-page murder story because Weber was an important foreigner killed by a professional team. The Germans will be pressing the British police for answers, and the EU politicians will want to look over the shoulders of the investigators. Everyone will be wondering about the motive and whether there is a wider threat."

"Then he should be very careful and get away as fast as he can after the heat dies down a little. He has three passports. He can stay with me for a week or so. He can grow his hair and a moustache in that time. He will get bored and drink himself silly, but I will cope."

* * *

Davis was interested in the news that Susan Robson was in Bristol. He was even more interested to hear that she had met a young lady at the railway station with whom she had walked to The Thistle hotel.

The people he had assigned to watch and protect her established that they were sharing a room, so the only name they had was Robson's. The surprising information was that she had also booked a single room and paid for it at check-in time. She had the key card, and it was under her name.

He phoned Ball and asked, "What do you think she is doing, Andrew?"

"Gathering her team around her, I guess, and preparing for the interview with Randall's fiancée. Has she left the children at home on their own?"

"Thank God, no. We are watching the house, anyway, but the kids are on a school trip. They'll be back tomorrow."

"That connection between the newspaper and Randall was one in a million, pure luck for us. And credit goes to Randall – he took the information to his boss, warned him of the impending disaster. All the time, he did not know how important it was to our project."

"Randall and Sawyer are both good guys. If we kill the story, our luck will also be their luck. We should go to Bristol and meet Robson. We will pick you up in half an hour. My driver will use a service car with lights and a siren in case we are held up by traffic."

"Okay. You can update me on my friend, Ricardo Denso, in the car."

Davis laughed and said, "He is in good hands."

* * *

Polish Peter, as Irina had named him (*the unknown soldier,* as Davis and Ball referred to him) reached Bristol without incident and found The Thistle easily with the help of a street map in the bus station. His journey from Brighton the previous day had been risky but necessary. He could not afford to waste time with the police, particularly if they decided he was a suspect. He did not know how it worked in the United Kingdom, but he guessed the system would allow him to be detained for a while under suspicion of conspiracy to commit murder.

Once he started noticing them on the way back from Brighton, he had been amazed at how many security cameras were in operation. Upon returning to London, he kept his face low and shoulders hunched, He hoped the police had not worked fast enough to watch all the London stations. As a precaution, instead of getting off at Victoria, he left the train at East Croydon and took a bus into central London. His aim was to get to the safety of Svetlana's apartment as quickly as possible.

Svetlana had texted him his room number in The Thistle and told him to walk past the lobby and take the lift directly to the third floor. There, she explained, she would be waiting in room 307 with Susan Robson.

It was the first time Robson had met her Polish ally. It was not love at first sight. In fact, she was unimpressed by his thug-like appearance. It gave her serious doubts about his intelligence, but he spoke English well and seemed calm. The warmth he conveyed towards Svetlana and his polite manners thawed Robson a little, and she decided to give him the benefit of the doubt. Still, she regretted that he had made himself so vulnerable by walking away from the murder scene in Brighton.

Robson's team, minus the dead Weber, was about to order dinner from the hotel restaurant when Davis, Ball, and a uniformed inspector walked into the dining room of The Thistle. Robson recognised Ball immediately and looked surprised.

"Mr Ball!" she exclaimed, "Why are you here?"

"First things first, Mrs Robson," said Davis firmly.

"This is Inspector Jones of the Sussex police. He would like to interview the gentleman sitting on your left in connection with a murder committed yesterday. He will interview him tonight and transfer him to Brighton tomorrow where he will be charged." He touched Peter on the shoulder and said, "Please leave the table and accompany the inspector. There are more police officers in the lobby, so don't try any heroics, please."

As Peter was led through the lobby to a waiting police car, he passed one of Steve's men. The man watched with interest from behind a newspaper. He waited until they were outside, and then he called his boss. In the street, another one of Steve's men climbed on his motorcycle and got ready to follow. Steve sent a short message to Denso: "Big man in Bristol. Seems to have a problem. Please call." He never got a reply, but it did generate some interest for the police technicians monitoring Denso's phones.

Inside the hotel, Davis took over the vacated chair and Ball signalled to the waiter to bring another place setting and chair. Davis introduced himself and announced their intentions, "We are joining you for dinner. We will be doing some plain speaking. You have not introduced the lady on your right, Mrs Robson."

"Svetlana is a good friend of mine and the niece of the man you have just removed from the chair you are now sitting in. What are you thinking of charging him with, Mr Davis?"

"Not my problem. The police will work something out over the next twenty-four hours. *Conspiracy to commit murder* would be my guess, however."

Svetlana was about to speak when Davis turned to her and said, "I hope you don't mind me calling you Svetlana. I don't have your second name. Anyway, I am sorry, Svetlana, that we took him away to be interviewed, but he has been either slightly stupid or very stupid."

"I think slightly stupid, Mr Davis," said Svetlana wryly. "He wanted Weber alive as much as we did. He did not lead Weber into a trap."

"I doubt he did, but the police may need a culprit. I will try and convince them to look elsewhere and be diligent in their investigation. There are only three or four groups that can organise that kind of assassination at short notice. I know them all and will help steer the police in their direction. In the meantime, your uncle is going to have a difficult time talking his way out of a serious charge." Davis then turned his head towards Robson and said, "And I will call you Susan since we are friends having dinner together."

"I am a lawyer, Mr Davis, and I do not mind what you call me, but I will use my knowledge of the law to protect my interests. And my friend's interests."

"My first reaction to that statement, Susan, is to say you obstructed the police in their enquiries and lied about certain documents being destroyed. Not very serious, but probably enough to get you struck off if we kick up a big fuss with the Law Society. We have many friends in that fine organisation, and a troublesome provincial solicitor is not going to get much sympathy."

"I doubt they will do that after the whole story is exposed. The revelations appearing on Sunday are sensational. And they are becoming more sensational as the body count grows," she replied confidently.

"Of course," he said, and he nodded his head. "By the way, six people multiplied by three shifts per day have been watching you, your house, and your office since yesterday, and three more people are in and around your son's hostel near Arundel, making sure they are safe. We are protecting you and your family in a way your knowledge of the law cannot. We believe we eliminated the threat earlier today by arresting a man at Heathrow, but we cannot be sure whether he left any instructions for action against you or your family. You referred glibly to a body count, but we do not want you or your children to be included."

Robson was visible shaken as she asked, "You think my or my family's life is at risk?"

"Yes. We have put a lot of resources into protecting you and your family. They are not ordinary policemen, and they have all the latest equipment. Did you really think you could play with this kind of fire without getting burned? Look what happened to Craig!"

Svetlana spoke in a defiant tone: "We think we will be safe once the story is out in the open. There would be no reason to try and harm us. Revenge is a possibility, but pretty pointless once the shit hits the fan."

Davis shook his head as he dealt the final blow: "The story will never be told. There's too much at stake, too many reputations on the line, too many institutions undermined. I took a call this evening, on the way here. The owner of your newspaper in Washington has killed the story and handed the documents to our ambassador. He has a few skeletons in his closet that we can easily overlook now that he has helped us with this little difficulty."

Susan Robson looked fit to burst with anger. She hesitated, faced Ball, and said, "You thought I was out of my depth? You were right." Ball nodded grimly. And then the food arrived.

* * *

Randall travelled to Penzance on Saturday morning feeling like a schoolboy going home with a bad end-of-term report. He was looking forward to the holiday, but not the embarrassment of Lisa knowing he was the ineffectual investigator in the Craig fiasco.

The train was on time and pulled into Penzance station with a final jolt of the brakes. Rising passengers were pushed back into their seats, and those already standing went stumbling forward in search of something to grab.

Lisa met him at the station. She was waving and jumping from foot to foot in an exaggerated greeting that was typical of her. He walked along the platform, sniffed the salty air, and listened to the loud call of seagulls. His spirits lifted. *Perhaps she will disregard Robson's criticism of the police investigation and me. Perhaps she will just tell me to toughen up.* He would know in a few seconds.

In short order, they hugged, and then she grabbed his arm and led him towards the exit. She said she was bursting to tell him some news. As soon as they reached the street, she almost shouted out what was on her mind, only lowering her voice when a passing traffic warden gave her a strange look. "You will never guess. That bloody woman has gone away for two weeks' holiday and did not keep the appointment. I am angry. She did not even have the decency to phone me and cancel."

"Strange," said Randall as a wave of relief spread over him.

"Then, just before you arrived, I phoned my editor. He told me that the story is dead, killed off, pulled. Something to do with high-level pressure put on our owner – State Department involvement, that kind of thing."

"And I thought America was the land of the free."

"Apparently not when money and high politics are involved. You would be surprised to know how often this happens in my wonderful profession."

Randall put his right arm around her shoulders and pulled so hard she squealed. Finally, she said, "I think you are really pleased to see me!"

He nodded as he looked her in the eye.

ABOUT THE AUTHOR

Duncan Pell's career in the steel industry spanned nearly forty years. During that time, he lived and worked in the United Kingdom, Netherlands, France, Ukraine, and the United Arab Emirates. He has travelled on business to many countries throughout the world selling steel products and developing sales networks. He is a frequent speaker at conferences and a well-known figure in industry circles. He lives in Ras al-Khaimah, near Dubai, and he is now an independent management consultant who writes in his spare time.